I0688531

Teachers Abroad Mysteries

#1 Revolution Revenge
#2 Oasis Assassin
#3 Turkish Delight Gone Sour
#4 Singapore Fling

Oasis Assassin

Phyllis Wachob

This book is dedicated to travelers and tourists.

Preface

Although some of the places and characters in this novel are real, for example, Siwa Oasis, the Shali, Amun's Temple, and the water holes, most are fictional. However, there is no Mr. David's Antiques or the American University of Egypt. In its essence, this is a work of fiction. Names, characters, places and incidents are either the product of the author's imagination or are used fictitiously, and any resemblance to actual persons, living or dead, businesses or establishments, events or locales is coincidental.

Cast of Characters

Barbie Falcon – English teacher at the American University of Egypt

Penelope Watson – English teacher at AUE and Barbie's roommate

Mitch P – Assistant Professor in Arabic History at AUE

Rachel – Mitch's wife

Cornelius Smythe – Professor Emeritus of Archeology at AUE

Thurman Hall – Professor and Head of the History Department at AUE

Mahmoud - local guide in Siwa

David (aka Ali Rafiq) – Antiquities dealer in the Khan el Khalili and Police Chief of Siwa

Winter Doern – Assistant Professor of History at AUE

Lisbon Truegood – Associate Professor of History at AUE

Schuyler Stanford – MA student at AUE

Dutch motorcyclist – world traveler

Chapter One: A Visit to Salt City

"Greed for power and prestige, defying the gods. It was hubris that created this!" Professor Emeritus Cornelius Smythe waddled to the sign that marked the beginning of the trail that headed upwards, into the labyrinth of crumbling buildings and teetering walls of the ruins they called 'The Shali'. "Made of salt bricks generations ago, cut from the crusted salty earth, stacked on top of one another, reaching for the sky in a symbol of the power of man conquering his environment. But now? It is a monument to the vanity of man. Hungry for power? Now a place of ruin," and he pointed to the remains of a gate that stood in front of the group.

"The inhabitants of Siwa lived in these houses, adding to them as their families grew, until one week in 1926, when it rained for three days." He paused dramatically as the group craned their necks to see the rounded stumps of walls and openings in the floors, showing only the wooden struts, massive palm trunks used for the ceiling materials. "It was then they had to flee because their houses…"

"Melted," shouted Professor Thurman Hall from the rear. "Hubris, damned right!"

Barbie turned to peer at the tall behatted man who stood slightly apart from the group. "Of course," whispered Barbie. "Salt bricks, they melted in the rain. Wow!"

Mitch, a colleague of Barbie's who stood next to her, clenched his teeth and muttered under his breath, "Hubris, that's a word he should be familiar with."

Professor Smythe continued, "What is left is no longer habitable, but is kept here as a reminder of the city as it once was. It will be lit in the evenings by floodlight, very dramatic. And now, my fellow AUEians, off you go. I no longer climb into the dramatic ruins of this isolated Egyptian oasis, but you must. Please go cautiously, careful of your step. In a few places there are warnings, so definitely don't go there, but anywhere can be a hazard. And when you reach the top of the ruined city, or village, whichever you prefer to call it, you may enjoy the sunset and the call to prayer from the myriad mosques in the town. I shall see you all at dinner."

Barbie, her roommate Penelope, their good friends Mitch and Rachel, along with most of the rest of the faculty members of the American University of Egypt who had come on this vacation trip to the isolated desert oasis of Siwa, began the climb upwards. Scattered all around them were the ruins, the broken floors, the toppled ceilings, the melted walls of this unique city of the desert. They had to pick their way through the crumbling walls as the path upwards was not always clear. Periodically the group stopped and gazed outwards to all parts of the desert. Directly at the base of the hill and oozing out into the dry desert, was the modern town of Siwa. The houses and buildings, invariably the same color as the desert beyond, dull browns and grays, were so alike each other it was hard to tell whether a building was a house, a store, a mosque or a school. The streets were sparsely used and the speed of most vehicles mimicked walking speed. Trucks, cars, donkey carts, and farm vehicles, all moved at a pace that was foreign to the bustling streets of Cairo that the city-dwellers were accustomed to. Occasional bursts of speed and noise invariably denoted a young man on a motorcycle.

Beyond the town lay the fields of waving palm trees and sun-dried colors of the olive trees, the only vegetation that grew well here. Scattered in among fields were the tops of houses, sheds and even tinier plots of vegetable gardens. Also to be seen were a few hills, topped with dun-colored ruins that Barbie knew they would see in the coming days. In one direction a bare hill was punctured with holes, tombs of ancient Greeks and Romans. Beyond it was another hill pancaked with layers of hardpan, a leftover from the time when Siwa was at the bottom of a sea. As well, in the distance, bodies of water shimmered in the breeze. These salt lakes were the sign of the blessing and the curse of Siwa. Water was everywhere, and no where. The salt water crept into the fields, rendering them unusable and the salt in the lakes kept increasing as the water evaporated.

Beyond the fields was the desert, easier seen the higher the group ascended. A real desert, dull brown and gray; it was pocked with hills and sand dunes, gullies and dips, not a flat wasteland, but dry; very, very dry.

Barbie and Penelope reached the topmost point on the opposite end from the highest point, which sported a flagpole. Barbie sat noisily, waiting for the cooling evening breeze, which she felt sure must come. She heaved in a big breath of fresh desert air and exhaled noisily. Penelope moved off, leaving Barbie alone with her thoughts.

Barbie's curly blonde hair stuck to the nape of her neck with the dampness caused by the heat of the day. She slipped off her light weight shirt, leaving her with bare arms and a plunging neckline. Up here, I feel enough alone to be able to flaunt my arms and chest away from the prying eyes of Egyptian men, she thought. She mused about her last eight months in Egypt. She was an English teacher by profession and had arrived in Cairo in August, ready to take up a position at the American University in Egypt, fondly known as AUE, the students and faculty were known as AUEians. It was an old college and in the wake of an expanding economy in Egypt had grown considerably in the last few years. The ESL department was large and Barbie, even at the age of 40-something, was still in demand as an experienced English teacher. She knew she could get a job almost anywhere in the world, but what brought her to Egypt was this very experience that lay before her, exploring the nooks and crannies of this superbly interesting country. However, the recent events, the 18-day Revolution which was now being hailed as part of the Arab Spring, had shaken her. The university had reopened and classes had commenced, but there was still considerable disruption in the teaching, and learning, in the university. Not encumbered with a family, the ex-husband had long ago drifted away (Barbie knew not where), and the one child grown and independent, she felt free to explore the world. The MA in Teaching English as a Second Language had given her the freedom to travel and explore. She thought over the last few years, each assignment more exciting than the last, and the number of wild and interesting countries she had visited grew steadily. She was a person who disdained the vacation to the same place every year, choosing instead to go as far as her budget would allow. She felt carefree and happy to be so. Her unconventional childhood, the sole offspring of hippies, was happy if somewhat abnormal.

The wind had increased earlier, but now suddenly dropped and the noises from the town rose up to greet Barbie; the honk of car horns and of donkeys, the clank of engines and machines, the soft murmurs of voices. The sun raced towards the horizon as Barbie tried to look, but not directly. She waited for the sounds of the call to prayer which she knew must be soon. She saw others in her group crawling over the ruins of the Salt City and tried to pinpoint them.

Twenty had come on this trip, filling up the seats of the small bus. The Easter holiday was long and ultimately boring if one spent it in Cairo. The university had organized this small excursion and Professor Emeritus Cornelius Smythe was their guide and leader. Other participants ranged from full professors to instructors like Barbie and her roommate Penelope. They had all been enthusiastic about getting away from the upsetting and dramatic events in Cairo, out into the desert, the clean air and hopefully, away from a poisonous atmosphere within the university ranks as well. Barbie thought back to the short organizational meeting that had been held in the past week, to make sure everyone knew where they were going, what they had to bring on the trip and general information. They had gathered in the Faculty Lounge in an informal setting and Rachel had acted as a secretary, taking down names, asking the participants about rooms and being a general help in planning.

Rachel and her academic husband Mitch were particular friends of Barbie and Penelope. They lived in the same building and shared adventures during the Revolution. During that time of chaos, they had felt free to wander into each other's apartments and raid each other's fridges. They had felt pleased to share this adventure as well. They had agreed that it was to be a 'tame' adventure, a jolly time being tourists and free of the hassles of teaching and the ongoing uncertainty of the political climate of the capital.

Barbie was happy to see that, so far, the trip had been a success in that sense. She watched the couple as they stopped and looked out at the scene.

The first crackling noise jolted Barbie from her thoughts. She heard the 'click' of a loudspeaker being turned on, and then a clearing of the throat. The first cry, the sound of summons to attention, was almost startling in its intensity and abruptness. Within seconds, another loudspeaker joined, seconds behind the first and keeping pace. They blended in with a third and a fourth and a fifth. Soon, Barbie was unable to tell how many mosques' muezzins had joined their calls to the first. The mosque at the entrance to the ruined Salt City was the loudest, if not among the first, and some, on the outskirts of town were mere whispers compared to those nearby. For more than ten minutes the competing sounds echoed over the town; blending, outdoing one another, pausing and then gradually, they stopped and died away.

The last had ceased, when Barbie caught a glimpse of two of the participants of the group walking away from her. She saw Rachel and Mitch try to round a corner, only to be blocked by a small barricade. She could see their faces and watch their mouths, but could hear nothing they said. They turned and disappeared behind a melted salt brick wall. She saw another figure, wearing a distinctive sun hat, come around another corner and then turn around sharply. Barbie watched

Thurman Hall, head of the History Department, lift his hands in surprise and then he spoke to someone out of sight. Two others from their group headed down and when Barbie looked over the side, she could make out the rounded figure of Cornelius Smythe at the bottom below, looking up into the Salt City. Penelope popped up in front of her, twenty steps away. She lifted her hand in greeting and waved at Barbie enthusiastically.

It was a typical gesture for Penelope. She was such a lovely roommate, Barbie thought. Invariably cheerful, always up for adventure and fun, Penelope acted as a rope that tethered Barbie to reality. Penelope had a secret passion for romance novels, and as a single woman of a certain age, occasionally confused fiction and reality. Her round face, framed by brown flyaway hair, did not tell the story of her demeanor in the classroom, where she was a kind, but demanding English teacher. Penelope was not much of an athlete and occasionally got caught in a physical situation she could not control.

As she waved at Barbie, Penelope slowly began to disappear. It was not as if she had fallen into a hole, rather that a hole had reached up and pulled her in. Barbie watched in amazement as Penelope's feet disappeared, and then her knees. Penelope's face grew a look of amazement, which rapidly changed to horror as she realized what was happening to her. The ground was obviously unstable here, but not full of open gaps. This one was in a slow collapsing state. Just before she was pulled under, Penelope raised her hands over her head and let out a mighty scream. At the same time, she reached out to the ground around her in an attempt to arrest her slow fall.

Mitch and Rachel arrived at that moment and as Mitch rushed forward to grab Penelope, Rachel joined her screams to Penelope's, hoping to attract attention to the accident. Mitch reached into the hole, and squatting as deeply as he could, jerked upwards and outwards while gripping Penelope's arms. Penelope's legs rapidly scrabbled through the dirt, dust and ancient palm tree trunks that made up the celling of the room she had fallen into. Her thin khaki pants tore quickly and her knees met the building materials in an encounter to her detriment. Blood oozed from gashes on her legs and Penelope's howls of pain added to her distress.

Barbie left her perch and quickly picked her way through the ruined city to the scene of Penelope's disaster. By the time she arrived, all was well, Penelope had been rescued and no one else had fallen into the hole. Barbie looked down at her friend who lay on the ground with her eyes closed, hardly daring to breathe.

"She looks like a bloodied corpse," said Rachel unhelpfully.

Barbie knelt beside Penelope. "No, she's not a corpse, are you? We can't deal with another corpse. Too many already. Penelope, dear friend, open your eyes and tell us all is well."

Penelope obeyed and her eyes flickered open. "I am not a corpse, not yet."

Chapter Two: The Dance Show

"Yuck, I need a shower!" said Barbie. "And so do you. Let's go for a swim. The pool is out in the back."

"Whoa, friend of mine. I do not need to go out there in the dark to an unknown place," Penelope answered. "I'll stay here and take a shower, you check out the pool."

"Suit yourself!" Barbie said as she whipped off her clothes and pulled on her swimsuit. She was a lover of swims, mostly in pools, but the sea was a good place to swim as well, as long as it was calm and not too cold. She carried her suit with her wherever she went and rarely passed up a chance to jump into water. "Tootleloo!" she called as she exited the room.

The girls' room faced the front entrance of the hotel, which consisted of a long line of single-story rooms split into two wings. In the center was a garden, the reception and a breakfast room. A walkway ran in a meandering fashion in front of the rooms and then swung to the rear behind the reception area. Barbie had been shown the path and noted the small sign "Pool" that sat next to the walkway. Tonight, the lighting was dim and Barbie almost missed the sign with the arrow indicating the path to the pool. As she made her way around the end of the building, she realized that the pool was not far away from their room at all, but was a two-minute walk. The odd-shaped pool sat in the midst of a dozen lounge chairs, some scattered tables and a number of wicker chairs set around the tables as seating. A large shallow section began with a series of wide steps leading into the main part of the pool. It had no square corners, only cemented sides to a natural pool.

Barbie threw her towel on a chair near a table and looked around. She felt, rather than saw, the presence of someone at the pool. In a darkly lit corner she saw a white stick rise, then a thin stream of smoke followed by the fall of the white stick. Barbie could not believe that anyone would dare come here to smoke when she was swimming. She stopped with only her feet on the top step in the shallow end of the pool. She peered into the shadows which were dappled by the branches of the trees and the uneven nature of the lights. She smelled the smoke, sweet and cloying.

"Yuck," she said loudly. "People smoking at the pool. How disgusting!"

The answer that came from the lounge chair in the far corner was a muffled "Huh". Barbie stepped out of the pool, slipped on her flip-flops and walked towards the noise. A few steps brought clarity.

Professor Thurman Hall, the Head of the History Department, sat on the farthest lounge chair in the pool area. Beside him was a small table strewn with personal effects. Barbie stopped. She thought swiftly of how she was going to respond to the obvious non-compliance of her complaint. He was quite senior to her in the pecking order at the University, but after all, he was just another faculty member on the same trip. She thought about what she knew of him and then thought better of pursuing the complaint. She retreated, gathering up her belongings and walked away, head held at a haughty angle. "Humph," she said loudly as she left. She did not linger for a reply.

Back in the room within ten minutes, she found the shower still occupied, so sat contemplating her behavior. Why didn't I say anything more, other than the wish that the offending cigarette be put out? She thought about what she knew of Thurman Hall, the not-so-old and definitely not loveable curmudgeon. He was not her HOD, but was one of the most visible and because of that, most powerful men at the University. It was definitely a man's world, as most universities are, and especially one in Egypt. He was visible and he was vocal. The rumors that had abounded about him were legion. He had complained loudly at faculty and at Senate meetings about 'uncollegial' behavior on the part of his own department members, but also of others in departments other than his own. Rumors abounded of his own uncollegial behavior. The word was about that he was not a good one to cross and not one to fight with. He always seemed to win. What Mitch had indicated at the Shali seemed apt in a way. Lust for power he certainly had, but so far, hubris had not been in the cards. She had not heard much of his private life, but knew he was unaccompanied in Egypt. That did not necessarily mean he was without a wife or partner, only that he lived alone.

When Penelope came out of the shower, she was surprised to see Barbie obviously NOT wet and asked what happened with her swim. She was told not to ask, but would hear the whole story later, when she could consult with Mitch about proper behavior towards the high and almighty Professor Hall.

Dinner was served in a venue across the road from the hotel, in another building, or an extension of their own hotel or a different one, no one knew. When they had gathered near the reception area of their hotel, they were directed across the street. The dining room was much larger than the small breakfast room that could only hold customers from the sixteen-room hotel. This dining room was much larger and as they were expecting a dance show, it could also contain more tourists from other tour groups and hotels. The dinner was served buffet style, as was usual in Egypt, and consisted of a variety of Egyptian dishes as well as Western. Penelope, Barbie, Mitch and Rachel had snagged a four-person table in the rear and as they settled down to the piled plates of food, Barbie leaned in for a good gossip.

"Mitch, please do tell me all about Thurman Hall, the Head of your Department," Barbie started the conversation in a loud whisper.

"Why the whispering and he is NOT the head of my department. I'm in Arabic Studies."

"But don't you teach History?? In the History Department?"

"Yes, but I'm only seconded to that Department. Technically, Professor Hall is not my HOD, nor will he ever be, Inshallah." Mitch finished with a common statement of Egyptians, that what has been said, will happen if God was willing, or in this case, never would happen.

"But tell us about him, oh please do," Penelope said. "He was at the pool, smoking, tonight and spoiled Barbie's swim, so we want to know why the nasty man has to do that and spoil things for other people."

"No idea," Mitch responded. "I have no grand psychological insights." He stuck his fork into a piece of tough chicken and began to wrestle with it.

"But this afternoon you talked about hubris, so you must have some ideas," Barbie persisted.

"Well, I'll tell you what Mitch has told me," offered Rachel. Still in a whisper, she reiterated the standard gossip, giving it all a colorful twist by adding nasty comments on his physical appearance as well as her interpretation of his psychological profile. "Well, It's obvious his mother treated him badly as a child as he hates women. And he hates men because he is going bald and he tries to hide it. Why do men do that 'comb-over' thing still? I thought it was passé and not done anymore. Also, of course, his buck teeth are the result of prolonged thumb-sucking as a child, and now he is terribly embarrassed by it, but simply cannot stop himself. That's why his wife left him, you know."

In the midst of a stifled laugh, Penelope demanded, "That's not true, is it? How nasty of you."

"Well, he is nasty, so being nasty back is his due. And look at him, sitting there with Cornelius and the Visiting Prof, who is he?" Rachel asked.

Mitch leaned forward and checked out the seating of the four men at the 'head' table, at least it was the one that was nearest the cleared space at the front of the room. Professor Emeritus Cornelius Smythe was well-known to those at the table. He was retired now, but had at one time been one of the most famous of Egyptian archeologists. He was the grand old man of AUE and was to be seen at almost any party he was invited to, whisky in hand. He sat in the center of any group, and called others to him, charming them with his raconteur's encyclopedic knowledge of Egypt, its history, including political history, of which he was present for most of the last forty years. He held the unofficial role of AUE historian as he knew the ins and outs of all the major players in the University as well as the country. He loved Egypt so much that he couldn't fathom living anywhere else, although it was rumored that he owned a family house in one of the tonier parts of Boston, from which he had come. A single man, of rumored proclivities, although no one spoke openly of it, he favored beautiful young women, especially intelligent ones and was a favorite of the female graduate students, the company of whom he shamelessly flattered. A round Santa Claus face was framed by an aureole of frizzy white hair, punctuated by twinkling blue eyes and a small, but lascivious set of pink lips. A man who had seen a lot of sun in his youth, Cornelius wisely covered his aging skin against further ravages from Father Sun. His hand invariably clutched a glass of the best whisky he could obtain in Egypt and in fact, there was a horde of it in his flat in Cairo. Barbie knew this as she and her friends had been the recipients of more than one bottle during the time of the Revolution, when many consumer goods were totally unavailable, even bread. But that stash of whisky was to be found in the flat downstairs from Barbie and Penelope's. Barbie adored the aging libertine and sought out his company, especially when she wanted to hear the latest gossip. Cornelius knew everyone and even though he was not always on someone's good side, he apologized for any unpleasantness so easily that it was difficult to dislike him, although many deplored his conduct.

The older man, Rachel's 'Visiting Prof' sitting at the table, was an enigma to Mitch, but the other two were well-known. Thurman sat sulking, sharing in Cornelius' whisky, although it had been decanted into a more innocuous bottle and was therefore more acceptable to the sensibilities of the Muslims in his company. The fourth occupant of the table was Mahmoud, their local guide. Although Cornelius may have known more of the ancient history of Siwa, Mahmoud was their local expert, especially as it related to the more current history and anthropology of the local culture. Mahmoud was in his late twenties, his brown face framed by the curly black hair of a typical Egyptian. He was also round and hearty as befitted a poor boy made good. A large stomach was the sign of success in Egypt, especially in the poorer parts of the country where having enough, and more than enough, to eat was a sign of success. Mahmoud was a success. A local boy who had graduated from primary school, been sent to Alexandria to study and who subsequently graduated with a degree in Hospitality and Tourism, he was a harbinger to the local boys and showed them how far they could go. He was revered among the locals for his education, connections to the University in Alexandria and his fluency in four languages. He was the 'go-to' guide in Siwa and had just finished writing a tourism guide to the town. He was deferential to Cornelius, but held his own in conversation with the other professors. He was a favorite of the tourists, as he was up for anything, solved any problems that arose and was full of suggestions of places to go and things to see. Besides, Barbie mused, he was ALWAYS cheerful.

At the moment Barbie noticed that the conversation at the four-person table had become very heated. The voices of three of the men were deliberately kept low, but Thurman's gradually became louder and louder, threatening the peace of the entire dining room. Finally, Thurman rose to his feet, stretching himself to his highest in a stance that many a psychologist would describe as 'threatening'.

"All these people should be dropped off the face of the earth. They have NO place in this university and I for one, am willing to sacrifice them. Forever." He threw his napkin down on the table and strode out of the dining room.

The entire room became quiet with embarrassment and dismay at the rudeness of the act that had been committed. This was NOT the harmony that the staff members had sought by taking this trip. After a thirty-second stunned and embarrassed silence, the whispers began, soon growing loud in a chorus of 'How dare he', 'How crude', 'What can we do with that man?' and general condemnation.

Barbie added her opinion. "Disagreeable seems the operative word here. I now feel justified in my negative opinion of the idiot."

Mitch leaned over to have a conversation with others at the next table. Pete and Sally, another new couple, sat with Lisbon Truegood, another member of the History Department and 'Trigger'. Barbie had met Lisbon, but 'Trigger' was unknown to her except by name. He was Eastern European, with a difficult name that sounded much like the moniker that everyone had given him. He knew that everyone butchered his name, but took it good-naturedly and responded to 'Trigger.' Mitch spoke for a few minutes with the group, then turned his attention back to his own table. Rachel demanded to know what had been said.

Mitch rubbed his hands over his face in a gesture of annoyance and as if he wanted to wash away all the unpleasantness. "They confirmed that he doesn't get along with anyone. The latest is an incredibly rude comment about Lisbon, in public, and something that should have been kept within the Department. But we all agree, he is an ass and we need to ignore all of this and get on with our jobs, and now, with our short holiday."

Barbie snorted in reply. "Who cares? I for one, do not. He's got nothing to do with me."

Mitch corroborated this opinion. "I don't like him, but again, he's not in my department. But this I can say. Trouble is brewing in that department. Everyone needs to beware of trouble in a department. We know that from the unfortunate events of January and February."

"Well, at least this time, it's only ex-pats fighting with ex-pats, not involving the Egyptians, is it?" Penelope asked.

"I think so, at least let us hope so. Lisbon, who's in the department, would rather everyone drop it all. Comments are only words and he isn't likely to fight it. However, he was urged to file a complaint against Thurman for maligning him. But he refused. And good for him, we need to ignore Thurman's bad behavior, not rise to the bait."

Mitch's last words were almost drowned out by the sounds of drums. A line of gaily dressed men ran into the room, pounding on large hand-held drums in a loud and insistent beat. Women out of sight ululated, adding to the cacophony that had erupted. Rachel laughed happily. "They have just saved us! Let the dancing begin! No more arguing, no more bad behavior from grown men!"

"What?" Penelope shouted at Rachel.

Rachel's response was to begin stamping her feet and clapping her hands in time to the drums and singing. The waiters bringing dessert had not finished, but now piled their hands with small bowls of sweet Egyptian desserts and dashed about, tossing four or five little bowls onto every table as they attempted to maneuver among the drummers and dancers.

Barbie leaned over to Mitch, "Better a Dance Show than an Adults Behaving Badly Show."

Mitch's response was a snort and a turn of his head towards the enthusiastic dancers.

One dance segued into another as the troupe sang, drummed and danced a variety of ethnic dances from various parts of Egypt and the countries surrounding them. The locals shied away from letting their women perform in front of strange men, but Mahmoud had managed to engage some 'loose women' from Alexandria to come for this special performance. The dancers were of course not immoral girls, but college students who did not object to wearing their tresses loose and shimmying a bit in front of strange men. To the locals, as long as they were not their own daughters, the dance was acceptable.

And to this end, the townspeople began to take up positions outside the doors and open windows of the dining room. The children of the staff, knowing that a dance performance was set for this evening, had gathered outside, waiting for an opportune moment to crowd into the room. Barbie glanced over at the uninvited group and noticed their smiling faces and clapping and felt impelled to join them.

As she looked, she noticed some tourists in the background, unmistakable blonde hair and bare arms. She looked closer, trying to make out what other tourists were here in Siwa. The Revolution had emptied Egypt of the swarms of tourists, and they had not yet come back in any numbers. So, who were these intruders on their dance show? She stood and inched towards the open window behind her.

A wave greeted her and Barbie waved back. Three unmistakable European heads appeared in the shadows, all of them waving and clapping. Barbie stared, then blinked, and finally waved enthusiastically. Three familiar faces, she thought as she sat down. I know them from somewhere. Then it occurred to her, they were graduate students in the Arabic Studies department. She had met them in Mitch's office one day. What were their names? She thought they had queen's names, all three. But what were they doing here? In Siwa? At the faculty's dance party?

Chapter Three: Taking a Nighttime Dip

"Barbie, it's really, really late. What do you mean, you want to go swimming now?" Penelope wailed.

"It's not really swimming, it's just a dip, a swift dip in and out. It will wash away all the cares and woes of the world. It will wash away all that has gone before." Barbie proceeded to snatch her suit off the back of a chair.

"This isn't like baptism," Penelope answered.

"I know, but it will do us good. We will go to bed relaxed and refreshed. And you know I can't go out there alone, not at this time of night."

"Okay, okay. I guess I can't sleep in any case. But let's get Mitch and Rachel to go too." Penelope whipped out the door before Barbie could answer.

Penelope reappeared almost immediately. "Otherwise occupied they said."

"Wow, I wish I could be otherwise occupied," Barbie said, slipping off her scarab bracelet and placing it carefully on the nightstand.

"Haven't heard from David?" Penelope asked in reference to the bracelet, a gift from David.

"You know I haven't. It's all finished. He's disappeared, that's that." Barbie sat on the bed and waited for Penelope to change into her swimsuit.

David was an antiquities dealer she had met a few months before during the Revolution. She had gone to his shop to purchase some gifts to take home, but had been sidetracked by the events of the 18 days of Egypt's Arab Spring. She had never had an opportunity to follow through with her purchases, but in the meantime had fallen in love with the handsome Egyptian. He had left abruptly, saying that he had 'enemies'. All she had left of her romance was this bracelet.

"I'll hurry so we can get this all over with." Penelope suited deeds to her words and within minutes the two were out the door, swinging their towels behind them.

Quietly they made their way to the pool. Barbie led the way confidently and soon they were at the pool enclosure. Barbie looked through the shadows at the previously occupied chair. "At least he isn't here again. That would <u>really</u> have spoiled it."

The only sounds were the whining buzz of mosquitoes and a faint rustle of the dry palm trees in the evening breeze. They threw their towels on the same table that Barbie had used earlier in the evening, and giggling at the foolishness of taking a midnight swim, slipped onto the first step.

"Woooooo," said Penelope. "You didn't tell me it was cold."

Barbie stepped beside her and shivered. "Yeah, you're right, it is cool. I guess I didn't get this far the last time I was here. Maybe it gets cold at night," Barbie responded.

"Or maybe it's cold all the time and you didn't know, or think to find out what we are doing here," retorted Penelope.

Barbie went in further, stifling whimpers of pain as the cool water touched her flesh. "I think it is quite refreshing. Weeeeee." Barbie launched herself from the step into the main part of the pool.

"Well, here goes. Better the water than being eaten alive by mosquitoes," Penelope said, also pushing off from the steps. With pants and moans she struck out to the far end using a breaststroke.

Barbie followed behind her and made noises of enjoyment to encourage Penelope, whom Barbie believed to be in need of more adventure and excitement in life. Barbie thought Penelope not adventurous enough, too likely to take the easy way out, not push herself forward at work, or sign up for the difficult things in life. Coming to Egypt was Barbie's idea and, so far Penelope had gone along with it all, including the camel trek with camping in the desert, as well as the camel race across the wild dunes. She had climbed to the highest point possible on every minaret in Cairo, at Barbie's urging. Barbie felt proud of her friend, now more confident and adventurous. However, this was hardly a high challenge.

Penelope screamed. Suddenly Barbie found herself extricating herself from Penelope's flailing arms as Penelope reversed herself in order to go back the way she had come. Barbie tried to see what had caused Penelope's panic but the lights and slight breeze caused wavering shadows and waves of black and reflected light to bounce around her.

"What is it? Why did you scream?" Barbie attempted to sound calm and collected, but inwardly trembled.

"There's something in the pool. There, there, I touched it!" came the terrified answer. "Maybe it's an animal or something. Maybe a branch. I can't see." Penelope again moved backwards causing Barbie to slip and go under.

"Ah, ah, it's after me," screamed Penelope again.

"No, it's just me," sputtered Barbie, pushing her way up to a standing position.

"I'm out." Penelope scrambled out and stood on the edge of the pool.

Barbie stood and squinted into the dark. "You're right. There is something here. But it's not an animal, at least not a live one. I think maybe it's a lounge chair cushion or something. It's white." Barbie reached forward and tugged on a white piece of cloth. "A sheet maybe," she continued. "It's heavy though, maybe a whole laundry bag. Penelope and a laundry bag. Wait till I tell this story!"

Barbie pulled again and the floating detritus moved and rolled. She pulled it with her towards the shallow end of the pool, near the steps where there was more light. She tugged again and the object, now larger than Barbie thought at first, came into view. It rolled over and a face appeared.

Water streamed off the face and left hair across the forehead. The mouth was open and Barbie thought she saw a grimace. Then she recognized who it was. Thurman Hall, Head of the History Department at the American University of Egypt. And he was quite, quite dead.

Barbie screamed.

Chapter Four: A Visit to the Police Station I

Barbie and Penelope huddled together on a lounge chair, having pulled their towels around them for modesty and the creeping cold. Mahmoud, the tour guide, hovered nearby, an occurrence for which both of the women felt immensely grateful. A friendly, known face kept them from freaking out, especially Penelope.

Behind Mahmoud was the hotel manger who, literally wrung his hands in consternation that such an occurrence could happen at his hotel. Behind the manager, lingering in the dim shadows and keeping their presence to a minimal volume in order to keep their front row seats, were some of the hotel staff and a few of the tour group who had heard the commotion. They were blocked from questioning Barbie and Penelope, but they sensed that all the commotion had something to do with a member of the group.

The body of Thurman Hall lay under a sheet on the cement deck of the pool area. A person with medical training, perhaps even a doctor, hovered over the corpse. He had recovered the body from the pool and summoned the manager. A whispered conversation ensued and then the manager hurried aside and pulled out his phone. This whispered conversation ended quickly and then the manager came back, bustling and in charge. He spoke rapidly to Mahmoud, who turned to his two charges.

"The Police want you to come to the Police station. They feel you will be more comfortable there, and of course they wish to talk with you. I will come with you while you get dressed. I hope that's okay?" Mahmoud smiled obsequiously.

"I do not want you to help me get dressed, thank you very much," huffed Penelope.

"No, no, you mistake me. I will come to the door outside your room and keep these people away from you, so that you can get dressed in comfort and without interference," he replied.

"And so, we have no time to talk with anyone else," Barbie continued, "in order to change our story or let anyone else corroborate our stories. Do they suspect us? Do they think we put Thurman Hall into the pool? Just for our amusement?"

"No, no, I'm sure there is nothing of the kind. They are being kind to you and to the hotel guests by making it easier for you and for them. Please, you must feel cold and a little uncomfortable…" Mahmoud looked at them pleadingly.

"Barbie, better at the police station than right here, don't you think? I for one, would like to get dressed and do all of this in a civilized manner." Penelope pulled on her towel and attempted to stand and wrap it around herself. She dislodged Barbie's towel which fell to the ground, exposing Barbie's charms.

Barbie had learned not long after she arrived in Egypt that a woman who wore a swimsuit at a place like a public beach, was almost as good as 'naked', and would be treated as such. She felt quite 'naked' now and pushed Penelope in an attempt to get her to move off of the edge of her towel.

At that moment, two young men with a stretcher appeared, bent on capturing their victim. They were dressed in a kind of uniform, but whose uniform was unclear. It could have been a hospital, a hotel or a general cleaners' garb. Barbie and Penelope stepped aside and watched in fascination as the two hauled the corpse onto the ancient army type stretcher. Barbie and Penelope pushed backwards into the shadows, tipping over three chairs in their attempt to give the corpse room to exit ahead of them. Shouts followed the stretcher as it made its way out to the front of the hotel, watched by all and sundry. As soon as the procession receded, Barbie turned to Mahmoud, "Please escort us to our room."

While Mahmoud stood guard, Barbie and Penelope hurriedly changed into clothes. They whispered to each other so as to escape the flapping ears of Mahmoud. "Do we have to coordinate our stories?" asked Barbie. "I know it was my idea to go swimming, and you went along. How do I explain that foolish idea?"

"Humph, that's your problem, but that is the truth and I think if we just give the truth to them, that's that."

"What about other things, should we volunteer anything, like that he had a fight at dinner or anything." Barbie continued.

"You know, that would be Mahmoud's bailiwick, not ours, so I think we tell the story straight. I don't think they believe we had anything to do with it. But what a bizarre thing to happen. How did he die? He was definitely dead, wasn't he?"

"I didn't really touch him, but there was no warmth left. And I saw his eyes, oh my god, his eyes. The eyes of a dead man. I'm going to have to take some sort of drug to make me sleep tonight. I don't want to remember looking into his face. Yuck! How can I get that memory out of my head?" Barbie sat in contemplation while Penelope looked for shoes.

"Don't worry about that yet," Penelope answered. "I think it may be awhile before we get to bed. Concentrate on getting through this encounter with the police. Hey, I thought they had done away with police after the start of the revolution, you know the nasty corrupt men who abused poor people and took bribes."

"Well, who is going to do their job? Maybe these are 'military police'. God, what a thought. I don't think I'm going to like this at all. Ready?" Barbie opened the door and they stepped out.

Mahmoud turned and faced them. "Are we ready ladies?"

Mitch jumped from the shadows. "What's going on here?"

Penelope burst into tears. "Mitch, have you come to rescue us? Please come with us. We need your support."

Despite Mahmoud's protests, Barbie and Penelope filled Mitch in on the body found in the pool.

"So, it is true," Mitch said. "I heard rumors and couldn't believe this. And you two found Professor Hall's body in the pool. Actually, IN the pool?"

"Presumably drowned, but that's all we know." Barbie straightened her shoulders. "It would be helpful if you came. We need our 'escort,' our 'man' to be beside us to protect us from the Police."

"But I will be there, you should not worry," Mahmoud protested.

"But you are an Egyptian man, it's not the same thing, we need our man." Barbie stood her ground.

Mitch dipped his head, took Mahmoud's arm and turned him away. He spoke gently in Arabic, smiling and agreeable. Mahmoud argued back.

Mahmoud turned again to the girls. "There is no problem, I will be with you at all times. There will be no possibility of bad behavior. You are honored guests in our country, and I will protect you. No need for you to go, Professor." Mahmoud turned to Mitch.

"He's right. If anyone touches you, the revolution will look like a Saturday afternoon practice game compared to what would be unleashed if there is any hanky-panky." Mitch reassured the girls.

"Hey, Mitch, what is 'hanky-panky' in Arabic? We might need the word." Barbie inhaled deeply. "We are off to give a simple statement to the police, accompanied by our esteemed guide and protector. You stay here and protect the rest of them. After all, he was the head of your department and you should be protecting the others from the same fate. Don't go near the pool."

"He was NOT the head of my department, and I don't think anyone else is going to go swimming at this time of night. You two are the only really foolish ones I know." Mitch raised his voice and sent them off with a loud phrase in Arabic that wished that they go with God. "Maasalama!"

"We'll need it," said Penelope

They followed Mahmoud who led the way with importance. He loudly shoved anyone who attempted to get in their way and rushed them through the scrum of others in their tour group. They reached the street and were ushered into an ancient Lada. The Russian-made cars were slowly being phased out of the country, but there had been so many of them that entire cars could be assembled from old parts. The old taxis were painted black and white and their drivers charged much less than taxis with air conditioning, seats with springs and windows that rolled up to keep out the dust of Egypt. This Lada looked as if it had served the pharaohs.

Barbie and Penelope got into the back seat, while Mahmoud sat in the front with a driver that may or may not have been attached to the police. They held a muttered conversation all the way. Penelope shifted in her seat, trying to find a place where a broken spring did not hit her in a delicate place. She eventually sat on Barbie's side of the middle, so the two were pressed against one door.

The drive started by going down the narrow street in front of their hotel, now very dimly lit, into the main square of the town. The lights still shown on the Shali, but mysteriously went out just as they passed. Time to roll up the sidewalks, Barbie thought. The ancient streetlights were few and far between, throwing pools of light around them, but leaving long stretches of street in semi-darkness. Lumps in the road occasionally uncurled and turned into yellow feral dogs, and late-night workers or revelers appeared and disappeared, their gallabeyas billowing around them as the wind caught the thin cotton material. The small shops, giving way to houses were uniformly flat-roofed, dull-colored and simple. As they made their way out of town to the police station, Penelope remarked on the sameness of small-town Egypt. "Like the outskirts of Luxor or Aswan. So much the same, so Egyptian."

They pulled up to a brilliantly lit open doorway and two young non-uniformed police men quickly approached the car in greeting. "Welcome, welcome," they said as the two women fell out of the car. They were led into the well-lit office and Barbie blinked at the white intense light. She wondered why this place was so brilliant and other places so ill-lit.

"I am Ahmed and this is my fellow officer…" one began.

"And brother, Mohammed. Pleased to make your acquaintance." The other continued, pulling out two chairs in the front room.

"No, no, my brother. We should seat them in our more comfortable room," Ahmed said, indicating a door.

"Oh, yes, of course. The most comfortable place for…" Mohamed began.

"Our lovely guests of honor," Ahmed finished.

The door was opened and the light switched on in an office that contained a desk and a number of cushioned chairs. Obviously not the place one would interview criminals, but guests of the police.

"Please have a…" Mohammed began.

"A very comfortable seat." Ahmed continued. "And maybe, a cup of…"

"Tea, or because you are Americans, maybe coffee?" Mohamed said, snapping his fingers at one of the young men who lingered in the outer office.

"Tea would be lovely," Penelope said, beaming at the brothers.

"So, shall we speak in English? I'm afraid my English is not so very good, maybe you would be more comfortable in another language, French perhaps? Do you speak Arabic?" Ahmed began.

"Of course, they don't speak Arabic," Mohamed said. "And you don't speak French," he hissed under his breath.

"Oh, English is good. And your English is perfect," Barbie said with an unctuous flattery that flowed easily off the tongue of an experienced English teacher that often had to inveigle private students with praise to get them to continue their lessons.

A kerfuffle ensued while tea was accepted, sugar added and cushions offered to 'the ladies'. The doorway filled with young men, whether assigned to the station, idle friends of the same or casual drop-ins, was unclear. The two policemen, Ahmed and Mohamed, did not chase any of them away, nor engage the services of any but the one who had brought tea. Mahmoud had to push his way into the now crowded office to stand behind his charges. Barbie noted that he, too, sipped a glass of tea.

"Now," Ahmed started.

"Please tell us what happened." Mohamed took out a pen and poised it above a pristine notepad.

Barbie looked at Penelope. "Serially, I think is the best way, not simultaneously as our new friends seem to do. Don't you think? I'll go first and if I miss anything, you can add, okay?"

Penelope nodded in agreement, clearly not comfortable with the arrangement of the men crowding in so close. "Mahmoud," she whispered. "Could we shut the door, maybe? The men…"

Mahmoud leapt to the door, pushed the young man in the front out and slammed the flimsy door with a 'crash'.

"Now, I shall tell you everything from the beginning. If I'm going too fast, let me know and I'll repeat or slow down. First of all, after dinner and the dancing, I got the idea to go for a swim. I love to swim and these pools are so special. I know that Penelope here is not so fond of swimming, but it doesn't look good for a woman to be seen going alone, so I talked her into it. Not that she needed a lot of persuasion, but she was a wee bit reluctant. Got this all so far??" Barbie cocked her head while she drew breath. Not waiting for a reply, she barreled on.

She gave so much information in the details that the lack of any real information was covered up. She gushed, she made asides, she told stories of what happened to her elsewhere in Egypt, all at breakneck speed. At the end of a fifteen-minute monologue, with no breaks, she announced. "And that's all I know. How about you, Penelope, anything to add?

The other four people in the office looked at Barbie in silence. Mohammed had only a few notes on his pad, Ahmed sat with his mouth open and Mahmoud stood in awe of Barbie's verbal prowess, at least in the amount she had to say. Penelope smirked in enjoyment at the response to Barbie's run-on commentary and Barbie sat, grinning and pleased with herself. "Well, if you have no other questions, we will be off. Chariot, my good man," she turned to Mahmoud.

Ahmed found his tongue first. "We need to check a few facts, just a few facts..."

"Yes, here, just when you find the floating body. What did you say?" Mohamed asked.

"Oh, I thought you took notes on everything? Well, Penelope 'found' the floating object, but I was the one who identified it. We were together. That is all, it's very simple. Do I need to repeat everything?" Barbie sat up very straight, bent down to pick up her bag from the floor where she had placed it and prepared to stand.

The door behind Barbie opened wider and a shadowy figure could be seen among the young men. He was dressed in a black uniform of the Egyptian police, now rarely seen in public. A crisp black wool felt beret sat jauntily on the side of his head, pulled down low over one eye. A dark complexion could not hide a very handsome trim mustache, riding above slightly parted lips that showed even white teeth, good enough for a toothbrush commercial.

The figure stepped into the light of the room and Barbie stared, her mouth opening in an astonished 'O'.

Barbie stood and faced the newcomer. She opened her mouth to say something, but only a silent 'David' came out.

He cocked his head, gave a tiny smile and lifted his right eyebrow slightly in a gesture that Barbie recognized well. A tiny flick of the head to indicate 'no' completed the communication, not recognizable by anyone else as conveying any meaning. But it conveyed worlds to Barbie.

So, this is where he disappeared to, she thought. She nodded her head in greeting. "Hello," she said.

Chapter Five: The Disappeared Reappear

With a nod of his head, David quietly dismissed the two plain clothes policemen and Mahmoud. He closed the door behind their retreating figures. He smiled at the two women sitting stunned in their chairs. Penelope, not understanding, sat open-mouthed.

"You do realize that you are being overheard, so you must tell the truth." David paused and stared at them both. "Do not reveal me," he continued in the barest of whispers.

"And this, the redoubtable Penelope Watson? And our very own Barbie Falcon." He smiled at them, but Penelope remained puzzled. She looked at Barbie for some answers, but Barbie was giving nothing away, yet.

"But sir," Barbie addressed him cheekily. "We have answered these questions, twice as a matter of fact. What more can we tell you? What can you tell us?"

David bent down to address Barbie, "I would like to have it all in order, nothing left out. As I see it, it was like this." He began to tell both of them their story, from the beginning of the ill-fated visit to the pool. As he carefully went over all their movements, he looked at them for confirmation. He paused often for them to assent or correct him, but he seemed to have absorbed the facts as related by Barbie quite well. The retelling took only one third the time that it had taken Barbie. In the meantime, he took concise notes, point by point, leaving nothing of importance out.

When he finished, he looked up at them and smiled broadly, "Anything else?"

Barbie looked at David and blurted out, "How did he die, did he drown?"

"Ah," David prevaricated. "All of this needs to be looked into. He was certainly very wet and very dead when taken from the pool, but that is all we know. Presumably, he drowned."

"Presumably?" Penelope asked. "Don't you know? When will you know for sure? But how else could he have die......." Penelope's voice faded away. In all the excitement, she had forgotten that a man was dead, someone who had been alive only hours before. And someone that they knew, someone they had seen and listened to, someone who knew and was known by dozens of people on their tour.

"So, are we finally done here?" Barbie asked, getting to her feet. She stood extremely close to David, violating the personal space rules of an American, but not one who just two months before had been helplessly in love with this man. As an Egyptian, the space was not the issue; the gender was. But he too, did not move away from the closeness.

"Yes, we are done, for now. I will personally escort you back to your hotel. You came with your guide, Mahmoud?" David was composed and suave.

Unctuous, Barbie thought. So sure of himself. He caught me unawares, but he must have known for at least a few minutes, if not longer. How did he know the whole story? Was he listening outside the room? Ah, what about that remark he made that all of our words were being listened to? I need to get him alone. I need to get him to explain a lot of things. A whole lot of things. Like why is he here? Why he left etc. etc. But Barbie also knew that he could be very closemouthed when it was what he wanted.

"Yes, we are done, if you say so. How can we get in touch with you again if we remember anything else? Will you be here, or where?" Barbie tried to bat her eyelashes, but he chuckled at her.

"I will not let you go so easily. I will give you my card. If you need me, you can call this number." He wrote a number on the back of the card and handed it to Barbie.

By this time, they had separated a few feet and were moving towards the door, which opened magically moments before they reached it, as if it were on an automatic door hinge; or someone was listening outside for their movements. They were greeted in the brightly lit front office by Ahmed and Mohamed, the police brothers, and Mahmoud. The young man who fetched the tea lingered and collected tea glasses and another group of young men moved back in a pack, curious hangers-on. Not much to do in a small town like this at this time of the morning. Since the Revolution, the video parlors were carefully watched for idle young men and the shopkeepers, although not forbidden, shied away from selling them liquor. Life had become even more boring in the small towns of Egypt like Siwa. But tonight had been an exception. Sudden death was like a shot of uppers to the small group of bored young men. Something had happened in their town, something that would bring them out of their ennui and excite them once again. They stared openly at the two women, and especially watched the handsome new police chief and his actions towards them.

David accompanied them out to the car, and watched as they stuffed themselves into the small Lada. When he realized that there was no room for him, and that they were safe in the hands of Mahmoud, he leaned into the car and extended his apologies. "I'm sorry, there is no room for me. But I will see you again. If you think of anything, anything at all, do not hesitate to call. You have my number."

Barbie looked up at him from her place pushed against the side window. "Yes, yes, I have your number and what is your position here?"

"Ah, I see that I need to introduce myself. I am Ali Rafiq, Chief of Police in Siwa. I am deeply involved in anything that is unusual here in our little city on the edge of the world. So, you can always ask for my assistance with whatever you need. Please, do call."

He stood and waved goodbye to them as they drove away. Barbie's last sight of him was standing in front of the lonely Police Station with a chorus behind him, who were waiting for the right moment to ask as one. "Who is this man? Where did he come from? What is he doing here?"

Barbie took the card and tried to read the name in Arabic. She could make out most of it and, after being told what the police officer's name was, she could then see it on the card. She turned the card over and looked at the phone number on the back. A faint prick of uneasiness arose.

"Barbie," Penelope began. "What was that all about?"

"Ah, my Dear Watson. Perhaps the answer comes with more investigation." She leaned forward and addressed Mahmoud. "Mahmoud, can you tell me anything about this Ali Rafiq?"

"Oh yes," he answered, turning around in his seat to address them. "He is our new Chief of Police. He came here after the Revolution, the 18 days. And he was very good. We feel so lucky to have him. He is not from here, so he is less corrupt. And he is so, how do you say, sophisticated. He has been overseas, you know. He has studied in London. The very best police techniques. And he is a kind and good man. I know that he will take care of all of this very well. Very well. It is always a difficult thing for a person not from here to die in Siwa. And a foreigner, from the US, oh my, this is a terrible thing. But I have full confidence in him to make everything right. You can trust him." He turned forward again.

"See, that's who he is, an outsider from somewhere else in Egypt. The new chief of Police, who solves all problems." Barbie smiled at Penelope.

"But don't you know him?" Penelope asked. "You..."

"Let's not discuss these unpleasant things now," Barbie dug her elbow into Penelope's ample waist. "Let's think of getting to bed. Ah, here is our street, I recognize it by the absence of any street lights."

They pulled up into the driveway and were deposited at the front door of the reception area. Mahmoud jumped out and opened the back door for the weary women. "I am so sorry you have been bothered so much. Please have a good night's rest. We will have to discuss what to do in the morning. This has never happened to me," he stood and shook his head sadly.

Barbie took pity on him. She stood close and said gently, "It's not your fault. Don't worry, all will be well. Dead bodies are just former people. All will come right."

Penelope wrinkled her nose at Barbie's words, "What's that supposed to mean? 'Dead bodies are just former people.' Have you gone bonkers?"

"Maybe," Barbie hissed back. "But he seems new to this, whereas yours truly has had some experience in the department of dead bodies who are former friends. I'm tired, I'm confused. And now I'm cold." She shivered in the cool night air.

"See you in the morning," she said to Mahmoud.

"Good night. Good night," he responded with a hangdog look.

"Barbie," Penelope began. "Who is this Ali Rafie guy?"

"Ali Rafiq, and keep your voice down. I'll tell you when we are alone." They walked as quietly as they could along the meandering walkway to their room.

Barbie fumbled with the lock, cursed the dim light and then found Mitch and Rachel by her side. Penelope shook her head, "You'd better come in. There have been complications."

Mitch had arrived with Barbie and Penelope in August of the previous year and shared in the orientation of the new crop of academics joining AUE. Rachel had arrived a few weeks later and they had all become good friends. Mitch was a wonderful help to the girls. His field was Arabic culture and history and his command of both classical and local Arabic was a godsend for the three challenged women. Mitch was drop dead handsome with twinkling blue eyes, blond hair and a square-jawed face. He sported a great set of abs and Barbie for one, was amazed at his physical strength. She dared not intrude to ask Rachel if he was also one with a lot of endurance, but suspected he was. He, of course, thought that he was not handsome, or strong or masculine enough, being only five feet four inches tall and a lightweight 160 pounds.

Rachel knew he was gorgeously handsome, but it did no good to tell Mitch that. Height and brawn he would never have, and these were the things he craved. He also was saddled with an unpronounceable Polish name, so he was affectionately known as Mitch P. Quiet and dependable, unflappable in the face of any disaster, he had been their rock during the chaos of the Revolution. If anyone knew what to do, it was he. He had ideas, knowledge of the Cairene culture and an unerring sense of what was important, and what wasn't. His wife Rachel was the opposite. Barbie thought as she watched them together, that the old saying about opposites attract, was true for them. The quieter Mitch got, the louder and more talkative Rachel became. Subject to attacks of morose depression, Rachel simply acknowledged his unhappiness, but pretended that all was well and jollied him out of his bad moods. She was the ideal of an Egyptian beauty, and had attracted far too much attention for her taste from the men of Zamalek, the neighborhood where they lived in Cairo. She was buxom, and pleasantly rounded fore and aft. She thought she was 'fat', but the men of Egypt thought she was beautiful and showed their appreciation of her charms, much to Rachel's dismay. Mitch laughed at her. She sported a frizzy halo of brown hair, similar to that of many Egyptian women and the sight of this hair, unbridled and not hidden under the headscarf of most Egyptian women, added to her charms. The attention paid to Rachel by the locals was a constant source of unhappiness for her. Mitch's presence at her side seemed not to have any effect on the behavior of the men, unless and until Mitch told them off in colorful local dialect. Inside, with her friends, Rachel laughed and was jolly, but outside, she acted like a different woman. This situation had become worse lately, and Barbie felt she needed this opportunity to get out and hang out with a group of expats in an attempt to deflect the unpleasantness of the harassment.

The four entered the room and Mitch and Rachel sat on the beds after Barbie and Penelope had swooped up their hastily scattered clothes and hung up wet swimsuits. Barbie went to the front window and checked to make sure it was tightly closed. She also checked to make sure no one was lurking outside, attempting to eavesdrop.

As soon as they felt secure, Mitch whipped out a bottle of whiskey from under his light jacket. "Glasses?"

Penelope disappeared into the bathroom and came out holding one scratched water glass aloft. "A treasure, but only one."

As Mitch poured a generous dollop in the ancient glass, Barbie asked, "Where did you get it?"

Mitch gave her a sideways look, "Who has whiskey, always?"

"Whoa, don't tell me you have been talking with Cornelius? And of course he brought whiskey with him. Oh well, I guess he figures that good stuff is hard to come by in Siwa. Locally made stuff is vile, and dangerous, and the imported stuff is probably VERY pricey. So, have you been talking with him? What does he think?"

"You first, what happened at the police station?" Mitch asked, contemplating the full glass of whiskey. He took a small sip.

"You don't drink, Mitch. What's up?" Barbie continued.

"Tonight, I do. What did the police say, what do they think?"

"Well, I told them EXACTLY what happened, in detail. But just the finding of the body. Nothing about the relationships around here, nothing that could make anyone look bad, even Him."

"You should have heard her," Penelope started to laugh. "She snowballed them all. She talked for fifteen minutes straight. She told them about the decision to go swimming, in detail…" Penelope went on to fill in Mitch and Rachel on the encounter at the Police Station.

Barbie stared at the glass as it came around to her. Suddenly she laughed and interrupted Penelope's telling. "Sorry, Penelope, just remembering the last time I drank out of a glass like this. Freshman year in college. Someone had a bottle of cooking brandy, half-full and we had only one glass, like this. It could have been a twin, or at least a cousin. And there was a handsome student sitting in the back of the group. I went to sit on the bed next to him, then we were holding hands and the next thing, the people I came with were leaving. Just like that. Well, I got pregnant, we got married and almost precisely a year later, he left. It took him seven years to get around to a divorce, and only because he found someone else to marry. My son, sweet, misguided kid, decided at the age of thirteen that he wanted to live with his dad. How can you tell a kid that possession of good looks, the right equipment and a blustering tone do not a man make? So, I lost my second man. And it all started with passing around a glass of liquor."

"Oh, Barbie, that's where your son came from? I'm so sorry to hear that," Penelope commiserated.

"Don't be sorry; he's a good kid. We're in touch, no bad feelings, only that I had no reason to stay at home anymore. So I started traveling. It's been a great life. But this," she gestured at the glass she held in her hand, "brought back memories." She handed the untouched glass to Mitch.

"No, no, I don't drink. I remembered why." He passed the glass onto Penelope and Rachel who gladly slurped some more.

"So that was all?" Mitch asked.

"Oh, except the Chief of Police gave Barbie his card. Ali Whatshisname."

"His card says Ali Rafiq. He said the usual, 'If you need to contact me etc. etc.' And then we came back. Poor Mahmoud is upset though. He doesn't know what to do with dead bodies!" Barbie laughed.

Mitch declined to join the laughter. "Oh, you might be interested in what Cornelius said," Mitch rejoined.

"Yes, what does our elder statesman have to say?" Penelope and Barbie both leaned closer. "Did you pump him for information?" Penelope asked.

"You could look at it that way. I felt as though we needed some perspective other than 'the girls screaming at the pool' version. He was agitated, and not very communicative. But he did slip that he thought the death was more than it looked on the surface. In other words, that someone drowned him, not that he drowned himself. He had little to say, having no evidence to support that idea, but that's when he gave me the bottle of whiskey. I am not sure what that was for, but it opens lips. And makes those who drink it get careless. I'll keep it and see if I can find others to talk to me." He smiled at them all.

"Why would Cornelius Smythe think that someone drowned Thurman Hall?" Penelope asked.

The three others looked at her. "He hated everyone," Rachel said.

"Everyone hated him," Barbie added.

"And it was public knowledge that he picked fights with his colleagues, his friends, his wives, his enemies. Everyone HATED Thurman Hall. There are so many people who wanted to kill him that looking for a motive is a very easy task. If this was an accidental death, everyone will be surprised. The real question is; who got to him first?"

Mitch and Rachel left then and Penelope and Barbie prepared for bed. When they were tucked in, with the light off, Penelope asked. "So, who is the Ali Rafie guy? You have been acting weird ever since you met him."

"Ali Rafiq is David. My David of Dawood's Antique shop. This is where he disappeared to. And the phone number he gave me is the same one he gave me over three months ago when I first met him. I had his phone number all along. Three months and I could have called him any time. And now, he shows up here. As the Chief of Police!"

Chapter Six: Why?

"So, he's come back to life!" Penelope stated.

"He never died; he just disappeared. Went into hiding is more like it."

"Disappeared, huh? He might as well have died. And he left you in the lurch. Are you ready to forgive him?" Penelope poked at Barbie's wound.

"I can't forgive him for something that he hasn't done. I mean, when he left, he let me know that he couldn't be contacted and that his life would be in danger. And with all the other events happening around us, I didn't have time to 'look' for him. I was afraid to ask anyone. I did sort of ask Cornelius once, but he didn't know anything, or at least he told me he knew nothing. You remember that time we went to the Khan, how I kept wandering around, trying to find the 'leather shop'. Well, it wasn't the leather shop I was looking for, but if I had found the leather shop, David's store was only three shops away. I was 'guided' there. But the Khan el Khalili is an amazing warren of alleys and shops and so I couldn't find it again."

"And I thought you wanted a leather jacket! You cheat." Penelope laughed.

"I did and I do, but I thought if I could find the shop, someone might be able to tell me where he was or how to contact him. And now, I know that he never gave up this phone number. How to hide in plain sight!"

"So how did you two communicate this evening? I mean, I was there with you all the time, I didn't hear you guys say anything. I just sensed something weird," Penelope quizzed Barbie.

Barbie chortled, "Little things with his eyebrows, a nod, a shake of the head, a little lowering of the eyelid. Oh, he is very good at that stuff. He has a whole language when he does that stuff. He told me not to let on to anyone that it was him or that we knew each other. Obviously the 'Ali Rafiq' is a disguise. I wonder if he's been here all this time? How did he get here? Did he know someone? And really, he could have called me!"

"But as you pointed out, you had his phone number all along. Why didn't you try calling him?"

"I never thought of it. Not once. I thought he left the country."

"Siwa is as good as, don't you think? This place is soooooo back of the beyond. I think it makes a wonderful place to hide out. And being a policeman??? How did that happen?"

"You and me both want the answer to that question. I think it's a good disguise, change your name, your profession, your location. But you know, I really need to talk with him. I think he owes me some sort of explanation." Barbie reached for her phone.

Penelope reached her hand out, grabbed Barbie's phone and held it out of reach. "No! Has your number changed? He could have called anytime and he chose not to. Don't chase, don't act so eager. You need to cool it!"

"Says the woman who has had so much success with men!" Barbie lunged for her phone.

"Well, at least I don't have a string of failed relationships behind me. I have had a few men in my life, and I didn't hang onto them by 'chasing' them like a puppy. Don't call, let him call you! You are here now, he knows where you are, let him do the chasing." Penelope put the phone down.

Barbie rubbed her temples and said, "Headache! Oh, that whiskey was not a good idea."

"So, I have one good question for you. Why didn't he contact you? He just went."

Barbie picked up the phone. "Or said he went. Maybe he couldn't contact me!?"

"Or didn't want to. Maybe you were reading more into this relationship than there was?" Penelope twisted her lips in a semblance of pity.

"But he is here now. He is obviously in police uniform. People know him, he has a name, a profession. Somebody must know he's here. Someone must have arranged this out of the way place. But why? Why here? And why, in all of the places did he walk into my tour group?"

"Is that a mangled line from 'Casablanca'? 'Of all the gin joints, in all the towns, in all the world, she walks into mine...'" growled Penelope in a bad imitation of Humphrey Bogart. "Pretty lame. But I get the connection. He might have stayed lost forever if you hadn't found that body. Correction, if we hadn't found that body. But trust me, I'm right on this one. Let him contact you. You might put his disguise in jeopardy if you call. Let him chose the time and place."

Barbie laughed, though not wholeheartedly. "Tomorrow I'll ask Cornelius. He will find out if he doesn't know already. He must know, or know how to find out. Oh, I'm tired."

The two settled down and pretended to sleep by closing their eyes.

"Penelope," began Barbie again. "Do you think there is anything to what Mitch said? About someone doing him in?"

"Barbie, what's got into you? What makes you think that something is wrong? The man drowned. What are you trying to do, create something that isn't there?"

"Watson," Barbie started again.

"No, no don't go there. I am NOT your Watson and you are not Sherlock Holmes. You need to leave it right there."

"But Mitch is right, how could he drown? It's a pool for heaven's sake!" Barbie sat up and faced Penelope in the semi-darkness. "He wasn't swimming, he had his clothes on, didn't he?"

"Lots of ways to die, especially in a cold pool. Heart attack, stroke, drunk and fell in. Lost his balance and hit his head. Maybe he is a diabetic and had an insulin attack. Maybe he has a pacemaker and his battery wore out. I don't know. What makes you think it's murder?"

At the word, Barbie shivered. "So, you think it's murder, do you? You heard what Mitch said, no one liked him."

"You are trying to create something that isn't there."

"Am not! There is something there. Even if it was natural, it wasn't really natural was it? People don't go out to their hotel pool, fall in and drown. He could have been pushed."

"If everyone who hated their boss pushed them in the nearest swimming pool there would be no bosses left in the world. Everyone hates their boss." Penelope sat up too.

"Ok, Watson, we need to think. We need to not let others tell us what's what, we need to think about this. I don't trust anyone to get it right."

"Why do we need to think? Can't we let the cops do their jobs?"

Barbie snorted, "The cops in Siwa are number one, an antiquities dealer, and number two, a couple of brothers who think they are comedians. They can't think their way out of a glass jar."

"Mixing metaphors again. 'Think their way out of a paper bag.' What is it that you want us to think about?"

"David, or rather Ali Rafiq, asked us if we thought of anything else to contact him. So, what is it that we could think of..."

"So, you have an excuse to call him!"

"'Kill two birds with one stone?' Or have I got that one wrong too? What we need to do is to lay it all out and then think of anything else, or anything new, or anything..."

"With which to lure the handsome David, AKA Ali Rafiqi..."

"Rafiq, the pseudonym is Rafiq. I wonder what it means..."

"Okay, Sherlock, here goes. Who saw him last? When did we know for certain that he was alive?"

"My dear Watson. At dinner, that we know of. We saw him storm out after having some sort of altercation with someone at his table. Number one suspect is someone who was sitting with him."

"Cornelius Smythe, Mahmoud the guide, and some distinguished visitor. Name unknown. Hardly likely, don't you think? They sat on until after the dance show, so if they were going to push him in the pool, they needed to rush right out and catch him there and push him under. Not enough time. By the time we got there, he was cold, dead and cold."

"Ten minutes, fifteen minutes from the end of the show until we found him. That doesn't rule out anyone at the show, but it does make it a lot less likely. So, let's see, who wasn't at the show?"

Penelope counted silently on her fingers, staring at the ceiling, checking with the little camera screen she kept in her head. "Wow," she concluded. "We were all there except Thurman. He was number twenty in the group. And unless someone snuck out in the middle of the show..."

"That is a possibility. But the possibility that someone would have seen them is also very high. Remember, the dance show took place in the dining hall across the street from the hotel proper. And the pool is in the back of the right-hand wing of the hotel. To get there, you have to pass by the reception desk. So, we need to let Ali Rafiq, I mean David, know this. Also, there is the idea of someone hearing them. We aren't the only ones in the hotel, and although all of us were at the dance, maybe someone from one of the other rooms wasn't. Maybe they saw or heard something."

"Barbie, that is so obvious. I'm sure that he's thought of that."

"You've forgotten. David isn't a policeman. He may not know how to conduct an investigation."

"And you do?"

"Don't forget that I have read all of Sherlock Holmes, at least three times, Agatha Christie, all of them including the plays, Dorothy Sayers, Ngaio Marsh, Dashiell Hammet, Tony Hillerman, Sue Grafton, Dick Francis…"

"Okay, okay. But remember, they are not police, they are authors, make believe. We could use some professional advice here," Penelope grumbled.

"Okay, time of death. We can narrow it down to from the time he left the dance show until we found him. One and a quarter hours, maybe one and a half. How cold was his body?"

"Hey, you touched it, not me! But I think it was pretty dead. Cold dead."

"But the water was really cold as well, and that might have made the body go cold more quickly. But that is only if he drowned. He might have died somewhere else and been taken there?"

Penelope once again rolled her eyes in the dark at Barbie. "What are you thinking? How could anyone have taken a dead body to the pool? No, I think he died there, either in the pool or next to it. Smoking. Wasn't he smoking when you saw him?"

"Yes, he was smoking and that might have something to do with it. Sometimes people smoke because they see someone else smoking, or smell the smoke. So, maybe he went out there to smoke and someone joined him. Or maybe someone said 'Let's go have a smoke,' and Thurman said, 'I know where a good place is, no one will bother us because no one goes there at night except weird English teachers, and they are all at the dance show. So, we can have a good long smoking session without interference.' And that's what they did. And then things went wrong. Thurman had a heart attack and the person didn't notice. No, that's silly. Thurman insulted him and the person pushed him into the pool where he had a stroke. And the person ran away. Or maybe it was after they smoked and the person left and Thurman decided to go for a swim? No, no, he was fully clothed. He wouldn't do that. Penelope, what about it? Is this death suspicious or not? Penelope? Penelope?"

Penelope's answer was a soft snore

Chapter Seven: Hangover

Barbie woke with a start, her head pounding. She groaned, turned over, and tried to ignore the shower noises from the bathroom. Do I have a hangover, she asked herself? I didn't drink that much and I wasn't drunk or even impaired when I finally fell asleep. She reached for her glass to get a drink of water, but it was empty. Maybe that's why she had a headache. No water, too much thinking and too much thrashing about in her bed.

Penelope burst from the bathroom and shouted at Barbie, "Don't want to miss breakfast. It's over at nine and it's 8:45 now."

Barbie dressed hurriedly while Penelope gathered her things and checked her phone to see if she had any email. After the terrifying 18 days of the Egyptian Revolution, Penelope had insisted upon getting a smart phone that could also get email. She reasoned that even if the government shut off their access again, a simple phone was no longer good enough for such an adventurous English teacher as she. The phone gave her a sense of safety, false though it may be, but she felt better able to handle the stress the outside world imposed upon her if she could occasionally access her emails. The small hotel in Siwa had remarkably good wi-fi connection and it was free!! Unheard of, Penelope remarked when she was told that she could access her phone's system in her room.

Barbie declared herself ready as she finger combed her wild curly blonde locks as they dashed out the door. Arriving in plenty of time, this was Egypt after all, they filled their plates from the buffet table. Barbie favored the fruits, Penelope the breads. They found seats at the table with Rachel who was nursing another cup of tea. Mitch had gone back to his room to 'work'.

"Oomph, I have a headache," Barbie said, gulping down a large glass of sugary water that was labeled 'orange juice'. "Maybe this will help. You, Rachel, no hangover?"

"No, but not a good nights' sleep. Every single sound outside caused me to sit up and pay attention. Mitch slept like a log, as always. In here," she indicated the dining room, "has been buzzing with your trip to the police station as well as the news of the demise of our dearly departed friend." She sat up and looked around. Many sets of eyes were focused on their table, trying to figure out the conversation this morning.

"Why don't I get up and make an announcement? Just let everyone know what happened and how it went. Maybe I'll even let slip a little nugget about long lost loves. Maybe even I could give a blow-by-blow description of…" Barbie halted as Penelope had an alarmed look on her face. "What?"

"Quiet! Have some respect. Announcement." Penelope murmured.

"May I have your attention," Mahmoud said, standing next to Cornelius Smythe. "We have an announcement." He turned to Cornelius.

"Humph, well, yes. As you may have heard, we have lost a colleague. Last night, our head of the History Department, Professor Thurman Hall, was found drowned. May god rest his soul. The hotel management are well in control of the situation and you may rest assured that there is no danger to anyone else. We are all very safe here in Siwa. In order to allow the hotel staff extra time this morning, we ask all of you to stay here, or outside your rooms until your room has been finished cleaning. Our departure for the day's activities will be slightly delayed, but we will soldier on with our program. So, instead of leaving at 9:30, we will depart at 11:00. Please enjoy your morning at leisure. And the dining room will remain open with coffee and tea until then."

"Please enjoy your time," Mahmoud said. "I can point the way to shopping or whatever, if you'd like."

The three women made faces at each other. "Really?" "Was that news?" "Delayed, not cancelled."

Rachel spied Mitch standing at the doorway and waved. Mitch greeted Cornelius as he passed him, but instead of joining the ladies, Mitch followed him out into the sunshine.

"I'm going to enjoy my coffee," Barbie muttered, rising to get another refill.

Rachel jumped up and headed out the door behind Mitch. Penelope noticed.

Barbie sat down with a contented sigh and began to slowly eat the rest of her breakfast. Penelope interrupted. "Cornelius, Mitch following Cornelius, Rachel following Mitch. I wonder what is up?"

"Yeah, I saw that too. We need to talk with Cornelius. At least we know where he is."

"We, we? Do you have a bird in your pocket? No, you can talk with Cornelius. I'm staying out of this." Penelope pouted.

"Penelope, you found him too. You went to the police station. You are involved whether you want to be or not. Ah, here comes Mitch, that was short. Mitch," Barbie waved him over.

"So, what did Cornelius say?" Barbie asked before Mitch could even sit down.

"Just a short talk about watching out for everyone. Not a consultation per se, but a questioning of what everyone is thinking and feeling. He felt a bit squeamish about canceling the tour, but seeing as how we have to stay here anyway, the best thing was to continue with the tour, keep everyone together here and see what comes of the police inquiry."

"Does Cornelius think the same way we do? That it is not so simple?"

"Precisely."

Barbie leaned forward to whisper to Mitch. "David," she said.

Mitch's eyebrows flew into his hairline and he cocked his head inquisitively at Barbie. "What?" he whispered back.

"David is here in Siwa. I met him last night." Barbie's lips curled into a tiny smile as she knew her revelation created more than a ripple of interest.

"Where? How? Does he have anything to do with this tragedy?" Mitch moved his chair closer in order to keep the conversation private.

Penelope looked at Mitch and smiled, "Not my secret to tell, don't look at me."

"Why are you telling me now?" Mitch demanded.

"Because you have Cornelius' ear and I think there is more than we know. Maybe he knows."

"Knows what? What could Cornelius know? I take it you asked him about David disappearing at the time. And what did he tell you?"

"That he didn't know. But I think he may know something now and pretty soon, if he has any dealing with the police, he will find out about David. Maybe he already knows."

"And what do the police know about David? Does this have anything to do with your visit to the police station last night? Did you know something about David last night, but you waited until this morning to tell me?"

Barbie looked ashamed. "I just wanted to… You see, David is the police."

Mitch's eyebrows once more reached into his hairline. "Police. He is the police."

Barbie took the card out of her pocket. "You see, he is Ali Rafiq, head of the Siwa Police Station."

Mitch snatched the card from Barbie and read the Arabic. "This is David? Are you sure?"

Barbie pursed her lips and gave him a smug smile. "I know him."

"I'll leave that alone. What's he doing here? He's not a real policeman, is he?"

"I can't imagine it. But if this was the place he managed to hide out, I'd say it was a good one. And after the Revolution, police were needed. Maybe he's a good one?"

"Wait, slow down. He questioned you last night? Do you think there is any connection between his disappearance and this? Surely not."

"Let's hope not, but it is all very strange. Now you know why I want to speak with Cornelius. Two things, really. One is David, the other is this. What do the police know that we don't? There is something strange about Thurman's death, isn't there?"

The conversation had been carried out in whispers, but as people left the dining room, bored with endless cups of coffee and sitting on dining room chairs, the friends had raised their voices slightly.

"I think this morning tells us that. Contrary to what we have been told about 'cleaning' our rooms, the police are actually searching our rooms." Mitch reported.

"No!" Penelope jumped up in alarm.

"Sit down." Mitch commanded. "There's nothing you can do about it and if anything is amiss, the hotel and," he looked at the card, "Ali Rafiq will answer for any disturbances."

"You knew Thurman Hall, Mitch. He was the head of your department, you can tell us about him," Penelope requested.

"Number one, he was not the head of my department. I'm in Arabic Studies, Arabic History, yes, but he was the head of the History Department. Occasionally I teach a class in that department. When I first got here, I used to go to all the departmental meetings so that I could learn who was who, and what was going on. I had no say, could ask no questions, but I did get some impressions, knew some dirt, heard some gossip."

"So, what gossip? What impressions?" Barbie and Penelope leaned in.

Rachel appeared in the doorway. "Oh, that's where you guys got to. The rest of them are off shopping or have gone across the way for a beer, or whatever. You do know that the police are here again?"

"David?" asked Barbie. "I mean Ali Rafiq, the head of the Siwa Police?" Barbie filled Rachel in briefly on the latest development regarding David and his whereabouts.

"So," Penelope intervened. "You were telling us about Thurman. Was he married, girlfriend, kids, where did he get his degree, what was his field etc. And why do we think someone drowned him."

The others looked at Penelope. This open use of the active form of 'drowned' was disturbing.

"Okay, here goes the short story. He's had two wives, no kids. He is a bit of a loner as far as his family is concerned. No one has ever even heard the word 'mother' or 'father' pass his lips. It's as if he were born of the primal universe. From what I can tell, he was only sociable to people who could help him with his career. He was blunt and unhelpful to others who he saw as beneath him or unable to advance his career. He was a bit of a slob, as you know. He was beginning to lose his hair and there are two things you can do when that happens. One, you can cut it short or shave it; give in to the inevitable. Or you can do a comb-over. He wasn't twenty-first century enough to do a short cut, so he combed his increasingly thin locks over his bald pate. Unbecoming, I thought. But he covered that up with his ubiquitous Panama hat. I'm sure you have seen him, walking around the campus, anywhere, with that wide-brimmed hat. It's not that it's silly, although that it is, but that in Egypt, no one wears hats.

"And he was a slob, or at least that what secretaries and others who worked with him in administrative capacities said. He claimed he knew where everything was, but his office was, pardon me porcine family, a pig sty. He left papers, books, reports, and leftover food everywhere. I only saw the mess through the doorway once, but boy, what a mess. People didn't dislike him because he is messy, forgetful, not organized and so forth but because he didn't have anything good to say about anybody. He didn't have close friends for that reason. Like, last night, he was sitting with Cornelius.

Professor Emeritus Smythe can help or hinder someone's career. Ipso facto, suck up to him. Mahmoud, the guide, is expendable. Do you see what I mean? Did you see the sneaky, overly-proud, smug nasty snake? That's what people thought of him. And some were scared of him, because he wielded power."

"Any other vices?" Barbie asked.

"Smoking, if you can call that a vice. He had lately moved to e-cigarettes because there was push back in his department about the smell. I guess he thought that the apple smell, or whatever, would mask the cigarette smoke. Actually, it's vapor, so it's not the same. Anyway, vices like chasing women, no. Drink, no more than any other expat in the university."

"Which doesn't say much. We all drink waaaaay too much. But did he do things while under the influence? Say or do anything that might get him fired, for example?" Penelope chimed in.

"You said he was proud; did he have reason to be? Definitive PhD thesis for example, groundbreaking book? Brilliantly-mentored grad students?" Barbie continued the questioning.

"No, to the first two, but maybe to the last one."

"Hobbies?" Rachel questioned.

"You mean did he play chess, collect stamps or play the violin? No, he was always listening to classical music, but my impression was that he didn't want people to think he favored rock and roll or country-western, so he always had his computer tuned to some Boston classical station. Or so I heard."

"How did he get to be HOD?" Barbie asked. "I mean, in our department we vote, so an unpopular person has little chance of becoming the head of the department. Did they actually vote for him?"

"They certainly didn't want him, but by some historical glitch, he was their only choice. There were a couple of guys retiring, so they were out. Some newly hired assistant professors, one up for tenure, so also not eligible. There were others, a few that were on terminal appointments, so again, not regular members of the department. So, he was the only choice. Fait accompli."

"Gosh, I hope that never happens to me," Barbie said. "Maybe academia isn't where I want to be. Sounds horrible."

"So, if someone was going to do him in, who would you say would do it?" Penelope asked.

"Winter Doern," Mitch answered without hesitation.

"Winter, who lives across from you guys in Hatshepsut's' Mansions? That Winter?" Barbie cried.

"She threatened him. She was denied tenure, and that is another issue whether it was fair or not, but she blamed it on him. And threatened him, in public, in a departmental meeting. She said that he should burn in hell for what he did to her and that if she had anything to do with it, he would be righteously punished. So, there you have it. Suspect number one."

"I heard about that too, but that was months ago. Why wait until now? And there is one little problem. She isn't here. She didn't come on this trip. She never comes on organized tours. I have heard her say so, many times. So, we know he was alive last evening after dinner, how could she have done it if she isn't here. Hired someone?"

"As I said," Mitch continued, "if you ask me, and you did, I would say that Winter Doern is your lady. She didn't like him, she hated him, had a reason and threatened him. What more could you want?"

"Motive does not make a murder," Barbie said with finality. "I need to talk with Cornelius."

Chapter Eight: A Visit to Professor Cornelius Smythe

Barbie tried to be inconspicuous as she tiptoed through the hotel grounds on her way to Prof Smythe's room. She was not certain he would be in, but she had checked at the hotel reception and discovered that the 'room cleaning' was finished, and so thought she might find him 'at home.' Maybe he is across the road having a beer, she thought. Barbie had joined him at the Marriott Hotel in Cairo on more than one occasion while he sipped his expensive tall glass of beer at the famed Cairene hotel on a Friday at noon.

Knocking gently at the door of room sixteen, she was answered with a faint, "Come."

Barbie cautiously opened the door and peeked in. The interior was darkened, but she saw Cornelius arise from his bed and face her. "Oh, my dear girl, how lovely to see you. Come in, come in."

Barbie came in, flipping the switch at the door to throw a pale aura over the room. She did not want to open the curtains and expose the visit to prying eyes.

"Good idea, keep this visit to ourselves. A splash, my dear?" Cornelius asked, pulling out a bottle of whiskey from a cupboard beside the bed.

"Oh, no, too early in the day, but thank you anyway. And thanks for the whiskey last night. It was much appreciated," Barbie replied.

"I'll have some, the start to the day was a bit stressful." Cornelius poured a sliver of whiskey into the twin of the much-used glass from their room. "But I am glad you are here. And once again, my dear girl, you have discovered a body." This last was in reference to the adventures Barbie had had during the Egyptian Revolution.

"Yes, unfortunately. Actually, it was my friend Penelope who found the body. I only turned it over and discovered who it was. And the last time, it was my cat, not me, who found the body." Barbie sat and remembered the moment a few months before when her cat, Badboy, had escaped from her apartment and run into the alleyway behind Hatshepsut's Mansions. There Barbie had found him, standing watch over the brutally murdered body of her student and assistant doorman. "This time it was totally different." Barbie thought that it might not have been totally different, but did not want to say this out loud; she wanted to avoid any bad luck. "I came today to ask if you knew anything about all this."

"About the dead or the living?" Cornelius smiled.

For a moment Barbie sat mesmerized. Did Cornelius know about David? Was this all entwined?

"I meant, did you want to know about the living Thurman Hall or the dead Thurman Hall? Were you planning on a memorial service and in need of fodder for a eulogy, or do you want to know how he died. You, of course, know where. Or at least where his body was found."

"Well, both actually. I think one leads to another. I think he died where he was found. It's a pretty obscure place, and seeing as how he was alive only a little over an hour before he was found, surely no one was sneaking around carrying a body from place to place. And, if someone was covering things up, his body probably wouldn't have been found until the morning if it hadn't been for my harebrained idea to go for a swim at such a late hour."

"Ah, you have suspicions about the manner in which he passed away."

"That's what I have come to ask. Do you think it was suicide?"

Cornelius leaned forward and in a sibilant whisper asked, "And why are you asking?"

Barbie sat still, not daring to breathe. "Because I'm a cat."

"Curiosity killed the cat," Professor Smythe intoned in stentorious tones.

"I'm not dead, yet."

Barbie waited while Cornelius leaned back onto the bed pillows which he had stacked up behind him.

"It was no suicide; of that I am sure. An angry man like Dr. Hall does not do himself in because someone doesn't like him or he begins to feel remorse for his past misdeeds. No, that kind of man, a disliked, but never remorseful or sorry man, never does away with himself. But others do. But could it have been an accident? We must surely hope for this. It will make all our lives easier."

"Most specifically mine. Remember, I found the body and so I feel I'm all mixed up in it. Which I don't like."

"But you admit you are curious."

"It was Mitch who said it. He said it out loud and that, I think, is the problem. Once you have it out there, then the idea grows and grows. And never really goes away. He said that lots of people would be happy, or relieved, that Thurman Hall was no more."

"Ah yes, quite a few. Life will be different for some. Too late for others, and others, who may believe that his passing will make a difference, will be sadly mistaken." Cornelius sipped his whiskey.

"Winter Doern."

"For her, it is too late. The deal is done. Tenure has been denied and I don't believe that anyone wants the decision taken back. It is a can of worms to reopen tenure decisions. There is a medieval aura that surrounds academic tenure. No open decisions, no looking again, no appeals. It is the last remaining bastion of medieval dons in the modern world. The process is changing in America, but this is not America. This is a tiny sliver of America on Egyptian soil, and unfortunately, the old-fashioned way of doing things has an appeal for the hidebound Egyptians and wayward academics. This place, this university, is a backwater. It is a romantic job, but surely not in the mainstream, unless you are in the fields of Egyptology, Arabic History or Middle Eastern Arts, Music and so forth. For the rest of you, it is just a playful interlude to a real job. And so those of us who are here are more often here because we couldn't make it at home. If we could, we would go there. As I said, for some, I would include myself, an Egyptologist, it is a good place, but for others; they are hiding out, running away."

"But Mitch said there were others, you have admitted it too. Students? Colleagues?"

"Stealing papers from a student is a nasty habit of professors. Young minds, lots of time to explore, to research, to find all the obscure nuggets of information. Time to talk, to argue and then time and energy to write papers. To have a professor, an experienced researcher, help a student with a paper is what we are asked to do. Thesis advisors need to add, to question, to help rewrite. That is our job. And when we see that the resulting paper is so much better due to our input, we naturally do not like the idea of giving the student all the credit. And besides, it is more likely to be placed in a better journal if it is couched in the right terms. And even a few well-chosen words to editors cannot help. Blind reviewing is not always so blind. And students do not often write really good papers that cannot be improved by their advisors. So the accusation of 'theft' of a paper is to be taken with a few grains of salt, or rather a whole shaker full of it. Don't believe all you hear in that regard.

"And colleagues who are chastened may need to be brought up short. Cries of 'uncollegiality' are rife in the academic world. Often there is a nugget of truth, or more than a nugget of truth. It is an ugly thing to call someone out, especially in public, but sometimes it needs to be done. And I'm afraid Thurman Hall did his share of calling out. He was not a kind man, and perhaps not always fair, but to ask for his resignation or to file a grievance is a serious matter. A very serious matter indeed! And again, circumstances are not always what they seem on the surface.

"Let us say that Thurman Hall had an accident. You know he was quite drunk at dinner, slurring his words, couldn't sit up straight. Angry, blind angry. And let us say that he went to the pool. It was dark. It was late. No one was there. Let us say that he met with an accident, tripped over a chair, fell and hit his head. Not being of sound mind, or body, he fell into the pool, unconscious. He couldn't breathe, he inhaled water instead of air, or was prevented from breathing, and he died. Then we can have an end to this story. Let us hope it is a short story."

Barbie sat quietly during this monologue, absorbing all the facts, nuances and prevarications thrown her way. "You told us that Siwa, the Shali, was destroyed by rain. And you mentioned hubris." She looked at Cornelius, but he only blinked innocently in return. "Let us hope it is a short story, and in fact, it has nothing to do with me. At the heart of it, it is not my business." She smiled at Cornelius.

"And now, on to another topic. What happened to our friend David, the antiquities dealer? He disappeared, but where to?" Barbie lifted her chin and directed these questions to Cornelius.

He met her gaze with one of confusion. He harrumphed twice and then said, "He disappeared, melted into the fabric of the Middle East."

"But he is here now." Barbie said.

"Here? Where? In Siwa?" Cornelius gaped at Barbie in a manner that showed he truly was astounded. "And how do you know this?"

"I met him at the Police Station last night. He is using an alias, Ali Rafiq, and he is currently the Head of the Siwa Police." Barbie smiled smugly. For once I have told Cornelius something that he did not know. What a twist.

"Are you sure? This is most unusual."

"It may say Ali Rafiq," Barbie said, handing the card over to Cornelius, "but believe me, it is David. In uniform no less."

Cornelius answered with a sly smile. "And does he look good in his police uniform?"

Barbie tried hard not to smile back, "Oh yes, quite good."

"Posing as a policeman, that is excellent. I would never have thought it of him. But in Siwa, how interesting. And you are sure of this?"

"Oh yes, although I was unable to speak with him, he definitely recognized me as well."

"And the phone number?" Cornelius had turned the card over and read the number on the back.

"I haven't tried it yet. I am assuming that there are 'ears' surrounding him most of the time. I thought I would wait until he called me. What I have to say is personal."

"Hiding in plain sight, what a clever idea."

"I wouldn't call Siwa in plain sight. It is off the beaten track and presumably that is why he is here." Barbie stopped and looked at Cornelius. "And you had no idea about this?"

"No, my dear, I didn't delve into it. I don't think anyone would torture an old man to find out things, but I like to keep knowledge on a 'need to know' basis. I knew he was safe, and that was all. I thought perhaps he had gone abroad. Much safer actually." Cornelius chuckled again and shook his head. "A slippery character for sure, to disappear like this. In Siwa…" Cornelius sunk his head onto his chest and steepled his fingers under his chin.

Barbie waited for a full minute, knowing that the older we get, the longer it takes us to figure things out, mainly because there are so many different 'things' that occur to us. "A penny for your thoughts?" she finally said.

"Who helped and how he might have come here. There are so many answers to those questions. If you want to know, you need to ask him. I cannot fathom this one. There are so many ways it could be answered."

Cornelius rose to his feet. "Well, we must get ready for our little excursion. We are scheduled for the Temple of Amun shortly. Oh, one more thing. Is he actually acting as a policeman? I mean, is he taking part in this investigation? I do not know the answer to whether he could be a policeman or not, but if he is in hiding, he must do something to earn his 'cover' so to speak."

"He did ask me to contact him if I had anything further to add. But I don't know if that was to be able to speak to me and give me his card, or whether that was for real." Barbie sighed with frustration.

"Never mind, we must be off to our latest appointment, which is perhaps the single most important monument in Siwa. Alexander the Great, you know. Off we go." He shooed Barbie out of his room.

Barbie softly retraced her steps past the reception area to go back to her room. When she came to the intersection of the path that led to the pool, she stopped. The small sign now seemed ominous. "Pool" it read with a small arrow pointing to the left down the shady path. As if a monstrous whirlpool pulled her, Barbie turned her footsteps down the path. As she got closer to the pool, she expected to find her path blocked, by police tape or a person. Nothing stopped her progress and soon she found herself once more at the pool.

The chairs and tables looked as though they had been rearranged by intrusive police, but the general scene was the same. In the corner, deep in shade was the lounge chair on which Thurman Hall reclined early last evening. A small table sat beside it. Barbie closed her eyes and tried to recall the details. There was less light then, but Barbie envisioned the recumbent Professor Hall, and a scattering of cigarette paraphernalia on the table bedside him. Perhaps there was also a book, or a phone, or some sort of square object on the table. She couldn't recall if there had been an ashtray or not, but she remembered vividly the flash of a white 'cancer stick' as he lifted it to his lips. And the smell. She remembered the smell, like a shisha pipe, sweet cloying fruit mixed with tobacco.

She approached the lounge chair and looked around. The small round table had been moved away from the chair and was now much closer to the gently lapping water of the haphazardly shaped pool. A high cement lip had been built around the natural spring and Barbie leaned over to see how high it was. She noticed that the bricks, at least on this part of the pool, had been built with a small cavity between the bricks and the cement of the pool deck. Perhaps it was to let the water drain, or a miscalculation by the builders, but it looked like a good place for garbage and nasty things. Barbie bent over to inspect the slight indentation and suddenly saw the white stick.

Without thinking, Barbie reached into the small depression to pick it up. It was a cigarette, but a mighty strange one. It was not made of paper, but of hard metal or plastic. Barbie had heard of this new type of cigarette, but not being a smoker, and one who disliked the smoke, she had never actually seen one this close before. As she looked at the e-cigarette in her hand, she realized that this is what she had seen the evening before. Now that she thought about it, the tip, the smoke, all seemed strange, like a parody of a man smoking a cigarette.

Then the folly of her strange search in the gutter outside the pool, the touching, the holding of this object that had belonged to a man now dead came to her. This was missed by a police search, or perhaps the police had not searched far at all. If they thought it was an accident, then they had looked around, moved the tables and chairs, perhaps taken away anything here that belonged to Professor Hall, but they had not conducted a thorough Sherlockian Holmes (or was it Sherlock Holmesian) type of search.

Barbie looked around. No one was here, no one had seen her touch the e-cigarette. Hastily she tossed it back where she had found it. Maybe it didn't belong to the dead man. Maybe it belonged to someone else. It could have been there for days, or weeks. And so what if it had been Prof Hall's? What did that mean?

She threw her head back, and clapped her hands together in a gesture of wiping away dirt or the dramatic gesture of wiping her hands of the matter. A strange sticky substance clung to her fingers where she had touched the e-cigarette. She dipped her hands into the pool and scooped up a handful of water. She rubbed it over her hands and let it fall back into the pool. She repeated the gesture for good measure, then walked away.

Chapter Nine: A Visit to the Temple of Amun

"It was in the year 525 BCE that the Persian king Cambyses, the son of Cyrus, invaded Egypt and put an end to the 26th Dynasty. It was while Cambyses was in Egypt that he decided to expand his empire by sending three armies to conquer Ethiopia, Carthage and the oasis of Amun, present day Siwa. The first campaign was a total disaster. The second was also a failure because of allies who refused to fight. The Phoenicians saw the Carthaginians as brothers or cousins and refused the alliance against them.

"It is not much of a stretch of the imagination to see why someone might covet Ethiopia and especially Carthage, but Siwa? It is speculated that Cambyses was angered that the Oracle of Amun had predicted failure and a tragic end to Cambyses' Egyptian adventure. To prove the oracle wrong, he launched a campaign. Now, most of the information we have is from Herodotus, so consider the source. It was said that Cambyses arrived at Thebes with a force of 50,000 soldiers bent on revenge. After seven days they reached the Kharga Oasis, directly opposite Thebes in the desert. They again set out towards the Amun Oasis and, so the story goes, were halfway there when a huge desert dust storm overcame them. The soldiers were sitting down to their midday meal, and so the sand covered them completely. No trace was ever found of the soldiers, their camels and mounts or indeed, anything of the invading force. The priests of Amun rejoiced that their enemy had been vanquished and the prestige of the Oracle of the temple of Amun went up considerably.

"Now the details are bit in question, 50,000 men, at their midday meal, but the facts are undisputed, Cambyses disappeared with a large army in 524 BCE. Of course, the archeologists and treasure hunters have been looking ever since for a remnant of this expedition. Of the fact that a desert storm could bury an army, there is proof. In the year 1805, there was a caravan of some 2,000 people with their camels and trade goods coming from Darfur in Sudan to Asuit. They were overcome by a desert storm and were buried in this very same desert. Other tales of lost armies and caravans come to us from the great Siwan manuscript, a compilation of the history of Siwa. However, there is no further proof of other armies and caravans lost in the vast empty desert."

Cornelius paused and waited for the bus to stop. Then he turned to the bus load of AUE staff and faculty, "And now we have arrived at the Temple of Amun, the very temple that Cambyses wanted to destroy and the very temple visited by Alexander the Great himself. Today you may stand at the very spot where he stood 2300 years ago. I will tell you more as we climb the hill to visit this incredibly important temple. Watch your step!" He stood, placed a well-kept but gently used Panama hat over his sparse white hair, gripped his cane with a stranglehold and descended at the head of his own modern warriors.

Out of the windows as they awaited their turn to climb down from the bus, Barbie and Penelope saw the village girls standing at the ready with trinkets for sale. Bracelets made from colored shells and gaudy string, handmade dolls, miniature baskets like the ones in their own kitchens were thrust at all those who descended. When the tourists had made their way through the scrum of little girls, the young boys approached. "Mister, madam, postcards?" This was accompanied with an out thrust arm and then a quick 'snap' that sent the package of twenty or thirty postcards folded together into a fluttering downward cascade that was immediately caught by the wind. The cacophony of the screaming children was embraced by some and sent others screaming to the entrance to the Temple complex.

"Ladies and gentlemen, this way please. The children will not follow us; I will forbid it." Mahmoud shouted from a short way off, directly underneath the dramatic rock where the Temple of Amun had been built centuries before. He shouted to the children in the local dialect and they scattered, only to regroup some ways off.

The group drifted towards Mahmoud and Cornelius. Normally, Mahmoud would have done the lecturing himself, being a qualified guide and quite knowledgeable. But Cornelius was an Egyptologist and had asked to take on the guiding duties for this most important site himself. One lone girl, the picture of sweetness, sidled up to Cornelius and softly tried to cajole him. It didn't work. "Imshee," he hissed. "Go away." She turned, squared her shoulders and sauntered to join her friends, tossing her head as if she hadn't a care in the world. She'll be back, thought Barbie.

The group from AUE gathered with Mahmoud and Cornelius at the beginning of the steep sloping entrance to the monument. Cornelius turned to face his group. "The Oracle at Amun was well-known to Cambyses, and through the next few centuries, many more famous persons had their fortunes told here. Athletes, poets and generals all had good fortune confirmed by the Oracle and so its fame grew. By the time of Alexander, the Oracle of Amun was truly one of the most well-known, and feared, oracles in the Greek world. In fact, it was better trusted than the Oracle of Delphi and temples to Amun cropped up in many Greek towns, trading on this famous temple. Suffice it to say, the very superstitious Alexander simply had to come here. He believed in Oracles, and the prayers, presents and visits he made to the various gods and temples reflected this. He needed to hedge his bets at every turn.

"He came here to Egypt in 333 BCE after conquering Syria and Palestine. He conquered Egypt easily, as the Persian Satrap surrendered Memphis without a fight, handing Alexander the garrison and the treasury. The Egyptians welcomed him with joy as the great deliverer from the Persians. He made sacrifices in all the important temples and showed great respect to the gods of Egypt. This characteristic of Alexander was, I believe, a sign of his great leadership abilities. So when did he come here? Why? And what was the result? These answers are to be found at the top of the hill." Cornelius looked up the slope and sighed. "Let us gather in the great courtyard, just outside the temple proper for the next part of the story."

Barbie looked up the walkway and put one foot in front of the other. Penelope groaned and said, "I'll see you up there."

Halfway up the slope Barbie stopped to take in the views, which were becoming grander and grander the higher she went. She had initially thought of Siwa as a depression in the ground, and hadn't thought about all the hills, and their advantages as viewpoints. She noticed another mini-bus pull up down below, which set the children off into another frenzy of calling to the would-be customers and snapping of packs of postcards. She couldn't see who they were, but presumed she would see them later. Siwa was, after all, a rather small town and the sights were limited.

As she reached the portal to the top of the courtyard, there appeared to be a bottleneck. Barbie waited her turn, and then realized that there were benches that lined the passageway through the gate. Two toothless men sporting dirty turbans and rumpled gallabeyas lounged on the rug covered benches. They had engaged both Mahmoud, their guide, and Mitch in conversation. They appeared to be gatekeepers and wanted the entrance fee due them. Mahmoud argued and became red in the face. Mitch tried to keep a smirk off his face as he listened to the reasons for payment from Mahmoud's tourists. Rachel stood beside Mitch and argued for paying the old men. "They haven't anything else to do. Why not give them a few pounds? We're rich, we can afford it."

Barbie listened to Mitch's answer. "But that is exactly what they are counting on. A little like a bribe to the men who stand guard over parked cars. Parking is free, but if you don't pay the parking boys, your car will have its tires slashed, its paint scratched or a window broken. Much cheaper to pay. That's their attitude."

Barbie was intrigued by what Mahmoud would do. Give the old men their bribe, or stand his ground? Just as he was about to give a final shout and push his way through, Cornelius appeared. A brief exchange with Mahmoud produced a 100-pound note from Cornelius' pocket. "We'll bill the University, my boy. These men would not dare to disrupt our tour now." He turned to his crowd, "Come all, come, come. Hear the story of the Temple of Amun."

As they entered the courtyard, a handful of the AUE tourists wandered off to take in the views from the parapet over the city of Siwa. Therefore, Cornelius waited a few minutes before commencing with the story of Alexander. He pointed out the various parts of the temple complex and how it had changed over the years. Near the gate was a mosque, made with palm logs for a ceiling. They were hundreds of years old, testament to the dryness of the desert. Also on the mostly flat top of the mound were other buildings, newer than the temple itself.

Finding most of his entourage reassembled, Cornelius resumed his story. "Alexander went to the present-day site of Alexandria and decided that it was to be 'his' city. Therefore, he founded it and named it Alexandria. He intended that this be his final resting place, and indeed, history tells us that a grand tomb was built there and that Alexander's body, hauled back from the Middle East where he died, was interred here. There are disputes of whether the body of Alexander lay there, but the tomb was certainly there. And it was a great spectacle.

"But at the same time, he wanted to visit the great Oracle of Amun in Siwa. What his real motives for doing so remain clouded in mystery. But he set off from Alexandria and followed the coastline to Marsa Matrouh. This is the very same route that we took to get here, although of course, we traveled much faster and in greater comfort. From there, he marched south into the desert, heading in a straight line towards Siwa, again, using the same route that we used. However, there was only a vague road and the desert winds blew strong, blowing sand over the faint tracks that were there. He got lost. There are two stories, one includes two snakes, and the other crows. The snake story is that they appeared before the column of soldiers and slithered across the sand to show the way. The other story, with the crows, is that the crows flew towards the oasis, slowing down and even sitting on the sand, waiting for the soldiers to continue on. In any case, in February of 332 BCE, Alexander reached the Oasis.

"Let me paint the scene for you. Imagine if you will, the people of the Oasis, learning that the new ruler of Egypt is approaching, come out of their houses, bringing fronds of the palm trees to wave, women ululating, crowds lining the roadways as the great man approached. Alexander was handsome, and young, and he was the conqueror. After paying his respects to the town officials, praying at the main town temple and offering sacrifices, as he had done in the temples lining the Nile, he made his way here, to the Temple of the God Amun. With his entourage, dressed in their finest, with the priests of the temple, also dressed in their priestly robes, they mounted the walkway, cheered by the local crowd. And processed to the temple."

Cornelius turned and led his group slowly across the courtyard, now strewn with rocks, pockmarked with the detritus of destroyed buildings and leavings of archaeological digs. They all needed to watch their steps as they meandered together towards the temple, which could be seen on the highest part of the hilltop. The stones had been finished with fine tools and were the work of fine craftsmen, a fact not lost on the group, who resolutely followed their erudite leader. Suddenly, Cornelius stopped.

He turned to his group. "You do realize, all of you, that today you will walk in the very footsteps of Alexander the Great. This is the only place where we can definitively say that we know exactly where he was. The day, the very place."

As they reached the temple entrance, all stopped and each person entered one by one, led by Cornelius. When they had all assembled inside, Cornelius stood off to the side, so that they could see the niche, still intact, where the statue of the god Amun would have ben placed. It was a rectangular temple, like so many of the temples they had seen before. In fact, this could have been an early Christian church, or for that matter, a later Christian church. Tall walls reaching to the open sky gave it a majestic appearance and a hush fell over the group. Barbie turned to see if all of their group had arrived. She gave a quick count, but stopped when she counted over twenty in the crowd around and behind her. But, she thought, we came with only twenty, and one is now gone, so who are these tourists? They look familiar…

"We are not exactly sure what Alexander asked the god," intoned Cornelius. "He wrote a letter to his mother in which he said that he would tell her in person when he next saw her, but sadly, that day never came. He died far from home, never again returning to Macedonia. We do know that he was very superstitious, or rather, he was a very religious man who believed in the gods and the oracles. It was said that he wanted to be seen as a god and that he tried hard to distance himself from his father Philip, not wanting to be seen as a man, a mere mortal, born of a man. He longed to be a real god. And of course, he wanted his fortune told."

A noise from the entrance stopped Cornelius in his telling of the story. A gaggle of young women pushed their way into the temple, followed by a tall, handsome figure dressed in a white bed sheet wrapped like a toga, an olive branch wreath wound with gold ribbons perched on his head of dark curls.

"I am Alexander the Great," he said in a mock BBC voice.

Snickers of surprise greeted him. More tourists squeezed in behind him. The king-like figure strode forward to the space immediately in front of the niche. He raised his head and preened, knocking his crown of olive askew. "I have come to consult the great oracle in the Temple of Amun," he intoned.

The crowd fell silent, even Cornelius smiled indulgently at the spectacle.

The ersatz Alexander threw his hands up and shouted, "Oh mighty Oracle, answer my question. Are you my father? Am I the son of Amun, the god?" He paused for effect.

A sound emanated from the direction of the niche. So silent as to barely be heard, but drawn out and insistent. "Yesssssss," came the reply, like a sibilant snake's hiss.

Alexander's hands dropped slightly and the actor hesitated. He turned around and quickly scanned the crowd. "Humph," he cleared his throat. Resuming, he again threw his hands into the air. "Oh, mighty Oracle of Amun, I have another question." He paused, but no sound came from the niche. He once more cleared his throat and took his position. "Will I be the conqueror of the world?" He threw his head back. The olive crown slipped to the dusty ground.

"Yes, but not for long." The sound unmistakably came from the empty niche.

Alexander stood for a second, then whipped around, causing his toga to slip off his shoulder. His eyes were wide and questioning, "Who said that?" he shouted in alarm.

"My dear boy," Cornelius stepped in. "Someone is having you on. They are playing a very old trick. There is a side passage that connects to the back of the niche. This isn't the only temple in Egypt equipped with a priest's passage. Look here," Cornelius gestured for the Alexander to come with him. The group followed and Cornelius pointed out, on the right-hand side, the entrance to a very narrow passage, only wide enough for a slender man to slip in between the inner and outer walls of the temple. The entrance was strewn with rubble, but the narrow opening looked passable.

"Quick, find out who did this!" 'Alexander' cried. One of his followers, a young man wearing black jeans and a black shirt, with a wild mane of hair, quickly volunteered. He scrambled over the rubble and gingerly entered the passage. The crowd took their places around the entrance, trying to see where he had gone. Within a few seconds, a shout was heard from within, "Gimme a flashlight, it's dark in here."

A short consultation produced a mobile phone with the light turned on, and the owner cautiously entered the tunnel, emerging without his phone. Murmurs of concern and surprise, mingled with some laughter could be heard among the crowd.

Barbie looked around at the crowd and felt a tingling sensation that she had seen these young people before. Where could they have come from? Cairo, presumably. But the few tourists who visited Egypt these days after the Revolution made tour group operators skittish about bringing clients to the land of pharaohs and the Arab Spring. Then she saw the three graduate students and realized that this was a graduate student group from AUE.

The young man in black emerged from the passage, covered in dust and looking like a Halloween mummy. He wore a look of puzzlement. "Did you see anyone come out?" he wheezed.

"No one." "There wasn't anyone." "You're the only one we've seen." The replies came from all around.

"If there was no one there, who gave the answers? Where was the priest?" Alexander asked. "A phantom prophecy."

Cornelius looked around and then questioned the intrepid explorer, "Are you sure? No one there? Then how…?"

Chapter Ten: Lunch at the Island Tea House

The group debouched from their bus at the trailhead. A sign pointed to 'Tea House and Pool' down a muddy walkway. A rim of salt lined the pathway. All around the trail were palm trees, slowly dying from too much salt. The fresh water lake had slowly become a salt water one and the salt leached into the land. Huge palm fronds hung from the trees, brown and dried. They crackled and snapped in the breeze, singing a death rattled song. Ahead the group could make out palm-thatched gazebos with cement benches and tables set within. Also, some lounge chairs sat off to the side, near the rim of a pool, now derelict. Beyond that, smoke ascended from a barbecue pit.

The twenty passengers crowded onto the path and tripped over themselves in an attempt to avoid the worst muddy parts. "Lunch," shouted Mahmoud. The group's pace picked up. Tourists always have time for meals, especially if they are included in the tour price.

"Good," Barbie said. "I'm starving. And we are later than usual, I'm sure, having left well over an hour later than normal."

"Food, glorious food," sang Penelope. "I see the mezzes table. Over there. Shall we grab a seat first and then load up, or go straight for the table?"

Rachel came up behind them and laughed. "There will be more than enough food, ladies. Let's get a good seat. Hah! I see Mitch has found the food first."

The women grabbed a four-person gazebo and draped their stuff over the chairs and table. There was little need to worry about theft in a place like this. They ran to join the crowd at the tables with salads and nibbles meant to ally the hunger pangs before the real food was served. The word 'mezz' was given to these and the plural was translated into English as mezzes. It was one of the first words a foreigner learned in Egypt, if he or she was interested in food.

Rachel ran after Mitch and Penelope hissed at Barbie, "So why did you do it?"

Barbie's head jerked around, her eyes wide and with pretend innocence. "Do what? What are you accusing me of doing?"

"Pretend to be the priest of Amun."

"Penelope, I did not do that! Humph!" Barbie looked her most offended.

"Of course, you did. Who else could have done that?" Penelope insisted.

"Penelope, look at me, look at my face." She pulled at Penelope to look at her directly. "I. Did. Not. Pretend. To. Be. The Priest. Of Amun. It wasn't me. You were there. I was in plain view of everyone the whole time. How could I have done that! Someone would have noticed, surely. I didn't do it."

"But you're the only one who could."

Barbie looked at Penelope and raised her right hand. "I had nothing to do with the whole spectacle. It wasn't me."

Penelope sighed, "Yeah, I guess so, if you say so. But…"

"But nothing. Let's go get something to eat." Barbie marched off.

Penelope finished, "Who did?"

Barbie thought as she walked to the mezzes table that of course Penelope would suspect her. Barbie had learned to throw her voice from her Dad. When her parents discovered that Barbie not only could sing, but had powerful lungs, her father had extended his magic trick repertoire to include ventriloquism and Barbie was his assistant. They were a great hit at her friends' birthday parties. But Barbie had gone on perfecting her skills to an extraordinary level. It was known only to her closest friends that Barbie could throw her voice to anywhere and everywhere she pleased. No wonder Penelope suspected her. But the appearance of the Alexander was a surprise to Barbie, not part of any plan of hers.

They got into line and Barbie hung back to check her phone, wanting to know if David had called. No phone calls. I should call him, thought Barbie. On the other hand, he knows where I am, what I'm doing and when would be the proper time to contact me. But I don't know about him.

Rachel had dipped into the hummus and had stuck a piece of bread in her mouth which impeded her announcement, "Look, look whoosh her." She swallowed the bread, coughed and then repeated herself. "Take a look at who has just arrived!"

Penelope laughed as the ersatz Alexander walked into the courtyard, black curls gently raised and fluffed by the wind. His entourage followed him, consisting of the three young women who had accompanied him to the temple and a gaggle of other young people. Included was the young man, still covered in white dust, who had tried to find the 'priest'.

"So, who is he?" Barbie asked.

Mitch looked and whispered, "Alexander, aka Schuyler Stanford, aka 'the wronged student'."

"Whoa," Barbie whispered. "Now I want to hear all about it."

When they were seated at the gazebo, separated from the rest of the party, Mitch launched into the story. "Schuyler was a graduate student of Thurman Hall's. He has been here a few years, comes from one of those moneyed families in New York that can afford to send their young folk off for a few years to do a European Tour or, in this case, at least three years in Cairo. Anyway, he had been doing some research, don't quite know the topic, but it was Thurman who put him onto it, gave him leads, people to talk to, books to read etc. Well, the young man actually produced something, something publishable. And so Thurman helped get it published. But when it came out, last month, guess whose name was on the paper?"

"Thurman stole his paper?" Barbie asked, remembering what Cornelius had said.

"That was the accusation, and it was made in a very public manner. Some of the other profs tried to talk to Schuyler, trying to explain to him that it was a normal thing for professors to put their names on papers that were substantially theirs. Schuyler's name was on the paper as second author, so it wasn't as if he was given no credit. But he certainly felt aggrieved. He filed a grievance against Thurman accusing him of theft. Schuyler was really, really pissed off, and let everyone know it. He seemed to be behind a move to make all the faculty and grad students take sides. Of course, the grad students supported him. They only heard his side of the story, and look at him! The Golden Boy, playing at being Alexander the Great. Now, how could you, if you were a student, vote against that, and in favor of the much-hated Thurman Hall? He even had the faculty split. It is never easy to tease out who contributed what in a paper, so how could any of us know the facts? It is not my department, I had no say in the matter, but I certainly knew all about the controversy. At the very least, I think that Thurman should not have sent the paper himself, put his name first, as it were. And the journal was a pretty low level one, not an 'A' journal. Thurman didn't need a publication in a journal like that, I shouldn't think. It couldn't have added to his CV or publication record. Unless he was just being mean, I think he should have given the damn publication to the student. It could be crucial to the student, getting into a PhD program, but peanuts for an academic like Thurman. Unless of course, his publication record is very thin. I don't know about that. But we all know what happens when you get tenure, you stop publishing. The number of Associate Professors swells the ranks of many institutions. The big push for the thesis, a job search and then the long six-year slog to tenure. It wears a body out. Maybe Thurman was at that point. Worn out, and needed a paper, any paper. Stealing a student paper is common. Sadly. So, there is the story."

"Wow," Barbie said. "Academia is that cutthroat? I had no idea. Hey, Penelope, let's stick with our MAs, jobs where people tell you what to do, no real research, nobody cares if you publish, just teach. But did it ever come to 'blows'?" Barbie turned again to Mitch.

"I was there at the meeting when it was openly discussed. It wasn't supposed to be, but Schuyler had made it so public that it couldn't easily be ignored. I kept my mouth shut, but Thurman did defend himself. He pointed out all I told you, about the research, the shaping of the paper, the theoretical position, all of this either given or greatly influenced by him. He made a very convincing case. But two people were dead set against him. One was Winter. She lit into him and called him lots of names. It wasn't very pretty. She also revisited her earlier denial of tenure and then went at Thurman. Called him unprofessional, said he should be dismissed from his position, dismissed from the university, debarred, but that's only for lawyers. Anyway, the last thing she said was that he 'ought to be shot.' He balked at that and asked her if she was going to pull the trigger. We were all taken aback. The other person who defended Schuyler was Lisbon. He has had issues with Thurman as well."

"How did you vote, Mitch?" Penelope asked.

"Oh, this wasn't a voting thing. And besides, I don't belong to that department, I couldn't vote even if I wanted to. I feel very strongly about the relationship between professors and graduate students. Students are due our care and we need to make sure that we are models of professional probity. Stealing material, especially among colleagues, is fraught with pits and potholes. Never easy, that's for sure. But I would not want to call out someone without more information, and that was not forthcoming. I kept my mouth firmly shut."

"But the system surely cheats young people, don't you think?" Rachel asked. "We ask the grad students to pay a lot of money and then they work for you, slogging hard work, and then to not give them credit, that's unfair." She turned aside to Penelope and Barbie. "I was working in the graduate student office when I met Mister Doctor P here. I heard a lot of gossip, and complaints and things that were unfair."

"But we can't really say about this case. And of course, now we will never know the truth. Thurman is dead," Mitch said with finality.

"And Schuyler, aka Alexander, is free to do what he wants with his papers in the future. He won't have to share any of it with Thurman, ever again." Barbie looked at Schuyler at a table on the far side of the courtyard, laughing with his three followers. "He is not sorry his supervisor is dead."

They finished their lunch, all but Penelope refusing dessert. The small group waited for Penelope, then wandered over to Cornelius' table, where he was holding forth on the history of the salt lakes of Siwa. He pointed to the small berm that had been created to keep the salt lake waters at bay around this small tea house. It was less than five years old and in that time, the waters had risen, threatening to flood the land. The pool that the tea house had been built next to had been destroyed by the salt water incursion. "Many of the fields of Siwa have been likewise threatened, forcing the inhabitants to go further out into the desert. Imagine if you will, an oasis in the desert, threatened by the rising water of its pools and lakes. Water everywhere, but too salty to drink. Ah, it is time to go, has everyone lunched? Good." Cornelius turned and started down the walkway, now churned to mud. The small group, swollen by the additional tourists, followed.

As they neared the roadway and the parked buses, Barbie watched as a car pulled up. It was painted black, and had a small gold and white shield on the side. With a sick feeling in her stomach, she recognized it as a police car. She watched as two men got out, one in plain clothes and one in the black uniform of the Egyptian police. The plain clothes policeman she recognized. It was one of the brothers. She couldn't remember which one. She put her head down and continued walking towards the bus.

The plains clothes policeman stood and scanned the crowd. Barbie tried to find a space on the opposite side of the crowd from him in which to walk. Hurry, she thought to her herself. If I can make it to the bus, I can avoid them. She pulled her loose scarf over her blonde curls.

"Miss Barbie, pardon me, Miss Barbie." The crowd of tourists parted as the policeman stopped in front of her. "Please Miss Barbie, come with us!"

Barbie faced them and stood her ground. "What, why? What do you want?"

"Please come with us to the police station. We need you to come with us now."

Barbie saw no smiles on the faces of the two men. She knew this was not a friendly request to come quietly to have a chat. There was something wrong. She turned to Cornelius and Mahmoud. They needed to protect her. Neither was to be found; they must have already got on the bus. The men stepped closer and the plainclothes man reached for her.

"No," she cried. "No, wait." She flipped her bag off her shoulder and dug into the the depths of the small knapsack. She found the slender rectangle and clutched it. "I need to make a phone call."

She turned her back to the men and quickly flipped through the phone numbers. "David, I do not give a shit who you are calling yourself these days. I do not care where you are and what you may be doing. I need to talk with you NOW!"

Chapter Eleven: A Visit to the Police Station II

David stood outside the police station as the car carrying Barbie pulled up to the front. Barbie noted that his expression, while attempting to be neutral, somber or stern, was instead sad. Damn right, she thought, you had better feel something. And this had better be good. She got out of the car by herself, but was immediately surrounded on both sides by police. They took care not to actually touch her, but were mighty close.

Barbie approached David and stood in front of him, looking directly into his face. "Ali Rafiq," she said. "What do you want, again?"

"Please," he pleaded, "come inside, have a cool drink and maybe you will feel better." He stepped back to let her enter first, and deflected the two police at her sides. He took command of the visitor. "Here, this way," he pointed to a door that had a shiny new brass plaque squarely attached in the center. "Please come to my office. Shai (tea)," he called over his shoulder. They proceeded into the office and he shut the door.

"Please sit down. And please accept my deepest apologies. The officers were rude, abrupt and out of line. They were supposed to ask you politely to come. But from your reaction on the phone, I think that was not the case? Am I right?"

Barbie was unable to immediately answer this question. David's tone was so conciliatory and Barbie knew that the police were more used to rounding up criminals than politely asking a witness to return to the office, and that he was right. "The least you could have done was telephone me, let me know before sending the goons. They were very impolite." Barbie looked at David and saw his eyebrows drawn together in thought and she felt the concern he had for her. "You made a mistake in the way you got me here. But," she paused for dramatic effect. "now I am here. I have obeyed your summons. And what can I do for you?" The brief phone call had quieted her fears of being kidnapped by the police and that it was David himself, in the guise of Ali Rafiq, who had asked that she once more come to the aid of the police.

"I wanted to see you again. I wanted to see your smile, listen to your voice, angry, sad, happy or any way, so I asked you to come." David's brilliant smile was accompanied by a twinkle in his eyes.

Barbie felt herself being drawn in even as she tried to keep a stern visage. She was a sucker for this kind of talk, but it was obvious that he was genuine in his declaration. If only she could resist a little more, she could keep the upper hand. She pursed her lips, and forced a haughty look onto her face. He laughed then, and she knew that she had failed. She smiled at him and shook her fist. "Heavy-handed, they were, not polite, you should chew them out," Barbie said between clenched teeth.

"I have already done so. Even now, they are being cautioned. Ah, here is the tea," he said in answer to a knock at the door. A tea tray with two glasses and a small dish with sugar cubes appeared in the hands of the driver of the police car that had come to pick up Barbie. Aha, she thought, he has already been punished. She knew that being the deliverer of tea was the lowest occupation, save that of toilet cleaner, in all of Egypt. She smiled sweetly at him and said, "Shukran." She hoped that her acknowledgement of him would be the icing on the cake of his humiliation. He dropped his eyes and quickly backed out of the room.

"I hope you don't mind tea; their coffee is atrocious. If I want coffee, I have to make it myself." David said, offering her the sugar dish. Barbie took one cube of sugar and watched David do the same. "Salut," he said raising his glass and slurping noisily in order to cool the hot tea. Barbie sipped more daintily.

After the ritual of the tea, Barbie felt calmer. "And now, Mr. Ali Rafiq, what can I do for you today?"

David in the persona of Ali Rafiq stated boldly. "We want to know what you and Dr. Thurman Hall argued about last evening."

"What? I didn't argue with him at all. I have almost barely spoken to him. I really don't know him, except by sight. I just saw him by the pool."

"And you said nothing to him? And he said nothing to you?" Ali Rafiq asked.

"I said something like, 'Smoking, how disgusting' and left."

"And did he say anything to you?"

"I don't think so, maybe he said something to my back as I left. But the message was conveyed that I didn't like his smoking and that I was leaving because of that. I didn't argue with him at all." Barbie looked at Ali Rafiq. "Who said I did?"

"There were reports of an argument at the pool. Your name was mentioned as you went to the pool; the front desk confirmed that. You did go to the pool, earlier, didn't you? Did you mention this in your account of last evening?"

"Number one, I did not argue with Thurman Hall. I did go to the pool, after we returned from climbing the Shali. I saw Professor Hall at the pool, I saw him smoking a cigarette, I smelled the smoke. I said something about smoking and then I immediately left. That is all there is to that. If he argued with someone else, that may be. You know he argued with everyone."

"Really?" Ali Rafiq said. "No one has mentioned this to us. We had no idea that he was that type of person!" He hesitated. "The report is that someone, a woman, was heard arguing with Professor Hall at the pool, shortly after you all returned from the trip to the Shali. As you were seen going there, it was assumed that this person must have been you. But now you tell me that you didn't argue with him, that the exchange was short, so it couldn't have been you. But who? Who else went to the pool?"

Barbie looked at David, for she had trouble thinking of him as Ali Rafiq, the policeman. At the moment, he was definitely Ali Rafiq. "It could have been almost anyone. The hotel is so full of bushes and trees, lights not working, nooks and crannies to slip into, that it would be extremely easy for someone to go there and not be seen. I am surprised that someone saw me. I didn't look for anyone else, but I didn't see anyone. That's not to say that someone else wasn't there at the pool. I stayed only a minute, less, and then left. I only saw Professor Hall because he was smoking, I saw the cigarette and the smoke. I didn't hear him at all. Someone else could have been there. Who told you that we argued?"

"A member of the staff. And the only thing she said was that it was a woman, the voices were raised, they spoke in English and she heard 'cigarette' and 'smoking', but didn't know what else was said. Her English is limited and she did not see who it was. She assumed it was you, because you had gone to the pool about the same time."

"Well, if that is all, then it might have been me. But I did NOT argue. I might have raised my voice; I do have a tendency to do that. My father smoked, and I hated it. I thought that it was a nasty thing. And so, I get agitated. But Dav…" she stopped as the object of her address put up his hand.

"Ali Rafiq, Captain of the Siwa Police Force. Please, do not forget!" he smiled at her, the same wide grin that she had fallen in love with.

"Yes, Captain. But you must realize that Dr. Thurman Hall was an argumentative man. Anyone can tell you that. In fact, there are people here who might be quite pleased to have him dead. And they may have argued with him about smoking and cigarettes too. He was a nasty piece of work. But I did not push him into the pool and drown him!"

David looked at her. "So, you must know that this was not an accident."

"Really! No, I am not surprised. Was it," she hesitated to say the word, "murder?"

"I will take you into my confidence. He did not die a natural death, nor was it an accident. We believe he was poisoned."

"Poisoned," Barbie squeaked. She thought of the food at the buffet table the night before. The spread of dishes laid out on the long table, everyone scooping huge portions of salad, meat, vegetables, grabbing at rolls, tiny plates of dessert. So many dishes, so many hands. She tried to envision what he had eaten, but as she had not sat near him, nor saw him in the buffet line, had no idea what he had eaten. "Dinner?" she asked.

"No, no one else was ill and there did not appear to be anything wrong with the food or with anyone else. No, we do not think it was dinner."

"Whew, then I guess I'm off the hook. I mean, what could I have done, way before dinner, to poison him? Because at dinner, he was fine." Barbie leaned forward, "Unless he had already been taken ill. You know, he was acting weirdly at dinner. I mean, he was arguing with others, even then. And that's when he left. We all stayed, to watch the dance show. So maybe someone put something in his glass? Or his food?"

"No, we don't think that. I mean, our doctor here, and he is not a trained forensic investigator, just a humble village doctor, said that it looked like nicotine poisoning."

"You mean, he smoked himself to death?" Barbie was startled. A novel way of going, she thought, but was it suicide? "But not an accident? Not accidently smoked himself to death? I thought that you had to smoke a lot and then you got lung cancer or emphysema, that is how you smoke yourself to death."

"No, not smoked himself to death, but too much nicotine, which is extremely difficult to get through regular cigarettes. No, you can easily get nicotine poisoning through an e-cigarette, though, which is what he was smoking. So, the cigarette he was smoking was an e-cigarette, wasn't it?"

"Yes, I guess it was. I am not familiar with e-cigarettes though. I can recognize one when I see it." Barbie began to feel very hot as she remembered that morning's adventure.

"It is rather easy to refill e-cigarettes. They come apart and you refill them. It is also easy to use something other than the liquid that is manufactured to go into the cigarettes, something that smells like and smokes like the real thing, but that has a higher concentration of nicotine. That way, if a person becomes ill, or in this case, dies, the cause of death could be attributed to too much smoke inhaled. In this case, the doctor believes that it will be found that the amount of nicotine found in the blood is excessive, even for someone who smoked a lot. It would have been extremely difficult for Dr. Hall to have smoked enough to have poisoned himself. Therefore, the doctor thinks that his e-cigarette is to blame; that someone refilled it, perhaps with an excessive amount of nicotine. It would have caused heart failure. And we might have thought that he died of natural causes. But the finding of the body in the pool, with few signs of violence on it, including bruising that may have happened as he fell into the pool does not rule that out. At the moment, this is all conjecture. It is one of the many scenarios that we are looking into. But I asked you here to talk about the argument. And that you have answered. Don't worry, I believe you. A mistake, someone else arguing, not really an 'argument', whatever. We can dismiss all of this."

Barbie had become still as she listened to Ali Rafiq tell his story. Her heart had begun to race and her face had turned hot, then cold, then was left with ugly red blotches all over it. She played the scene back over again and again. She envisioned her hand reaching for the e-cigarette, picking it up and then returning it to the hiding place under the lip of the pool. She thought of her fingerprints all up and down the shiny white surface. Fingerprints that would be over those of the killer, if the killer had not wiped the cigarette clean. Yes, that was it, the killer of course would have wiped fingerprints off of it. So that would leave Thurman Hall's prints. And hers.

Barbie smiled at David as he looked at her curiously. Barbie's throat closed up and she could say nothing.

Chapter Twelve: "I need a nap"

The strong midday sun was past its peak, but the heat it had generated still radiated down onto Barbie as she wended her way back to her room. The interview had been good and bad. Good in that she had escaped the clutches, for now, of the police for something she had not done. Bad because she had still not talked with 'David', only Ali Rafiq. And there was the little problem of fingerprints on the e-cigarette. On the other hand, who was to say that that was THE e-cigarette. The police should have looked around before Barbie had returned. In fact, the absence of any barriers to her return, crime scene tape, guards etc., made her believe that this was not the e-cigarette that had been tampered with. Then again, the Egyptian police were not known for being the brightest on the block. Even if Ali Rafiq had been in charge, he would not have done the 'looking,' would he?

Barbie stopped at the reception desk and found out that the key to her room was not on its little hook, and that the group had returned. Penelope would be in. She hoped. She did not want to retrace her steps and…

Barbie knocked briefly on the door, "It's me." She found Penelope sprawled on her bed, checking emails.

"Wow," Penelope grinned at her. "I thought you were gone, gone. As in locked up this time. I know that you talked to Dav… I mean the Chief of Police, but the whole thing had me worried. Don't worry, I didn't send out any SOS emails yet."

"Locked up? You thought they were gong to lock me up? Whose side are you on?" Barbie threw her bag on the floor and flopped on her bed. "God, I could use a nap. I need to rest; I need to process information."

"Not before you tell me everything," Penelope demanded.

Barbie started with her visit to Cornelius that morning. It was hard to summarize all the vague things he had said, but it seemed important to try. She mentioned her trip to the pool and the finding of the e-cigarette, with the proviso, "Hold that thought in your head." Then she picked up the story when she had been whisked off to the Police Station. When she got to the part about the poisoning by e-cigarette, Penelope immediately jumped in.

"They suspect you! Your fingerprints are all over it. They'll arrest you for sure."

"Whoa, Penelope Watson. Number one, they do not have my fingerprints, unless they ask the US government for them. I don't think they will go to all the trouble to do that right now. What makes you think they have the wherewithal to do fingerprint identification anyway? There was no talk of taking everyone's fingerprints. NO mention of fingerprints at all. But I am a little concerned. I will NOT tell the police, or Ali Rafiq, that I touched an e-cigarette that could have been the fatal one. We will just leave it. I do not have the means or the knowledge to do that. Someone who knows about e-cigarettes could have done it, but a ding-dong like me who knows nothing about them? No way."

"Then the only reason why they hauled you off was because someone 'heard' an argument?? They must be thinking of something else!" Penelope said.

"Why did David, I mean Ali Rafiq, let me know how Thurman died? That is not done if you suspect the person, don't you think? But then why are they targeting me? I'm sure they are keeping eyes on me. Maybe you are right, maybe they do suspect something about me. I know that I didn't argue with Thurman Hall, but now they have someone who said I did. David doesn't believe it's me, he said so. And I believe him, but what about the other police? And is David really in charge, or is he just a pretty face?

"You know me, Penelope. I am curious and I want to know things. But this is different, I think I need to find out before they start blaming things on ME. Especially because of the e-cigarette, now they have some sort of evidence they think might tie us together. So, I need to be Sherlock Holmes, and you need to be my Watson. Also, we could use more help. Get Mitch and Rachel."

Soon all four were assembled, sprawled on the beds. Mitch had checked the doors, the windows were shut completely, the air-conditioning on high, and the curtains tightly pulled. No one was listening and no one could hear, even if they tried to.

When they were set, Barbie went over the evidence. She recalled her conversations with Cornelius, with David and admitted the finding of the e-cigarette. "So the police are now looking at murder, nicotine poisoning, with most likely a tampering of an e-cigarette. I don't know if they have a time frame or not. If he started smoking a tampered e-cigarette before dinner, could the effects be felt during dinner? Maybe that is what made him so argumentative. What do we know about nicotine poisoning? Could someone have tampered with the cigarette in Cairo? Or did it have to be here? And if it was here, when was it done? We didn't get here until yesterday afternoon, so there was little time to tamper with anything. But I do know that he was smoking yesterday evening, before dinner, and that he was fine for well over an hour after that. Was it the same cigarette? A different one? Oh, there are too many questions." Barbie shook her head in frustration.

Mitch sat thinking, his head sunk on his chest. He looked up. "Before we can really figure out what happened, we need to know more about the poison and who might have tampered with Thurman's cigarette. How do you get nicotine poison? Do you collect it from the liquid that you can buy? Or do you have to get it wholesale as it were? These are questions that I don't think we can answer, unless Watson here can look it up on her internet."

"I could try to do that. But I have a better idea. Why don't we look at the people who wanted Thurman Hall dead? I mean, when we said he was dead, we all knew who wanted him dead, but it seems a real stretch to say that Winter Doern fiddled with his cigarette." Penelope Watson weighed in. "It seems unlikely. Even though poison is a woman's choice of getting rid of someone, and you don't even have to be there for it to work, it still seems a long stretch to accuse poor Winter. I mean, she isn't here and how would she know that it would work. Maybe he'd just get really sick."

Rachel jumped in, "But even if he didn't die from it, getting really sick is nasty and maybe that might have been punishment in itself. Maybe it would scare him, make him think twice about doing something to anyone else. Maybe that would have a point. And if he died, well, better yet. Gosh, that does sound awful!"

"Schuyler Stanford," Barbie muttered.

"What?" Rachel said, "Alexander the Great?"

"We do know that he was very, very angry with Thurman Hall. And he is quite clever," Mitch said. "But Thurman Hall was his supervisor for his thesis. It does not do you any good to bump off your supervisor. It simply delays things horribly. If he had another supervisor lined up, who had read his work and was willing to take over right away, then maybe. But however much you hate and loathe your supervisor, it is not only bad form to do him or her in, it is against all logic."

"This wasn't a crime of logic, I fear," Barbie said. "most crimes are crimes of passion. The Mafia does killings to get rid of rivals, but this is not that."

"But he is here, in Siwa. I don't know what hotel they are staying in, but he could have gotten to Thurman's cigarettes and tampered with them. It would be easy to say, "Hey, supervisor, you're here, can I come and see you? I have a question to ask about my work." Mitch added.

"But I thought they were fighting about the stolen paper. I mean, if you are mad at someone, even your supervisor, surely you wouldn't go looking for them at a more social gathering. And how would he do it? And for that matter, how would anyone do it?" Penelope asked. "Well, here it is, nicotine poisoning, all you ever wanted to know about how to poison yourself with e-cigarettes. Whoa, little kids smoking them?? No, no." She went quiet as she read on.

"You'd have to get ahold of the cigarette or cigarettes. We presume the one Barbie found was an extra, that it didn't have 'extra' nicotine in it. Did it look tampered with?" Mitch turned to Barbie.

"Wow." Barbie looked at Mitch, then all of them. "Maybe it did. When I picked it up, there was something sticky on the outside. I washed my hands immediately, but it kind of burned. I mean, I was busy and my mind full of other things, but there was something on the outside. I thought it was gunk from the gutter. Maybe, oh gosh. Do you think it could have been nicotine? How I would I know?"

"You would feel funny, like you had been smoking cigarettes. Your heart rate would go up and in fact, skin poisoning is the worst kind, worse than smoking and worse than ingesting. Because when it gets on your skin, it goes straight into your blood system. So, Barbie did you feel like there was burning on your hands, where the 'gunk' was, or did you feel like you had been in a café with a hundred other smokers, in other words, like you had too many cigarettes?"

"Yes, that's why I washed my hands and wiped them on my pants. It did burn a little. And then I went to talk with Cornelius. I felt a little hyper, you know, anxious and all that, so maybe it was the nicotine poisoning me. It did feel a little like that time we went to the shisha café to watch the soccer game. You know, everyone was smoking like chimneys and I got an awful headache and couldn't sleep all night. I did feel funny, but this whole trip has been weird and…"

"You touched the murder weapon?" Rachel asked in a whisper.

Barbie sat thoughtfully twisting the ends of her hair. "Maybe, but I hope not."

"C'mon," Penelope said. "I think these websites aren't going to tell us much. There are ways of filling the cigarettes that means that you can leak the stuff all over instead of pouring it into the right place. Someone would have had to have something more than the regular stuff, added nicotine or something like that. Who would know how to do that?"

"A chemist," answered Mitch. "Someone who knew how to add more nicotine so that there was too much. A good inhale of added poison might do it. And if you knew your chemistry, maybe you could brew it up yourself."

"So, we need to look for someone who hated Thurman Hall, was smart and had the opportunity to put poisonous nicotine into his e-cigarette. Means, motive and opportunity. Who fills the bill?" Penelope asked the group.

"Lisbon Truegood." Mitch said softly as he pulled at his lower lip, as if he didn't want it to come out.

"The guy's a dork, but is he a murderer?" asked Rachel. "I only met him once, and didn't much like him, socially inept, a bit of a buffoon, can't hold his liquor, and did not have much time for his HOD."

"You know this?" asked Penelope. "Wow, I didn't know you were so interested in the teachers and profs at AUE."

"I'm not just a pretty face. I am a faculty wife, a position of importance. I need to know a lot of things that can help my husband's career. And I go to a lot of faculty parties, where I do not drink much, socialize with the other faculty and deport myself with decorum at the same time as I collect dirt."

"Collect dirt, what's that got to do with it?" Penelope asked.

"Gossip, lady, the juicier the better. We need to know all the down and dirty things about others, and keep them from knowing anything about us. It's an important job, as I said. And when I quit my job back home and followed Mitch out here, I decided that I would do what needed to be done. And I've been good at it, haven't I?" Rachel asked Mitch coquettishly.

"The best," he answered, reaching over to plant a quick 'smack' on her cheek.

"Hey guys, can we cut the cheap physical shit and get back to the problem? Where were we?" Barbie asked.

Rachel simpered, something Barbie had never seen her do before. "Jealous," she mouthed.

"Lisbon Truegood. The professor everyone loves to dislike, but we can never figure out why. He is socially inept, he says the wrong thing at the wrong time, blurts things out and makes enemies."

"So why is he a suspect?"

"Because he and Thurman Hall had a falling out. It blew up into an enormous typhoon-like fight, again during a departmental meeting. Things happen in departmental meetings." Mitch shook his head as he told the story. "I wasn't there for this one, but I heard an almost exact accounting from two reliable witnesses who were there. Pete and Trigger both heard the whole thing. The matter at the heart of it all was rather trivial, but the disagreement wasn't. On the one hand, you have Thurman, head of the department, acting as if his word is gospel, his opinions always correct and come from the highest of intellectual deliberations. Everyone else's ideas or opinions must be wrong. And enter Truegood, or rather, Truegood doesn't want to lick Prof Hall's boots any more. In the end, the HOD position was between the two of them. There is no extra money for undertaking the job, or hardly any, and lots more responsibility, but it was the prestige, and Thurman really wanted the job. Lisbon had arrived the year after Thurman and got his tenure the year after Thurman, a year behind. And the feeling was that Thurman, being 'elder' should get the job. No one liked him, except those up the food chain, but Lisbon can be a bit of a wild card, so everyone thought Thurman should get the job, do it better, irritate fewer people. I don't think that Lisbon was angry so much about the job as the continued sniping from Thurman."

"So get on with the story, what happened?" Barbie demanded.

"Thurman accused Lisbon of not being collegial." Mitch leaned back and let the statement percolate.

"Not collegial? Whatever does that mean?" Penelope asked.

"It covers a multitude of sins and is a reason to deny tenure and ultimately, can get you blacklisted and make your life so miserable that you voluntarily leave. Being labeled 'uncollegial' is the mortal sin of academia. That and not publishing."

"But what does it mean, not being nice to your colleagues?" Penelope insisted.

"Much more than that, it means being uncooperative, the worst sin that an academic could commit." Mitch swallowed and looked uncomfortable even being near the word.

"But I thought that if you got tenure, that meant that you couldn't be fired, right? So, Lisbon is safe, if he has tenure. What could Thurman do to him, he couldn't get him fired, and all the other petty things that are done to people, well, academics often work alone, teaching, researching, hanging in their offices." Barbie looked puzzled.

"It's not the reality, it's the accusation."

"So, what did Lisbon do when accused of being 'uncollegial'?"

"He was quite upset, sputtered a lot and told the whole group that Thurman was not fit to be Head of Department, not fit to be a human being, and would be better off dead, rid the human race of his vile character. And those words are ones I believe can be put in quotes. He was a little off his rocker with anxiety, frustration and humiliation, to have petty disagreements aired in public. And he already didn't get along with Thurman."

Silence fell then, but Penelope soon broke it. "But because he said those things doesn't make him a murderer. Besides, when was this?"

Mitch thought, "About six months ago, last fall."

"And he has been biding his time since then, waiting for his moment to poison an e-cigarette?"

"Yeah, I think it is a stretch. As I have said before, if you are looking for a villain, I would say Winter Doern. She threatened to kill him. Right there in a meeting. I heard it. And that was last December."

Barbie looked thoughtful. "This is all speculation. I mean, we can say 'kill him' or 'murder him', but could you ever murder someone? I just can't see myself doing that, unless I was defending myself. But attack?" Barbie lay back on the bed and stared at the ceiling. "Plunge a knife into someone, put arsenic in their tea, take a rock and bang someone over the head. For what reason? Avenging honor, passion, money. Calculated murder?" Barbie closed her eyes. "I'm really tired. I need a nap, or a swim!"

"Nap," her three companions said at once. They all got up and left her alone.

As she walked out the door, following Rachel and Mitch to the lounge, Penelope muttered, "To think that she wants to go back to that pool!?"

Chapter Thirteen: Sunset at the Tombs

"Barbie, wake up, we're going to the Tombs. You can't miss this!" Penelope shook Barbie's shoulder.

Barbie's blond curls shook as she reached for her watch on the bedside table. "Wow, what time is it?"

"Time for the tombs. They are the famous tombs and Cornelius is going to tell us all about them. Everyone should be there because we can watch the sunset."

"I've got to shower!" Barbie stumbled into the bathroom.

"You have less than five minutes, don't do your hair," Penelope advised.

"Arhghhhhh," Barbie yelled as the cold water cascaded down on her. "It's waking me up."

When she emerged a few minutes later, Barbie looked at her hair and slumped back on the bed. "I don't think I'll go. I need to think some more, try to figure out a way to stay out of jail. If I can figure out whodunit, then I'll be better off than seeing some old tombs."

"But everyone will be there. If you want information, this is the place to get it. We can talk with everyone, see if anyone else knows anything. I'm mean, discreetly of course. Casual conversations about how awful it all was and what will happen now. Who might be the next HOD, who smokes e-cigarettes, things like that. Could be useful. You can go one direction, I can go another and we can casually talk to a lot of people. Casual, you know. Not interrogating. And we can get Mitch and Rachel to snoop a little as well. What are friends for if not to intrude on each other's business?"

"Wow, you'd do that? It might be dangerous. You are right, I'm not thinking straight, I need to enlist the aid of my friends." Barbie finished dressing and they headed out the door and towards the bus.

"Jackets everyone," said Mahmoud as the group began to gather. "Even though it seems warm now, it can get cold after the sun sets. We hope it doesn't get cold, but you never know."

The two women did an about face and raced back to the room. They encountered Rachel and Mitch on the way and relayed the information.

"We have ours," Rachel announced.

"Good, I'm glad we met you," Barbie started.

"Barbie needs your help. Now that everyone will be coming to the outing this evening, we can use the time to gather information. Like who knows what kind of gossip about politics, about e-cigarettes, who smokes them etc." Penelope said.

"Maybe we'll even run into the graduate students and their tour group. I mean, Schuyler and his followers were there this morning. If they know that Cornelius will be lecturing about the tombs, they may even try to go and piggyback on the lecture. But even if they don't go, we can talk with the others," Mitch said. "Good thinking, Barbie."

"Oh, it wasn't her idea. It was the great Watson. Okay gang, here we are, everyone knows what to do? Let's split up." Penelope took charge as Barbie looked around distractedly.

As they filed on the bus, Barbie deliberately chose a seat next to a someone different this time, trying to mingle. She was told the seat was taken. She sat next to Penelope, again. "Try number one down the tubes."

"Oh, hi, Barbie," said one of the faculty wives who had climbed on the bus. Barbie thought furiously. Name, name. Oh, now I remember, she is the wife of Mitch's colleague Pete. Her name is Sally. You must try to remember names better, she told herself. You are a teacher; students hate it when you forget their names. And you have met this woman before today, so try to be friendly and ask, politely.

"Oh, hi. Please forgive, I'm a little distracted today, could tell me your name again?" Barbie put on her widest grin.

"Sally, it's Sally. I know, it's such an old-fashioned name, no one can remember it. My husband is Pete."

"That's right, Sally and Pete. And what is his department again?" Barbie continued as Sally took the seat across the aisle, opposite Barbie.

"History. History of Biology. I don't know anything about it, but he is the smartest guy in the world and I just fell in love with that, you know?!" Sally gushed as she looked over at her handsome, but dorky, husband.

Barbie thought that Sally was a pretty smart woman too, to hook up with an intelligent, capable PhD who could be a university professor, or go into business. Much better than a used car salesman.

Sally gushed a minute more, then leaned over from her seat opposite Barbie's and whispered. "You must be really distracted and upset. And the police today, oh that must have been awful. It wasn't anything bad, was it? I mean, you're here with us, aren't you?"

"Yeah, no problem, only routine stuff. They wanted to check my name. They thought they had got it wrong, but…"

"Good afternoon, ladies and gentlemen, scholars and lovers of Egypt," Cornelius' voice interrupted the inane conversation with the beginning of his lecture.

Barbie mouthed silently to Sally, "I'll talk with you later." Barbie thought to herself, this was a good start. She probably knows a lot of people and loves to gossip. If she hasn't got a lot to do, she probably hangs around the gym, and coffee shops and knows all the players, at least in her husband's department, and among the wives. I must speak with her more.

"We are now headed for a hill on the outskirts of Siwa city proper colloquially known as 'The Tombs,'" intoned Professor Smythe. "But the proper name is Jebel al Mawta or the Hill of the Dead. The hill was used for burying the dead as early as the 26th Dynasty, but many are also from the Ptolemaic Dynasty. The Romans used them, robbing the earlier tombs and reusing them. The bodies were mummified, of course, but in a much more haphazard way. They were Egyptians, after all. Very thoroughly Egyptian. We will be able to see the Temple of Amun that we visited this morning and the sunset should be rather nice. I urge you to watch the time, however, as you do not want to be caught out after dark. There are no lights and many tombs, which are only holes in the rock, are not clearly marked or roped off." He stared at Penelope pointedly.

Cornelius paused for a few moments as Mahmoud took over the microphone in the bus. He laid out the plans for dinner this evening and a lecture about Siwan culture that was promised for after dinner. Then he handed over the microphone once more to the white-haired guru of all thing Egyptian.

"As the tombs are Egyptian, although built by the Romans, they contain Egyptian motifs. But because they are Roman, they also contain styles and motifs that are Roman. This blending of styles can also be seen in the tombs in Alexandria. You have all seen them, haven't you?" He turned around to face the bus riders and bullied them into nodding in the affirmative. Barbie nodded automatically at Cornelius' glare. It was best not to argue with him.

"The last time I was here, there were still mummies, not so neatly wrapped, but recognizable mummies, in the tombs themselves. I do not know if they have been disturbed or stolen since then. We can all go take a look or I can tell you where to go. As well as some rather nice paintings on the walls, there is a magnificent crocodile painting that has given the name to the tomb, aptly known as the Crocodile Tomb. As well, the well-preserved tomb of Si-Amun is the best-known example on the Hill.

"The extent of the necropolis was not known until the Second World War, when an exodus from the town sent the inhabitants to temporary shelter in the tombs. In their desire to have more space, or accommodate more families, the earliest arrivals tossed out the mummies, confiscated the grave goods, and then started to dig a little more. It didn't take long for them to find extra rooms in the back and sides of the existing tombs. Many discoveries of new tombs were found at this time. It happened like this. The Italian air force arrived and bombed the town. The townspeople, about 4,000 at the time, moved into the tombs for safety. They stayed for three years and the blackened ceilings in the tombs that can still be seen are from that time. Unfortunately, there was destruction of the tombs as well. The Tomb of Si-Amun was found at this time, and was damaged by soldiers, who attempted to take the cave paintings by hacking away at the walls. So misguided. The individual tombs will be described when we get there. But at this time, are there any questions?"

A voice called out from the back, "Professor Smythe, this morning we saw Alexander, will we see walking mummies this afternoon?"

The bus erupted in laughter and Professor Smythe turned around in his seat, looking for the jokester. "I don't know about that, but you had better be careful what you wish for young man. You might get it." He lowered his voice, but Barbie thought she heard him say, "We don't need any more corpses."

When they arrived at the Hill of the Dead, they were met by a row of touristic goods spread out on the barbed-wire fence that surrounded the hill. Young and old men, boys and a few girls, approached the group and started their spiels. "Postcards, shawls, beautiful shawls, authentic Siwa baskets, hats, hats." Fistfuls of souvenirs were thrust at the group and whenever a pair of eyes strayed to look at something, the intensity of the sell became urgent. The touts had never been to school to learn this, but they were astute readers of the human face.

The group had to walk the gauntlet of pesky sellers before they reached the steps that led up the hill. Mahmoud bought tickets and handed them out as they all entered the enclosure and started up the hill. Even though Cornelius was one of the first to start up the hill, he was quickly left behind. Barbie lagged behind with him.

"How are you doing?" asked Barbie, watching Cornelius huff and puff as he pulled himself up the staircase.

"Oh, I will make it, never fear. I do so love this place, and the tombs here, so special to me." He puffed a few more times, then stopped to catch his breath. "And you, my dear, how are you doing? The police weren't too harsh with you I hope?"

"No, no problems there." She thought about revealing to Cornelius her conversation with David, but he preempted her.

"I assume you met our friend Mr. David again?"

Barbie hesitated for a moment. "Yes, I did."

"And is he in charge of this investigation?" Cornelius looked sideways at Barbie.

"I spoke with him, and so I know that he is deeply involved, but I am not sure he is 'in charge'. He..." she stopped as a few stragglers caught up and passed them.

"Well, you will be well-treated if nothing else. Let us go. No, no, you go on ahead and tell them all to wait for me at the sign. We can gather there and I will tell everyone about the tombs. Rush off young lady!"

Barbie did as she was told and soon caught up to Rachel and Mitch.

"I'm glad I caught up with you. Now, this is what we need to know, so please ask as many as you can, very casually, you understand. Where were they last night after dinner and before we found the body?"

"Barbie, we can't ask that! Just like that, 'Where were you last night?'"

"I know, you need to be circumspect, do it in a roundabout way. You can ask them to give a critique of the dancing, or who they sat at dinner with and whatever, get as many people talking as you can. And Mitch, you are a smoker."

"Whoa, was, Barbie, was. I don't do that anymore."

"Well, you did during the Revolution!"

"That was then, I had reason to. Two dead friends, the whole country in an uproar, why wouldn't I smoke? Anyway, I stopped as soon as things calmed down." Mitch's lips twitched.

"But now is the perfect time to think about taking it up again. You can ask around about e-cigarettes. Has anyone tried them, how do you do it, do you know anyone else who smokes them, etc. That should lead to a few ideas, don't you think?"

Mitch sighed and nodded his head.

"Good, you are true friends. We can meet up later to exchange ideas. Now, Cornelius told me we should meet at the sign for our introduction. I'll see you there."

The roar of a motorcycle reached their ears as they saw a dust cloud float up from the parking lot. They watched as a large motorcycle pulled up beside their bus and a black clad, helmeted figure dismounted. The slender person whipped off the helmet and shook his bald head.

"Who's that?" asked Barbie, trying to keep the hair out of her eyes as she squinted to get a better view.

"He's a crazy Dutchman," mumbled Mitch.

"I heard some of the others talking about him. It appears that he arrived last evening, late. He's motoring around Africa," Rachel said.

"Is he crazy because he he riding his motorcycle around Africa or is he crazy because of something else innate? Surely we are not saying 'crazy Dutchman' as if all Dutch are crazy?" Barbie responded.

"Who but a crazy man would travel around Africa on a motorcycle, alone?" Mitch opined.

"Sounds like interesting fun to me," Barbie said wistfully.

"Look, we can see the Shali, with the lovely late afternoon light on it. And over there is the Temple of Amun. This is a glorious place for sunset!" Rachel said, turning in all directions to see the views. A sea of dusty green palm trees was broken by hills; ones they could now recognize as they had visited them.

"Hey guys, they are gathering up there near the sign, time to make a move," Barbie said, striking out for the gathering point.

"Lady, postcards? Want buy postcards?" The gallebeya-clad man approached Barbie speaking in a low, seductive voice.

"Oh lord, not again," Barbie said, more to herself than the postcard seller.

"Ah, madam," the turbaned seller said again, approaching closer and dropping his voice. "These are special postcards, perfect for you!"

Barbie's head whipped around and she looked, really looked at the man.

She recognized the smile of even white teeth, the dark mustache skimming his upper lip, and the handsome figure. Once more, she felt the siren call of the romantic heroine tucked inside her. She stepped off the path and reached forward to touch the packet of proffered postcards.

"Barbie, where are you going? The lecture has started," Rachel called.

Barbie faced her friends, putting her body in between them and the postcard seller. "Just going to buy some postcards, I'll come soon. Catch you later!"

She turned back to the salesman who had moved off the path and was disappearing behind a large boulder. Barbie followed him, the antiquities seller David, aka the Siwa Chief of Police, Ali Rafiq.

Chapter Fourteen: A Meeting with David

When they had rounded a corner and were out of sight of the rest of the tourists, Barbie reached out and touched David's hand. He turned and clutched her other hand, allowing the stack of postcards in his hand to fall to the ground. They stared into each other's eyes. It was the first time they had touched each other since that magical moment months earlier in the Gezira Club when they had kissed.

"Oh, I have missed you!" Barbie said, her eyes filling with tears.

"It is so wonderful to look at your face, hear your voice again. I do apologize for not contacting you. I thought it was the best thing. This life, this hiding, this thing that is all mixed up with politics, is so difficult. My friends in Cairo do not know. I knew that it was only a matter of time before I had to leave again, but I wanted to stay in Egypt. You understand, it is my country and I could not abandon her. But you would have been in danger if you had known. So it was for the best. I have not forgotten you, though!" He smiled at her with the same genuine smile, while his eyes crinkled at the edges.

Barbie's heart melted and she thought, of course I forgive you. What is there to forgive? Our love, (was it love?), was momentary, a fling, a brilliant star in the dark night.

"But we have no time now for reminiscing. I came here to tell you that you are in trouble, only a little trouble you understand, but I need to keep you up to date, to help you if I can." David kept his hands on hers as he said this, even though Barbie tried to pull away.

"What do you mean by 'trouble'?" she squeaked in a whisper. "If they only knew how much trouble I have been in, or think I've been in."

"Who are you talking about, 'they', who is 'they'?" David asked.

"The police, of course. Unless YOU are the police. Are you?" Barbie asked more in control.

"Well, not really, but yes, I am. The police. Or at least acting police. And in this case, I am playing the part. I need to be seen as police, to complete my disguise."

"Disguise? This is all a disguise? I mean, the gallabeya obviously is, but the business card, the uniform, the office, that is a disguise as well?" Barbie opened her eyes wide to look at him.

"Yes, isn't it fun?"

"David, there has been a death, quite possibly a murder. This isn't fun."

"Yes, you are right, it is serious. But what did you mean 'how much trouble' you are in? Is there something you aren't telling me?" David pulled her closer.

Unfair, thought Barbie, he is using his wiles on me.

"You first," she said. "Tell me what the police know."

"Okay, I'll tell you and then you will understand why I am telling you. They are fairly certain that Thurman Hall's e-cigarette was poisoned, tampered with. It was probably filled with more potent nicotine than it should have been."

"Was this at the pool? Where he was found?"

David looked at her strangely. "No, in his room, there was a cigarette that was leaking some liquid. One of the policemen picked it up, smelled it and the liquid leaked on his hand. Just a few minutes later he fainted. They took him to the hospital. They are trying to find ways to analyze the cigarette. The idea that we are working on now is that someone tampered with the e-cigarette. If only a little on the hands can cause fainting, think of what inhaling could do. The autopsy hasn't been completed yet and I think it may take a while, so we are looking at someone who could have tampered with his e-cigarettes. That is the current scenario.”

“So, killed by an e-cigarette? Interesting. And the only one is the one in the room? More than one in the room? What about the other part of the paraphernalia, the plug, the extra nicotine liquid? Have you found that? Any other clues there? And what about the pool?” Barbie looked happy and innocently at David.

“Why are you so interested in the pool?”

Barbie hesitated and tried to look elsewhere. “The pool, the pool. I found him in the pool. I saw him smoking at the pool before dinner. This is where it all took place, so why wasn’t something found at the pool? Makes sense to me.”

“The theory is that he smoked the cigarette in his room and then went out to the pool area, where he was overwhelmed by the nicotine in his blood. Of course, someone could have taken the cigarette away from the pool and put it back in his room. But the keys to his room were in his pocket, the door was locked…”

“It’s just that there was another e-cigarette at the pool.” Barbie muttered.

“The one you saw him smoking before dinner?”

“The one I picked up, touched, left fingerprints on this morning.”

“What did you do with it?” David asked quickly.

“Dropped it, put it back where I found it. I mean, there was no one there, no crime scene tape, no one watching, so I looked around and saw it and picked it up. When I realized what it was, boy, I dropped it right away. But it has my fingerprints on it.”

David laughed. “Don’t worry about that. Egyptian police are not very adept at the fine arts of forensic detection. It’s more of the ‘round up the usual suspects’ kind of policing. Besides, if that one has your fingerprints on it, the one found in his room has the police officer’s fingerprints all over it. Obliterating any old ones, ones made by the killer. I think the methods we are using on this case are quite primitive. I think that the real suspects are one of the group, that makes sense, unless it was an accident. In which case, we would all be quite happy. It may come to that in the end. Easier."

They looked glumly at each other. "Besides," continued David. "Fingerprints are notoriously difficult to get right. If they do take your prints, try to get your hands dirty, try some fingernail polish or oil or something. It's not as easy as they make it look on TV. And, remember, this is Egypt. I'll find out how many cigarettes have been found, see if they found one at the pool. Take a look at it myself if I can, and obliterate any of my lovely Barbie's prints."

"You'd do that? Pervert justice? For me?" Barbie said surprised.

"You didn't kill him, so it is not a perversion of justice. It is maintaining justice. And what you can do for me is to try and find out who might have wanted him dead and how they did it, presuming it was in his e-cigarette. And also, we don't want any more AUE Professors turning up dead." David's face was stern.

"We have some ideas already. When we heard Thurman Hall was dead, we all know who wanted him dead; who would be dancing on his grave!" Barbie admitted.

"Tell all!" David picked up his scattered postcards and led Barbie over to a flat rock and invited her to sit down. He sat beside her, his arm touching hers.

Barbie related the list of 'possibles' starting with Winter. She told him of the incident with Schuyler that morning and then what Mitch had said about the stolen paper. She also whisked over the name of Lisbon Truegood, which Barbie felt was a long shot. "And there may be others. The rumors are incredible. No one seemed to like him, and no one seems to be mourning him. I don't think most of our group yet know that you suspect murder though."

"Oh, please do keep that quiet. And one more thing you can do for me. Please be on the lookout for more information. You are an insider in this. We, the police, don't know much. Please help us."

"As long as you keep my name off the list of suspects," Barbie laughed. "Besides, we are already doing that. I was afraid that the police would suspect me, so I have enlisted the help of my friends. Mitch and Rachel and also Penelope are out there even as we speak, trying to dig up information. And you know the source of a lot of this is the grand old man himself, Cornelius Smythe. You should talk with him. He knows you are here, by the way."

David rolled his eyes but said nothing. Did he imagine he could have kept his presence a secret for too long, thought Barbie.

Scuffling noises broke out on the rough hillside around the corner. Both jumped up from their seat and David pulled the end of his turban up around his neck, concealing his face.

"Lady, lady, very nice postcards. See, many photos Siwa," David thrust the postcards at Barbie, who had stumbled against him in her hurry to jump up from their seat on the rock.

Three young girls, their arms and legs bare in a California-girl style, but inappropriate for Egypt, rounded the corner. They hung to one another and giggled as they came. Barbie recognized them as three of Schuyler's fan club, that she had seen that morning at the Temple of Amun.

"Only ten pounds, ten postcards," whined David, thrusting them in Barbie's direction.

"Whoa, postcards," one said. "Can I see?" she asked, thrusting out her hand.

Barbie watched as David's clean long fingered hand snaked out from underneath his gallebeya. He proffered the postcards balanced on top of his palm, trying to hide his city man's hands.

"I'll take them," Barbie said loudly, snatching the postcards out of David's hand, before the younger woman could look at them. She fumbled in her small backpack for her purse.

"Do you have any others then?" asked another one of the would-be buyers, smiling directly into the face of the ersatz policeman.

A momentary look of panic crept into David's eyes and then he turned around. A small khaki bag lay on the rock and David pulled a small book out of it. "Book? You want book?"

"Does it have pictures? I want a picture book!" the second girl stated eagerly.

"Pictures, of course, pictures." David opened the book and showed them ancient poorly reproduced black and white photos of local people, the various archeological sites and local handicrafts.

The graduate student took the book and flipped through the pages. "But this is used, this isn't new. Look, there is writing in it," she held it out to David to show marginal notes, most in English and a few in Arabic that littered the pages. "Don't you have a new one?"

"Postcards, I have more postcards," David said as he rummaged in the bag, finally finding a dirty old dog-eared fold-out selection of postcards. Compared with the book, this series of photos could be classified as antiquities.

"Euww," said the third graduate student. "It's been through a lot of hands. You don't want that, Esmeralda. Take the book. Or why not wait until we go to the little book shop thingy in the village. We could go tomorrow."

"Pardon me," Barbie interrupted. "You girls are graduate students at AUE, aren't you? I've met you before. Aren't you Aida?" Barbie asked the shortest, darker haired one of the three.

"Yeah, that's right, we have met," said Aida. "Barbie Doll, right?"

Barbie groaned inwardly. Why did I ever start using that line, 'I'm blonde, I'm ditzy and my mother named me Barbie, what can I do?' to explain away the name. "It's Barbie, Barbie Falcon, not Doll. And what are you guys doing here in Siwa?"

"Like everyone else I guess, taking advantage of Spring Break," said the third.

Barbie racked her brain trying to think of this one's name. "So, did you come with a group? From AUE?"

"Yeah, graduate students and a few faculty members who couldn't get on your tour. We're staying at a different hotel, down the street from your group, but we are of course going to the same places. We just love the old guy, Professor Smythe," she emphasized the long 'i' sound in Smythe. He is a hoot! So, we are going to his lectures, or making sure we are where he is to get the advantage of his incredible knowledge of Egypt. I hear that he was in Egypt doing his digging before the last flood of the Nile. How cool is that?"

Suddenly, Barbie remembered her name, Roxana. How appropriate, to be named after the wife of Alexander the Great. And now, Barbie felt protective of Cornelius. To be referred to as 'a hoot'. The old guy was that, but so much more, she thought. How dare these little upstarts patronize him.

David intervened at this point, and held out another book to Esmeralda. "This, good book. See, no writing." He flipped the pages to show the girls that this was not a used book, and that it had good photos as well.

"Hmm, how much?" Esmeralda asked thumbing through the book.

Curious, Barbie looked over her shoulder to peruse the book herself. She read the chapter titles and headings and recognized the topics: 'The Zaggalah,' 'Clothes,' 'Baskets'. She sniffed and said, "Nice book."

"Look, photo from this place," David pointed out, sure now the girls would look at the book and not his hands as he rifled through the pages to find the view that they recognized. Soon they were bargaining for the books and the remaining dirty, rolls of postcards. He had let his turban slip from his face and now he smiled as he bargained, cajoling the girls into spending all their petty cash on books and postcards.

When they had bought all his stock, David said goodbye and waved at them. Barbie stood beside him as they rounded the rock and slipped out of view.

"You make a very convincing salesman. I thought you were a policeman?" Barbie laughed.

"After all, that is really my profession, salesman. Just not antiquities, but anything. Am I convincing as a Siwan?"

"They don't know the difference. So, where are my postcards?" Barbie asked, looking around.

"Sold them. For twice what you were going to pay." He looked at her again, the intensity had come back into his eyes and the dark pupils expanded in the dying light, making deep unfathomable orbs of mystery. "I need to speak to you again to get your report. Tonight, in the garden, we will continue this conversation. Go now," he said, dismissing her.

Barbie grabbed her bag and started off down the hill. She turned to wave to him, but David had disappeared as quickly as he had appeared. The sun dipped behind the horizon, and the shadows quickly faded. The call to prayer started in the distance and Barbie remembered the warnings of holes in the rocks where Romans had dug tombs. She looked at her feet and not the view, so she missed seeing the shadowy figure glide quickly down the hillside.

Chapter Fifteen: A Lecture on Siwa

Dinner was a subdued affair. The groups of AUE professors and staff were reminded that twenty-four hours before, there had been one more of their number. There was an empty chair at the table where he had sat the evening before. No one could be persuaded to add themselves to that table. Mahmoud invited a number of staff, but they had all declined. He sat fidgeting, looking at the chair, and finally he moved it off to the side with other unwanted and empty chairs.

Barbie noticed and felt guilty for the tension. She told herself that finding the body was not the same as making him dead. But if she hadn't decided to go swimming, would that task have been taken by a member of the hotel staff, a more neutral person, rather than someone who had known the victim, however slightly?

Before the guests were finished with their dessert, Mahmoud stood and announced, "This evening there will be a lecture by our own distinguished Professor Cornelius Smythe about Siwa. He will tell you about the history, the customs of the people and how they live. It will be very informative and we hope that you will all stay here for it. The lecture should start in about fifteen minutes. Maybe some other guests from this hotel or another hotel will join us. We want to be generous but please, stay in your chairs in order to have a good seat."

The AUE group stayed seated, or asked others to look after their chairs as they drifted out to go to their rooms, to use the facilities or to get a brief breath of fresh air. Barbie sat with Penelope, Rachel and Mitch. They bunched their chairs together and turned them to face the front of the room. They pointedly tried to keep others from placing a chair in front of their table. They dare not exchange any information in public and there had been no time before dinner.

Three young women sauntered into the dining room. Barbie looked at them, now wearing sweaters over their bare shoulders and she noted that their thighs were covered as well. She pointedly looked away as their eyes scanned the room, presumably looking for a place to sit. When they found a place at the far end of the room, Barbie told the others about her encounter with Esmeralda, Aida and Roxana.

"Can you imagine? Those names? And especially Roxana. Maybe it was she who pushed the 'Adonis' Schuyler into pretending to be Alexander." Penelope giggled.

"Alexander didn't meet Roxana until after he had visited Siwa, so the analogy is not apt. Sorry Penelope. Although I've met them, I really don't know much about them. 'The Three Graces', maybe?" Mitch said.

"The three stooges is more like it," said Penelope. "I know them because they were in my Arabic class last semester. I think they were taking the 'extra' class because they were finding the regular Arabic classes weren't enough, as in too difficult for them. I mean, they are supposedly doing MA degrees in Arabic studies or Middle Eastern studies or some such thing. Anyway, I think they need to pass an exam. They were the giggly girls in the back of the class. But their relationship with Schuyler, what do you make of that?"

"One, all, none?" opined Rachel. "I've met them before as well. They met when they got here, but it's like they are sisters or whatever. Schuyler is one of the MA crowd, so they only met him after they arrived. I think there is competition to be 'Schuyler's girlfriend', but it hasn't broken them apart. That's why I think it's 'none'. They call him 'Sky' and they think highly of him. I think his family has money, and of course, the guy is handsome and smooth, so what's not to like?"

"But what are they like?" Barbie asked.

"All alike. I kept forgetting which one is which," Penelope said.

"Same here, except I would say, 'the tall one is Esmeralda, the dark one is Aida', etc. That was the only way I could tell them apart. They melded. 'Sky' was their favorite topic of conversation." Rachel said.

"So maybe we need to speak to them as well," Barbie said.

They watched as others came into the room. One by one the newcomers were identified. Most were graduate students, but a few faculty members who had been late signing up for this bus trip, had come with the younger group. After all, it was just who was on which bus, the tour was the same.

Cornelius stood and harrumphed. The occupants of the room fell quiet. Behind them, the windows were being opened from the outside as a few people had complained of the rising heat from the bodies. The evening breeze felt better and was more convenient for the lecture than air-conditioning. Barbie turned to look into the darkness outside. A tree trunk glowed a soft white, but the foliage faded to black.

Cornelius gave a short introduction of himself and the topic for this evening's talk. Suddenly, the door to the outside swung open. Schuyler Stanford stood in the doorway, filling it with his presence. A few scattered whispers quickly morphed into a quiet chant of "toga, toga, toga."

Schuyler nodded and struck a pose. He was not wearing a toga, this time, but there was no doubt that the audience remembered his stunt of the morning. The chant grew louder and even Penelope joined in, but quietly. "Toga, toga, toga." Schuyler raised his hands in tribute to his admirers.

Cornelius looked at the young man standing in the doorway with a withering glance and nodded to Mahmoud, who disappeared. Within thirty seconds, a large Egyptian appeared behind Schuyler, dwarfing him.

"Alexander, my dear boy, how delightful you could make it. Now, please take your seat and we can get on with our lecture." Cornelius paused, but not long enough for Schuyler to make a scene seating himself with his admirers.

As Cornelius continued, a screen was placed behind him, and a projector and computer in front. A whir and fuss only momentarily interrupted the great orator, and then a PowerPoint presentation flickered to life.

"Now that we have covered the more ancient history of Siwa, let us turn to more modern times. I have told you of the 1926 disaster of the rain, the melting and eventual abandonment of the Shali. But there was one habit of the Siwans that continued long after that. There were then, as now, date palms, olive orchards and some gardens outside the walls of the city." Here photos that looked almost similar to the views of present Siwa appeared on the screen.

"So, what's new?" whispered Barbie to the others.

"To preserve the dignity and chastity of the women of Siwa, a law was promulgated, that no unmarried man could spend the night within the city walls. The young men, many of them migrant workers from Alexandria or the coast, or even from other oases, had to live outside the town. They created a bachelor's world unto themselves. This was called the 'Zaggalah', which means 'club-bearer'. These young men constituted a private army for the rich landowners as well as workers on the plantations. They spent their evenings in singing and dancing and drinking strong liquor made from the date palm. You can imagine the mischief they got up to."

Here Cornelius paused and smiled. Barbie imagined him thinking of young men, their good times, singing and dancing and maybe wishing he knew them when.

"Visitors to Siwa reported on this behavior and word got around. The rich, older men took young boys as 'brides' and the wedding ceremonies were great occasions for yet more singing and dancing. This homosexual behavior became quite well known and called attention to the lax 'morals' of the Siwans. In 1928, King Fuad made a visit, not long, but important for the running of Siwa. He made it quite clear that

Siwa was part of Egypt and Egypt did not tolerate this openness. After that date, marriage certificates between men were no longer made, but that did not stop the marriages and the partying.

"When the tarmac road was laid in the 1980s, and tourists started coming, the Siwan customs were quite well known and this attracted a number of the wrong kind of tourist, perhaps men who thought they were in San Francisco or Sydney, those modern-day meccas of open homosexuality. In any case, these latter-day tourists were disappointed to find the zaggalah had gone the way of all slightly dodgy customs and they returned home disappointed in the 'primitive' habits of Siwans. I will no longer talk about the Zaggalah as it is a touchy subject for modern day life here, and if anyone wants more information, they can ask me later.

"Now, I'd like to go on to talk about every day customs. Perhaps the one custom that can still be seen in Siwa is the habit of wearing the tarfottet. This is a blue cotton sheet, manufactured in the town of Kerdasa, near the pyramids of Giza. This shows the integrated nature of life in Siwa. The Siwan women are given these blue cloths at the time of their marriage and they sew them together and embroider them. You can still occasionally see a woman sitting on the flat bed of a donkey cart, her tarfottet pulled around her and held together by her teeth. She puts it in a peak, so that it appears as though a blue striped tent is riding on the donkey cart. Amazing.

"You can buy these embroidered cloths at some of the shops in town and they make interesting souvenirs. Also, other souvenirs that you might like to buy are the locally made baskets, decorated with multi-colored pom-poms, some round, some flat. The silver jewelry that you may have read about is no longer made here, but in Alexandria. The townspeople make the trip to buy large silver ornaments for wedding gifts. Carpets are another item that is for sale, both Bedouin carpets and those made here by young girls. You can visit the carpet factory tomorrow if you'd like.

"Now the Siwan language is Berber, as the language and the people arrived from the Maghreb, the West…"

Barbie's mind began to wander and she shifted in her chair, looking over her shoulder and out the window. She was surprised to find a man hanging over the window sill. He held a motorcycle helmet in his right hand and in his left, an unlit cigarette, the regular kind. He wore a motorcycle jacket of black leather. His nose was surmounted by a pair of small metal rimmed glasses and the sparse gray hair on his head stuck up in wild abandon. Barbie poked at Penelope until she got her attention.

"The crazy Dutchman?" whispered Barbie, nodding at the open window.

Penelope snickered and nodded. Barbie turned and stared out the window, trying to make out the faces of the other heads that melted into the darkness. Some wore headscarves, some wore turbans, others the ubiquitous baseball caps of youth all over the world.

One covered head turned to look into the room, but quickly looked away. Barbie thought at first that she had recognized the face, but then chided herself. She had faces and ideas on her mind. She was tired and stressed, wasn't she?

"Penelope," she whispered. "I thought I saw somebody. The grad students had faculty on their tour, didn't they? They're here now. They've been with us all along. So how many of them are there?"

"I don't know," came the soft reply. "We could count?"

Barbie looked out the window, but only saw the Dutch motorcyclist, alone at the window, no one stood behind him in the garden now. She quietly tried counting the tour group they came with and then the additional members. She quickly realized that she did not know how many there were on the grad students tour, and if all of them had come tonight. But in the end, she told herself, it didn't matter how many there were in the group. There was one person that was here, that she hadn't counted on. She knew her to see her. Barbie had seen her many times coming in and out of Hatshepsut's Mansions. She saw her at least every other day. Sometimes she saw her face, sometimes just the figure or the side of her head. But she recognized her when she saw her.

Barbie felt sure she had seen Winter Doern. She knew she was here in Siwa. Or was it her? Or was it someone who looked nondescript enough to be anyone?

Chapter Sixteen: A Meeting in the Garden

Barbie recoiled at the thought, but then turned her attention back to the dining room where Cornelius was beginning to wrap up his talk for the evening. There were a few lingering questions, but most of the audience seemed sated with information, of all kinds, and only wanted to go to bed. Barbie found Sally and Pete sitting at a far table and wished that she had had time to speak to Sally, but the events on the Hill of the Dead and then the mad rush to dinner precluded any more conversation. Maybe tomorrow, she thought, if it isn't too late.

As Barbie filed out with everyone else, she motioned to Penelope and indicated that she was going to the garden. She had told Penelope about the meeting, but still didn't know what she had to report, nothing more than this afternoon. Maybe David had had time to think of some questions and other lines of inquiry. Just as she was wondering where she was to meet David, he called.

"Go outside the reception area, turn right and walk down to the end of the block of rooms. It will be quiet there. There is a secluded gazebo with a couch, we will meet there." Then he rang off. Barbie did as she was told, wondering how he knew that the lecture had been let out and that she was now free for their meeting. Probably lurking in the bushes with all the other shadowy figures in this mystery, she thought.

She cautiously walked through the deserted gardens, glimpsing the gibbous moon overhead. It would be full in a few days and then all could celebrate Easter. She stopped at the entrance to the gazebo and peered inside. It was dark, very dark. Then she saw his teeth smile and his palm raised in greeting. He was dressed all in black, not policeman's black, but camouflage black. Slick, sexy, thought Barbie.

He rose from the low couch and took her hand, raising it to his lips and pressing moist full lips against the back of her hand. He smiled and turned her hand over, planting a kiss on the tender palm. Barbie gulped, not too loudly she hoped. He pulled her down beside him on the couch and looked into her eyes. Barbie thought it would have been nice to actually see him, rather than feel the heat from his body and the tickling sensation of his lips and mustache on her hand.

"We don't have much time," he said, leaning in to touch her arm with his. His voice was low and soft. Barbie did not want to be talking about murders and suspects, she wanted to be talking about the little bits of their lives, as they did at his antique shop in Cairo, or the stolen moments at the Gezira Club. She wanted him to tell her how he came to be here in Siwa and what he had been doing. She wanted him to tell her how much he had missed her, because she wanted to tell him how much she had wanted to see and talk with him.

"Thurman Hall almost certainly died of poisoning. They are still not sure how or what kind, but they are most suspicious of the e-cigarette, that is the official position at the moment. They have two e-cigarettes, I'm not sure where they found them, but I believe they both came from his room, or his pockets or bag. They have not tried to do anything with fingerprints yet. They don't know how, and frankly I believe that all the police have touched all the evidence with their bare hands, leaving myriad prints on everything. So, I think we can discount fingerprinting. Also, if someone did tamper with his cigarettes, I think they would have taken care not to leave traces of themselves. But any and all of this is still very inconclusive.

"As far as the Siwa police are concerned, you are still their main suspect, mainly because they have no other clues. Now, now, don't protest that it is silly for them to suspect you, but they are rather stupid. They won't arrest you as they have no evidence, and they won't arrest any one else unless they have some evidence. Which they don't."

"Okay, make sure that when they come to get me, you are there to tell them this," Barbie's voice shook as she imagined the rough and ready Siwa police force grabbing her from her bed, or off the bus. "In that case, I need to find out who did this. What do the police know about Thurman Hall?"

"Extraordinarily little. That's where you and your friends come in. We need to know everything you know about him, his friends, his enemies, who owed him money, who he owed money to, his wives, his girlfriends, his children, his job; we need to know everything. If I can get this information, then they will have something to run with, someone to pursue and deflect suspicion from you. I know you didn't do it, but they don't."

"Okay, how long do you have? Take notes. A lot of this comes from Mitch, so if you want to fill in the details, you are going to have to get him to tell you. Otherwise, try Cornelius. You know that he has been in Egypt since before the last flood, and at AUE for all that time. He is a fount of knowledge. Of course, you know that." Barbie hesitated and waited for David to acknowledge Cornelius.

"You are right, but I don't want to go to him if I don't have to. I need to keep him out of this if at all possible. You can ask him for me, can't you?" David said, hesitation creeping into his voice.

"Okay, here goes. Thurman Hall was a thoroughly bad character; everyone agrees to that. He has an ex-wife, maybe even two, but neither of them seem to be anywhere near Siwa, or even in Egypt, so you can rule them out. Unless they contracted his killing." Barbie said in a flat voice, as if retelling the information again. "He was not nice to many in his department. He insulted Lisbon Truegood in front of everyone, allegedly stole a paper from Schuyler Stanford and published it under his own name and of course, there is the case of Winter Doern, who has now lost her job because he 'denied her tenure'. Whether any of this is true or not, it doesn't justify murder, even though the factor of revenge comes on strong here. Money doesn't seem to be a factor unless someone owed him money. I haven't heard anything about money connected with Professor Hall. He earned a modest salary, not much compared to what he could earn in the States, but more than enough to live on. So unless there are investments or other money complications, I don't think this is about that. As I said, the ex-wife or wives aren't here, and I don't think he has children, so inheriting money is not in the picture. As far as any of us know, there is no 'love interest' in his life. As far as we know… So, there you have it, love, money, revenge. It's got to be revenge."

"Okay, motive is revenge, the means is by the e-cigarette, but what about opportunity? We know, no, change that to we strongly suspect, that the poison, some sort of distilled nicotine, was placed in his e-cigarette. Because it was leaking, we think it might have been done badly, by someone who didn't know how to properly fill the cigarette."

"Or by Thurman himself? Couldn't the person have prepared the poison and then substituted his refill for their own? Maybe he didn't know how to refill his own cigarettes? Maybe that explains the fact that the cigarette I found out by the pool was also leaking. Perhaps not as badly as the one found in his room, but I am sure there was some sticky smelly residue on the outside of it as well. I washed it off immediately," Barbie recalled.

"Poison is a tricky method of murder. In some ways it has to be opportunistic, or done by someone very close to the victim. A wife can easily poison her husband's food or drink if she cooks for him. And the other way around. A medical caregiver can give innocent-looking drugs, but they may have been substituted for one that is not. Just because the person giving the medicine may look innocent, or is innocent, doesn't mean much in the end. They may be suspected. It's usually when someone is a repeat offender that they can be caught.

One dead husband may be overlooked, or one dead old lady who leaves you her money, but not two or three. But is this the case? Wives, caregivers? None around." David sunk his head onto his chest and tapped his fingers on his knee.

Barbie remained quiet, not having anything to add to this cogitation.

Finally, David raised his head. "Okay, you mentioned three people this afternoon who might be suspect. Could they have poisoned his e-cigarette?"

"As you said, poisoners have the advantage of not having to 'be' there when the deed is done. But I do know that Lisbon Truegood and Schuyler Stanford are here in Siwa. But not Winter Doern. But this evening, I thought I saw Winter Doern. Everyone assumes that she isn't here, but I'm sure I saw her. It was just a glance, but…"

David shook his head, "Yes or no? Here or not? Never mind."

"Was Thurman smoking before last evening? On the bus trip? At the bus stops?" David cocked his head.

"I didn't pay attention. Another thing to find out. So many questions, no answers. But in a way, we all agreed that Winter was the obvious. I think you should look at her very carefully. We all thought that she had done a bunk after the fall semester. You remember, we were in our winter break when the Revolution descended upon us. No one saw her for those 18 days and we thought, that was it, she had done a bunk, gone home for good. But then she showed up, ten days late, but in time to take her classes before they were reassigned. She mostly kept to herself, she lives downstairs from us. But I would see her every other day or so, often enough to know that she was still around. She didn't go anywhere with other people, to meetings or Saturday events or whatever. She never did apparently, so that wasn't a departure from her usual routine. In any case, we all felt strangely upset. But the Revolution and the aftermath, all over the Middle East, has had us all on edge. We didn't pay attention to peripheral persons like Winter. She lost all 'celebrity' status and we stopped talking about her. But there are other people around. Nobody liked Thurman Hall."

"Others? What others? And what relationship do they have to Dr. Hall?"

Barbie stumbled in reply. "I really don't know who the others are. I mean, if you are looking for suspects, the three female graduate students have as much or more reason to do something to Thurman Hall. He was the head of the History Department and I think that some of them may have taken classes from him. And he may have had an even closer relationship being a supervisor or a mentor or whatever. I mean, I don't really know them. But I do know they are here. And maybe they did something to Thurman Hall to get back at him for what he did to Schuyler. They are rumored to all be in love with him. That's a bit of a stretch of the imagination to think one of them poisoned his e-cigarette. But you can't just say the field is limited and narrow. You need to dig some more."

"Me? How do I 'dig'? I have no reason to question anyone. 'Did you put nicotine poison in an e-cigarette? Why?' The police here would just as soon all this would go away. I think in the end, they may say he accidentally poisoned himself. People do poison themselves with e-cigarettes you know."

"Would you give up, just like that? Just because the local police couldn't be bothered? And if they did give up, would that let me off the hook?"

"I think so. But there is something about this death that bothers me. I understand that he was not a nice person, that others may have had reason to dislike him, even want him gone, disappeared. But to take someone's life is evil. I have had reason lately to feel as though I need to be more of 'my brother's keeper' and be aware of what is happening around me. I am not here on this earth to enrich myself, to enjoy my life and ignore the injustices that are committed by those around me. I need to be a better person. So, that is why I want to, no, I need to, pursue this. I can't just 'let it go.' Even if the police want to, I don't want to. There is this thing that is 'justice', that is NOT abstract when it comes to murder. I want to see justice done."

"It's an easy thing to say, isn't it? It's easy to say 'I'll do justice'. But justice for whom? Who gets to make that decision? I agree that taking someone's life is wrong, but so is ending someone's career, or stealing, or causing another person to be under suspicion unfairly. Not a reason to kill, but wrong. And how many wrongs like this can you shrug off and say, 'not a nice person'? Justice is not an easy concept, and even more difficult to put into practice," Barbie continued.

Barbie leaned against David and took his hand in hers. "You are a good person, a truly noble person. That is a reason to cherish you and our friendship. I will help if I can. I will help you in your quest for justice."

"Thank you," he whispered. "I feel guilty for the deaths of so many during the Revolution. I tried to stop some of it. I felt helpless. I found out that I have little personal power and in the end, had to leave. I felt defeated, a lost man. I came here and tried to do some good. I have tried to be a good policeman in Siwa. There's not much crime and not knowing the culture and the players, I have kept on the fringes. But this, this crime."

Barbie put her arm around his shoulders. She wanted to hug him, but was afraid that now was not the time. "You know, Cornelius spoke about lust for power and he also talked about hubris. I don't think he was specifically talking about Professor Hall, but warning all of us about arrogance."

In the distance, they heard a motorcycle roar and then listened as it came down the street quietly putt-putting. As it passed, Barbie sat up. "Could it have been done by an outsider? A person not mixed up with us, but a stranger? That motorcycle made me think of the person riding it. He isn't from here. Maybe he found Thurman Hall at the pool and had an argument with him, hit him and then he fell into the pool. If he already had enough nicotine in his system, maybe he was unable to get out, drowned. A weird accident?"

"I suppose, but why would you say that?" David queried.

"Maybe because I don't want to believe that it was done by someone I know. I want it to be an outsider, someone who is not part of us. A 'them' as it were. Easier to handle mentally. Just like you might want it to be an accident, not murder."

A rustling in the bushes stopped Barbie. She looked at David and saw concern in his face. "I'll keep in touch. Ask people things," he commanded. And he was gone.

The rustling became louder. Barbie stood and pressed her back against the side of the gazebo, in a position where she could see outside, but not be readily seen. The rustling continued. Just as Barbie thought it must be a stray cat, she heard a voice.

"He's gone. He can't hurt you any more," a male voice said, soft and low.

Barbie inhaled noisily. She recognized the man's voice. She listened and heard something that could be struggling, or noisy embracing. Since there was no protest, she assumed it was okay. Who could he be talking to? She thought.

"The Hand of God drowned him. He will not think of pawing me," said a female voice, close to Barbie's ear.

"No more," came the answer, amid more rustling.

"There you are! I thought I had lost you out here." This was a new voice and much louder. "Whoops, I thought you wanted to be alone. And here I thought that you were mourning one lost love?! In reality, looking for comfort in another's arms. Well, good for you Sky, eliminate the competition and you can have anything you want. Good luck!"

Barbie heard but did not see the figure leaving, smacking the cement tiles with a click-clack, click-clack, in retreat towards the reception area.

The rustling became louder, then softer and Barbie heard more retreat. She thought they had gone in the opposite direction because she could not see or hear anything more. A cat yowl sounded in another corner of the garden, as if simply waiting for all the humans to leave the cat in peace.

Barbie tried to think about what she had heard. Competition? Pawing? Drowning? Was there an accusation of sexual harassment? Was that a reason for murder? What was the Hand of God reference? One of the three was Sky, but who were the other two females? She could think of three, but which two were here, or was it someone else all together? Was this an angry exchange or merely snarky? The voices were clear, but no one shouted. Another mystery? Was it part of the main mystery, or was this a side issue. Why did she conceal herself? Why didn't she confront them? What was she doing here, listening to conversations in the dark? Barbie cautiously exited the gazebo and slowly, silently made her way towards her room.

Chapter Seventeen: Consultation

Barbie knocked softly on Rachel and Mitch's door. She knew they were still awake because a chink of light shone underneath the door. When Rachel stuck her head out, Barbie whispered that she and Mitch should join her in her room. Like a good friend, Rachel assented.

Still quiet, Barbie looked around the neighborhood of their rooms. All was quiet, no disturbances could be heard. The nighttime animal noises of the desert, nighttime birds rustling in the trees, feral cats seeking food, whether wild mice or domestic garbage, slithering denizens of the night; all were quiet in the vicinity. Barbie looked at her wrist and felt the absence of her watch. Don't worry, she told herself, time isn't important at this point, it's the thinking.

She crept back to her room and knocked quietly on the door. Penelope opened it immediately. Barbie slipped in, and quietly closed it behind her. She whispered to Penelope, "Turn on the TV, make a little noise. We are having guests in a few minutes."

"No can do," Penelope answered. "The TV doesn't work. I've already tried. It's broken."

"Plugged in?" Barbie asked.

Penelope looked startled and dashed to the TV set, finding the cord and picking it up. It had not been plugged in. She hurriedly plugged it in and started pressing buttons. She looked around for a remote box, but even that failed to light the screen. "Plugged in or not, it's broken."

"Do you have your computer? Turn it on and find a radio station. Low, not loud, only enough noise to cover us. I'm looking for little presents that someone may have left." Barbie fell to her knees and started searching the room, looking closely at all the lights, outlets, anything that could hide something small.

"Presents? What kind of presents?" Penelope asked. "I'll help if you tell me what I'm looking for."

"Electronic bugs," mouthed Barbie.

They searched for five minutes until the knock on the door alerted them to guests.

Barbie let Mitch and Rachel in while Penelope tried to find a radio station on the computer. She found one, classical music from Seattle, but it was useful as a static screen in case there was any one listening.

When they were settled in, seated on the beds, Penelope produced a piece of paper and announced quietly. "We need to make sure that Barbie doesn't get arrested. We need to see where we are, what everyone knows and what we can do. Start with you Barbie, I know you had a meeting this evening with the police chief, what did he have to say?"

"Well, can I tell you what I heard in the bushes after the meeting? I think that was just as important." Barbie retold the conversation she heard in the bushes after David left. "Isn't this just as important information? I mean, does it mean that one of the girls, I couldn't tell their voices apart, not that I know them well enough anyway, is involved? Or that she was involved in Thurman Hall's death? This puts a new spin on everything."

Mitch sat in silent thought. "Winter did it, that's all there is to it."

Rachel looked at Mitch, her mouth crunched into an 'O'. "You really believe that is the end of it? How can you be so certain?"

"Man's intuition." Mitch sat sullenly.

"But Winter's not here," Barbie said. "Except maybe she is. I think I saw her this evening, only a glimpse. At the time, I was sure it was her. But has anyone seen or heard of her being in Siwa?"

They stared at Barbie, saying nothing. "So, how does the man's intuition hold up here?"

"She didn't need to be here, that's number one. And number two, just because we haven't seen or heard that she is here, doesn't mean that she isn't." Mitch was obstinate. "We need to ask around a bit more on that point."

"But based on what Barbie heard tonight, I think we need to look again at Schuyler. Are you sure it was his voice you heard in the bushes?" asked Rachel.

"Fairly certain. I wouldn't bet my life on it, but he has this little New Yorky whine that I heard when he was being Alexander. Unmistakable."

"How do you know that Barbie?" Penelope asked.

"An ex-husband. Now, no more comments. I think we can go with the assumption that it was Schuyler. And then what was he referring to? 'He can't hurt you anymore?' It seems obvious to me that he was referring to Thurman Hall hurting someone, the one he was talking to."

"But you said that she referred to the 'Hand of God'. What did that mean?" Rachel joined in.

"Wow, it could have meant almost anything. I believe in fate sometimes. Maybe that's what she was referring to. That fate had taken the nastiness away."

"Hubris?" Mitch intervened.

"Be real," Penelope said. "When someone gets on the Hand of God trip, they mean something by it. Do you think that Schuyler, who didn't like Thurman for other personal reasons, took it upon himself to 'defend' his friend's honor by poisoning him?"

"Murder demands evil forethought. Poisoning someone means plotting to kill. Gathering tools and preparing things. Working out how and where and in this case, taking advantage. This was not an accident, nor the reaction of a moment." Mitch hung his head, as if the thought weighed him down.

"Barbie," began Rachel, "What did David tell you this evening? Anything new?"

"Not really. Only that they seem to have figured out something, such as that it wasn't a natural death, but they would rather have it be 'misadventure' or an accident. They could send all the evidence to a proper police lab, but they are dragging their feet. I mean, from the outside, it could just be an accident. Even if it was poisoning, he could have done it himself, accidentally. They would be happy if that were the case. Foreigners dying because of an accident. We had nothing to do with it. Crazy foreigners, coming to Egypt to have accidents. It would be better for everyone if this were the case."

"David would go along with this?" Penelope asked.

"He might not have choices. He isn't a real policeman, he has no authority and besides, this is Egypt. He spoke vaguely about not having as much clout as he thought, that he couldn't jeopardize his 'hiding place'.

"So where was Schuyler? Could he have done it? He had the motive, but did he have the opportunity? Do we know where he was when Thurman died? Or before he died?" Mitch seemed to abandon his man's intuition to help think through the murder suspect list. "We didn't see him until he showed up at the Temple of Amun dressed as the great Alexander. But presumably they, the grad student contingent, had arrived the night before. Do we know where they are staying? Do we know when they arrived?"

"Good questions," Penelope said, writing them down.

"And then, could he have tampered with the cigarette? What do we know about e-cigarettes and the nicotine stuff that goes in them?" Mitch continued.

The three women looked at Mitch.

"What are you looking at me for?"

"You smoke," cooed his wife. "You know about cigarettes."

"I don't know that much about e-cigarettes. There are two kinds, one of them is refillable, the other isn't, it's a one-time smoke. You have to plug them in and activate the small battery. They kind of look the same, long and slender, trying to mimic real cigarettes. But there are others, big square things, that are the refillable kind. They don't make you look cool or anything. They pack a wallop. It is possible to inhale too much nicotine and poison yourself. I mean, if you huff and puff and huff and puff, you might get too much. It causes your heart to beat way too fast. And if you have a bad heart, it could cause you to pass out, or have an accident while driving or something like that."

"Or like drowning in a cold pool?" Barbie asked.

"You mean we are sitting here saying it could just be an accident and not murder?" asked Rachel, looking at them one by one.

"Are we making a mountain out of a molehill?" Barbie asked. "Write that down Penelope. We need to find out how likely it was to be an accident. Were there bruises for example, or some other reason to suspect murder and not an accident?"

"We would feel stupid to be looking for a murderer and find only an accident," Rachel said. "But we also know that time is important. So, I vote to keep looking into the idea that it could be murder."

"Lisbon Truegood." Barbie uttered his name in a monotone. "We said that he was angry with Thurman."

"Lisbon, that old sweetie? Are you nuts, Barbie?" Penelope barked.

"Quiet," Rachel said. "We don't want all of them to know what we're doing." The four stopped and listened to Penelope's radio station for an entire minute, letting the outburst settle down before resuming in a quieter tone.

"By the way, I haven't had a chance to ask if any one found out any information this afternoon. I didn't. Lots of dead ends and solid walls." Barbie twisted her lips in consternation.

"Funny you'd mention Lisbon. Because this afternoon I mentioned to Tim that Lisbon's situation might have changed with the demise of his Head of Department. And Tim said something strange. Remember, I'm not IN the department, just a seconded member, so I don't always hear all the gossip in a straightforward manner. I wasn't at this particular meeting, but apparently Lisbon let fly some superbly nasty language at Thurman. He didn't threaten to kill him, but that's what everyone thought. I have never seen Lisbon blow up; this was unusual. Tim told me, when I made a slight mention of the HOD question, that this tiff was about that. Apparently, Lisbon wanted to be HOD, but was discouraged from throwing his hat into the ring, told that he was not senior enough, was only an Associate Prof and hadn't been one for very long, not long enough. The upshot was that Lisbon didn't even put his name forward. And then there is a vote and the only name on the ballot was Thurman's, so in he goes. Lisbon felt as though he was not encouraged. He may not have had a chance, but Thurman had only been at AUE for one year longer, so why was he the ONLY one? Anyway, it was a bit muddled on that account. But what was not muddled at all, but quite clear was the fact that Thurman questioned Lisbon's 'collegiality' in front of the whole department. I had heard about this meeting, but wasn't there and all I heard was the gossip. This time Pete did because it was over, the fight was over, he said. He believes that if Lisbon wants the job of HOD, he can have it. At this point, no one in the department even wants to think about it, but the winner, if there is one, is Lisbon Truegood. And everyone knows it. The 'uncollegiality' was a way to get rid of a rival. Everyone knew that, but it would have been even worse manners than those of Thurman's to say so. It's all about the gossip. Everyone thought that Lisbon was hurt, so he lashed out, perhaps inappropriately, in a meeting, but that he was justified in being angry at the way he had been treated."

This monologue was received with silence. The women, nonacademics, understood the petty bickering in the academic departments of universities, but they existed on the periphery. They now felt quite glad to be away from it. But they understood the gravity of the sentiments that Mitch talked about.

"I was sitting in the lunch room one day and I overheard a conversation that I have only now remembered," Penelope said. "I didn't think much of it at the time because I didn't know the persons involved and I didn't know who they were talking about. But listening to Barbie's story about the conversation in the garden reminds me. I want to tell you, even though it may not be relevant. Maybe it is. But this was it. One woman, I think a faculty wife, said that a person (they knew who they were talking about) had been complained about. There was some inappropriate behavior on the part of this person. And the other woman, a friend, I didn't know her, said, 'Well, couldn't she just have said, 'no?' And the first one said that it was a macho culture and that he was a superior and that it would be hard to prove. The good ole boys would only say that it was all in fun, or that she should think of it as a compliment, or he only asked and what's the harm in that? Is this relevant? Helpful? Maybe if I think hard I can remember who it was who said it. I don't think it was our graduate students, the ones in the garden, but maybe it was. After all, what I overheard was third hand."

"Even a faculty wife can know about such things," said Rachel. "Maybe it was about Thurman and one of the grad students. You know how vulnerable they can be. Especially the women in such a macho culture as this. I think the men here get infected with the dominant culture around them and latch onto it too much. They are the 'chosen' ones and it makes them feel good to be on the top of the heap. Not you, sweetie," she said to Mitch.

"But you are right. The Head of the Department has a lot of power over graduate students, recommendation letters, seeing their theses go through, not to speak of the courses they may take from a teacher. It's amazing how a little signature can delay things, make students miss chances, jobs, scholarships and so forth. It can ruin a career, or at least make it a lot rougher than it has to be. So, if even one of those students was being targeted, maybe all three of them are in on it?" Mitch thought aloud.

"You're right." Barbie followed through. "It would be easy enough for one of them to fiddle with the cigarette while another kept him busy. They could have done a hand-off to each other. And maybe if they were not all in on it, like murder, maybe there was an opportunity for them to 'get back' at Thurman for wrongs done. I mean, it is much more difficult for three of them to conspire to murder someone. More like conspire to give him a scare."

"They've been acting normally though. Wouldn't the weak link be scared? They have not shown any nervousness at all. They have all been laughing and happy. By that I mean as 'happy' as any of us feel after one of our party has died in mysterious circumstances," Penelope added.

"Do they have an alibi? Were they even here? We don't know when they arrived," Mitch said. "The same could be said about Schuyler. They all came together with the group of grad students. But then again, we don't know when the cigarette was tampered with. And we don't know if someone was needed to make sure Thurman drowned. Three of them together, or even two of them could have done it. Oh God, we are back to square one!"

"Maybe the police missed something. I know that I went back to look and found that cigarette. Maybe there is something else they missed. Isn't it worth a try? I'm going to look again. It is way too late for anyone to be there; I'll be able to do a thorough search. I'll take my flashlight and do a good job this time." Barbie jumped up and started out the door.

Rachel jumped up and stood in front of her, "No, Barbie, bad idea."

Both Mitch and Penelope moved and stood with Rachel at the door. "NO, NO, NO."

"You don't frighten me. And you can't stop me. In the end, I will do what I want. You guys are not the ones that the police suspect. It's me and I will go." Barbie thrust her chin in the air.

Thirty seconds passed as the four friends stood at an impasse. Mitch broke the silence. "Ok, you can go, but we are going with you and when you are done, you will come back with us. You will NOT go alone."

Barbie smiled and fetched her flashlight. "We had better leave the computer here, still on, make anyone think we are still listening to music."

"Can we turn it to country and western? This is fooling no one. Classical? Really?" Mitch groused.

"I'm going. Come with me or not. I'm off to the pool enclosure for one last try."

The four friends went as silently as four people can be, trying to shine flashlights, lock the door, and not trip over their own and others' feet.

Barbie led the way. The first part, from their room to the reception area was well lit. Lights shone in the bushes, throwing grotesque visons of long leaves swaying in the breeze across the walkway, hiding small animals and fears in the shadows. Barbie turned on Rachel and complained about Rachel's sandals which made a flipping-flopping noise when she walked. Penelope tried to contain her nervousness by breathing deeply which also created unnecessary noise. As they neared the reception area, Barbie stopped them to peer into the office to see if anyone sat at the desk, or was using the computer in the lobby. It was deserted, which gave her pause, but not for long. After the reception area, the pathway gradually wound its way far from the lighted areas. The cement stones became uneven and dark shadows spread across their path. Barbie turned on her flashlight which threw a feeble light directly in front of her feet but did not penetrate far into the inky night.

After thirty steps, the large bushes opened up to the pool area, which was almost completely in the dark. Trees overhung the pool and they created a moveable blackness that danced with unspoken and unseen dangers.

"This is creepy," said Penelope. "What are you looking for, Barbie? Why are we here?" She squeaked quietly.

"I'll know it when and if I see it. Everyone, take your phones or flashlights and shine them everywhere. Look for anything. The police are idiots; they might have missed good clues. They weren't honestly looking."

Rachel and Mitch used their phones, and Penelope, who had no light, vowed to watch their backs. "You two take that side, to the right where the lounge chair was sitting and his stuff was collected from," Barbie directed Mitch and Rachel. "I'll look to the left."

They spread out and flashed their lights in front of them in arcs. The scrape of chairs and tables being moved made Penelope hush them again and again. "Quiet, someone will hear!"

"Whew. Look at this?" Barbie held up a small rectangular piece of paper, which they all recognized as a receipt from a shop. The small white paper fluttered in Barbie's hand.

"Do you think this is important?" whispered Rachel.

"What are you doing here?" came a shout, causing them all to jump.

A bright light shone directly in Barbie's eyes and she tried to cover her face with the hand that held the receipt.

"Why are you here? Why are you making so much noise?" came the shout again.

"Mahmoud," Barbie recognized the voice. "Oh, how nice to bring a light. But I have found it."

"Found what? What is this all about?" he shouted again.

Mitch and Rachel stood close together, their telephone lights off, attempting to be inconspicuous. They let Barbie take the lead.

"It's a receipt that I lost. I need it. Yeah, I need it for my taxes. You know American get really, really funny about having receipts for everything. And this is important. I bought a book, see," she held it out and immediately snatched it back, shoving it into her front pants pocket. "Good, I've found it now. We can go back, gang. Thanks for your help."

Mahmoud dropped the light from Barbie's face and swept it around to reveal her three co-conspirators. "Well," his voice lowered. "If you need this. But it is late. The others have complained and you are making noise. Couldn't you wait until morning?"

"I have found it, thank you," Barbie answered. "I don't need to look any more. We are going."

"You are aware of the reputation of this pool? I don't know why they built a hotel here. Maybe because they thought that foreigners wouldn't know the stories and would think nothing of it. And of course, no one will tell you. But now I am telling you. This pool is cursed. No one from Siwa will swim here. Even the staff don't like to be around it. Now we know for sure. It is an evil pool."

Chapter Eighteen: Decisions at Breakfast

Brilliant morning sun poured into the breakfast room located next to the reception area. The mosquitos of the night had gone, and were replaced by small grey birds, small brown birds and buzzing insects that would not bite. The garden rustled with their meanderings, punctuated by the sound of morning watering by the gardeners. They silently moved hoses and watering cans, managing to irrigate the plants in the garden without spray or any sound but the gurgle of water. Barbie approached the dining room, listening to the soft morning sounds and wondering at the lushness of the garden here, in fact in all of Siwa, surrounded by harsh desert.

She heard the clink of forks on plates, coffee cups hitting the saucers and a low murmur of morning voices, not awake enough to sound above a whisper. She had left Penelope still asleep, which was an unusual switch for the two roommates. She spied Mitch and Rachel at the end table in an alcove at the back of the small breakfast room. She slipped in beside Mitch with a cup of coffee in her hand. She sat it down with a tinkle and confronted him. "Receipt translated?" she demanded.

"Good morning to you, too. And yes. It's for a bag of chips and a coke, dated four days ago in Cairo. I have no idea where it came from, generic as it were. Does that tell you anything at all?"

"Fingerprints?" Barbie continued, slurping her coffee.

"Yours, mine and could be half the staff as well. I suspect it came from a room's trash can and not from anyone in particular. Satisfied?" Mitch turned back to his breakfast, a conglomeration of Western and Egyptian breakfast. He dug his fork into a small bowl of ful, fava beans cooked overnight and spiced with onions, parsley, garlic and chili. Salt optional. He also had an omelet, sweet breakfast breads, and flat Egyptian bread called 'baladi bread' because it was literally 'country bread', or as Penelope was fond of calling it, 'peasant's bread'. He had smeared thick lumps of butter on it and topped it with honey. Barbie salivated.

"Okay, enough of that, dead end, don't you think?" Barbie said, eyeing Mitch's bread.

"Okay, take it," Mitch said, handing the bread to Barbie. "I can always get more."

"No, I'll get my own," Barbie said getting up and heading to the breakfast buffet. It was one of the most pleasant aspects of hotels in Egypt. Even the cheapest served breakfast, but the larger hotels always had buffets. The bigger the hotel, the wealthier the clientele, the better the breakfast. Sometimes Barbie felt she should choose hotels for the breakfast, eat that one meal, then fast the rest of the day. She piled her plate high with fruits, scrambled eggs and a bowl of cereal. She approached the basket of baladi with care. She did not see any that had been torn yet, but tried to avoid other's hand germs in Egypt. She took a whole round for herself, promising herself that she would share with Penelope, then put butter and jam on her plate. She was more relaxed when she sat again.

The three ate in silence. Then Cornelius Smythe stood. He waited until the diners became quiet. He harrumphed and spoke, "Good morning, ladies and gentlemen, I hope you are all well rested?" He waited until there was a murmur of assent. "As you know, we were originally scheduled for two more days of seeing the wonders of Siwa. However, due to the unfortunate demise of our esteemed colleague, there has been talk of cutting short our sojourn, in order to not to appear unseemly in our merriment. However, I do not detect an inordinate amount of unseemly behavior, and returning to

Cairo early would also appear unseemly to some. Hasty retreat, and all that. As well, our esteemed colleagues in the police division here feel as though they would like us to remain so they can talk with us again. There does appear to be some complications surrounding our friend's death and it would not be to our advantage, or theirs, if we left too soon. So, we will not be leaving early, or at least, we will not be leaving today.

"Our morning is free. I suggest you take the opportunity to go shopping, explore the village, visit the small but worthwhile folk museum or simply rest. Maps are available at the reception desk so you will not get lost. You can walk, but if you are not inclined to brave the sun, you may hire a donkey cart in the lane outside the hotel gate, or in the square. Don't be put off by the age of the drivers, but do check for comfort in the seating arrangements and the awning. The small boys and their brothers and sisters speak English well enough and if you point to the photos on the map, you should be able to get to wherever you need to go. Please make sure you set the price before you head off.

"We will meet again at 2pm, after a light lunch on your own. You should bring your swimming costumes if you wish to swim in the pool. We will also be visiting the Bedouin village and the Siwa water-bottling plant. Until then, have a relaxing time." Cornelius looked around the room to see if anyone had any questions. One of the professors jumped up and accosted him privately. Barbie overheard 'carpets' and turned away. Spare me looking at or buying any more carpets, she thought.

Barbie sat languidly over her breakfast and waited for Penelope. When she arrived, they discussed what they might do in the free morning hours. "Walk around town, see what's here!" Penelope said.

"Go shopping, in other words?" Barbie countered.

They headed back to their room to pick up their small daypacks for the morning's roam. They waved at Mitch and Rachel as the two sat outside under a tree. Penelope veered off course to talk with them. Barbie continued on to the room.

Five minutes later there was a knock at the door. Barbie heaved a sigh. Why can't she just come in instead of making me go open the door. Did I lock it, thought Barbie?

She ripped at the door and opened her mouth to protest. When she saw who stood there, she closed her mouth with a 'snap'. Ali Rafiq, resplendent in police uniform, stood on her doorstep. "Good morning, Ms. Falcon. Would you care for a ride?"

"Depends on where," she smiled.

"First to my office, then I'll take you wherever you want to go. I understand that you have a free morning."

"Come in, I'll get my things and I am yours!" Barbie couldn't help smiling at the thought of the handsome man whisking her away.

On their way out of the hotel, Barbie spied Penelope with Mitch and Rachel, still sitting under the tree in the cool garden. She called out to them. "I'm off. I'll call and meet you later."

"Where are you going?" Penelope asked.

"With," Barbie paused and looked around. David had disappeared, gone ahead of her. "Ali Rafiq, to his office. I'm getting a ride." She tossed the room key to Penelope and waved.

At the reception area, she found no one, so she proceeded to the street gate. Still she found no one. What happened to him, she thought, looking up and down the street.

As she peered down the street towards the main square two hundred yards away, a car approached her from the opposite direction. By the time she had noticed the noise and turned, it had stopped beside her. It was an old battered Lada, painted black, left over from the days of the Russians. It was the car of the Egyptian taxi driver and they had never gone away as spare parts and expertise in repair had constantly been available. Cheap. Barbie leaned over and saw that David sat in the driver's seat. She pulled and twisted at the door handle until it loosened and she got in. It took three slams to keep the door shut.

"I do apologize for the state of the transport," he said. "But we are in Siwa, in the farthest reaches of the Egyptian empire. We cannot choose our vehicles. We are going to take the scenic route," he announced. "I want to avoid prying eyes."

Barbie sat back and watched the street scenes of Siwa as they wound their way through back streets. Donkey carts were more numerous here than in the touristic parts of the town as whole families climbed aboard to be transported through the town. Some carts were piled high with produce from gardens in the suburbs, being transported to the markets in town, while others, coming in the opposite direction, had a variety of goods, watched over by a child or two and a blue tent. Barbie knew that underneath the blue and white checked cloth sat the mother of the family, holding the front part closed with her teeth. She felt amazed that in the twenty-first century, in a modern country like Egypt, that medieval scenes were to be found. At least the spring-less carts had rubber tires, lessening the impact of bouncing over potholes. The roads were mostly dirt and even now, approaching mid-morning, they were covered with a thin film of very fine dust which was thrown up by the tires of carts, motorcycles and a few cars. Barbie knew better than to roll up the window. The window probably wouldn't roll up, and even if she did manage to get the window closed, the dust would seep in through the ill-fitting windows and cover the interior with dust, and she would get hot. She reasoned, through experience, that open windows were preferable.

Before she realized it, they had arrived at the back of the police station. David parked under a tree which threw thin filtered shade on the vehicle. David got out and came to Barbie's side of the car. She had not been idle, but had been unable to push the door open. David did it with a flick of his wrist and a yank. He ushered her into a separate part of the police station, this part more private and more up to date.

"These are our private offices," he explained as he called for a 'boy' to bring tea. They mounted two steps, crossed a deep veranda and entered through a screen door into a spacious office. Mounted on the wall was an air-conditioning unit that would surely be used in the afternoon heat. At the moment, the inside temperature was pleasantly cool. There was a couch, three chairs and a massive wooden desk. On the desk was a small computer screen, a telephone, and two empty trays. Behind the desk was a tall book case, half full of books, the other half sporting Egyptian 'antiquities' and tourist artifacts. Barbie recognized Siwan baskets, carved basalt 'Bastet' cats, mother-of-pearl inlaid boxes and other tourist trinkets from the Kahn el Khalili. So David had brought some things with him, thought Barbie. He didn't completely leave his old life behind him.

Awkwardly Barbie strolled in the office, looking out the window, looking at the souvenirs on the shelves, looking at anything but the man who stood beside the desk. The tea appeared promptly and David dismissed the man who brought it. They sat, Barbie on the couch, David in a chair not far from her. They fussed with the tea glasses, and slurped the sweet liquid.

When the preliminary pleasantries had taken place, Barbie started the conversation. "I have some 'gossip' to report. It may be nothing, but if it can move the incident forward to closure, so be it." She relayed the conversation of the last evening in the garden, their speculations on it, and then Penelope's addition of gossip from the lunch room. "That's all. And you? What do you have to report?"

"As far as the doctor can determine, there were lethal, or near lethal, levels of nicotine in Thurman Hall's blood. If he didn't die of a heart attack, he died of drowning due to inability to control his movements sufficiently to crawl out of the pool. That still leaves us with a question mark as to whether this was murder or an accident. But coupled with the highly concentrated liquid on the outside of the e-cigarette, that 'poisoned' one of our police officers, we are going forward with the idea that someone else put concentrated nicotine into the cigarette. We don't think that Thurman Hall committed suicide this way; we think it was deliberate. However, we are still holding open the idea that it was an accident, just to be able to cover ourselves if we can't find a murderer."

"And you can't just 'round up the usual suspects' because this is not a local theft, a terrorist attack or other kind of 'usual' thing in Siwa. Hummmmm." Barbie sipped the rest of her tea and sat back in the folds of the couch. "I noticed that you keep referring to the Siwa Police as 'we'. Are you one of them? Really and truly?"

Ali Rafiq laughed David's hearty laugh deep in his throat. "I have gotten used to being Ali Rafiq, the Chief of Police in Siwa. Naturally, I have slipped into the royal 'we' when I refer to our department. I did study law for a few semesters at the university in London, but I did not fancy being a lawyer and was not able to identify a body of man-made law that I thought was fully encompassing of the idea of 'justice', so I quit. But coming here, even in the pretense of being a man of the law, I studied a bit." He gestured to the wall of books. "Some of these are Arabic law books, Egyptian law as it were, and some are how to manage a police force. And some, you may be interested to see here."

He invited Barbie to come around the back of the desk and peruse the books. A shelf contained books in English and Barbie laughed as she read the titles. "Sherlock Holmes? Are you crazy? This is going to help you in your cover of being a back woods policeman?"

"I'll have you know that Conan Doyle was a master detective. I think medical professionals have to be. 'Finding out' is what medical diagnosis is all about. Eliminating the improbable or the impossible and then deciding what a disease is and how to cure it. And when he wrote the Sherlock Homes stories, he used his knowledge of deduction for the edification of the rest of us. Specifically, me. I learned a lot. At least right away, I began to sound good. Bit of a problem translating it into Arabic, until I found a good translation. And a few other police procedurals, good for the grounding of the professionalism."

Barbie ran her fingers along the spines of a group of mystery novels. Agatha Christie, Ngaio Marsh, John Grisham,

Stieg Larson, Dashiell Hammett. Some she heartily approved of, but at one, she baulked. "Raymond Chandler? Really? Interesting, but maybe you could have learned better elsewhere."

"I've had a lot of time, sitting here in Siwa. Many boring evenings, many opportunities to read novels."

"You have a fabulous library. Do you have a nice place to live, at least? And TV? Internet or otherwise?"

"You are in my sitting room and I have a bedroom, ensuite. Not bad," he said nodding his head towards a small door in the corner that Barbie had overlooked. "But it is not as good as Cairo," he said looking up at the ceiling, letting his eyes wander into the distance.

"Do you miss Cairo? The hustle and bustle? It must be excruciating for a city boy like you?" Barbie thought of the long lonely nights David had spent in Siwa, with a closed business and a host of friends left behind in the metropolis.

"The Arab Spring has passed me by. I thought that I could do something for my country, but I was mistaken. My friends turned on me. To be fair, they needed to protect their businesses and their families. So as long as I am out of Cairo, no one bothers with me. I'm not so well-known as to need to be watched and am no threat to the present government. I am sad to see the 'Revolution' devolve into the Arab Spring. Such euphoria, such hope and promise. Now we only have the uncertainty of an 'Arab Spring'. I will stay here, keep up to date, do my little job…"

"And read novels," Barbie teased.

"And read newspapers, blogs and journals and anything I can. I will become knowledgeable about it all. Even though I am not physically in the center of things, I will remain committed. Now, you need to be a tourist. I will take you back to the center of the city, will that do?"

"Perfect," Barbie answered. She took out her phone and called Penelope. They were currently sitting in a café on the main square, in fact they had just arrived. "Order me a coffee! I'll be there soon."

The ride back to the city was more direct and within five minutes, Barbie saw the main square, dominated by the picturesque Shali, in the distance.

A motorcycle passed them on the road. It roared by and left a swirl of dust in its wake. David looked to see the sleek black lines, the shiny chrome and the expensive roar of the engine. He followed it with his eyes. Barbie noticed and laughed.

"Do you welcome motorcycle gangs in Siwa? Ever had any trouble with them?" Barbie teased.

"No, but this one I don't know. I assume it's a foreigner," he answered.

"Oh, I know who it is," Barbie said. "He's new in town, a stranger. They say he's Dutch and he's alone."

"A stranger," David repeated.

Chapter Nineteen: Shopping in Siwa

David found the café and dropped Barbie off. He waved briefly at her friends, but quickly left. She approached their table and sat down.

Mitch and Rachel looked at Barbie and smiled knowingly. Barbie smiled archly in return. Penelope ignored the lovelorn looks and started in on her ideas for shopping. Barbie's coffee arrived. It was Nescafe, made with lukewarm water and was highly sugared. She sipped distastefully and asked if she was now expected to pay for it.

"So, what did Mr. Ali Rafiq have to say?" Mitch leaned forward conspiratorially.

"Nothing much. Definitely nicotine poisoning. He hinted that the police may call it an accident, even though it definitely looks like murder. Everything is at a standstill. He didn't say anything more about me being suspected. I'm free to roam the city. Penelope, where are we going first?"

They looked at the map of the city and plotted their route to places of interest. Penelope wanted to buy some stamps and send some postcards. "I've never been to such an exotic place before. My mother would enjoy a postcard from a weird place like this. Anyone else for the Post Office?"

"A Siwan basket for me I think," said Rachel. "Oh look, there is one going by now." She jumped up from her seat, grabbed her camera and aimed it at the donkey cart going by. A small boy, hardly able to control the wild little donkey, sat in the front. On the back of the cart was a blue and white checked tent with one hand out, holding down an enormous basket. The huge globe was made from multicolored straw which made the main part look like a Dr. Seuss character's belly. Attached at the top and all the way around were pom poms of various hues and a fringe. The basket swayed and bounced like a giant cat toy on a spring. "Follow that basket, I want to buy it."

"Rachel, maybe she wants it, or needs it. Let's go look at the shops, I am sure they sell them." Mitch tried to restrain his wife from running after the dusty cart, now rattling down the street.

They gathered their things and started wandering. The main square was lined with shops selling olives and dates. The olives were displayed in extremely large jars, floating in briny liquid. They came in olive green, but also in black, dark brown, light green and every hue in between. It was possible to buy only a few, placed in a plastic bag with the top tied in knot, or the whole jar. Rows of all sizes lined the shelves of many shops. Olive oil was sold in giant square cans of ten liters or more. Other shelves contained dates. The cheap dates were placed outside in heaps, covered with flies and bees, and encrusted with sugar. Others were packaged in colorful boxes and wrapped in cheap plastic. The four browsed through the shops, but thought that buying large quantities was not in their best interests at the moment.

"We could horde them for the next revolution!" offered Penelope.

In the shadow of the Shali, steps from the dusty main square, sat a shop that screamed 'upscale'. They entered. The wooden floor and extensive wooden shelving enveloped them in a soft, quiet world. The smell of olive was strong, but not nauseating nor unpleasant. The shelves were lined not with dusty mismatched bottles of fermenting olives, but with elegantly shaped bottles tied with raffia bows. The labels declared them to be olive oil from the finest of Siwa olives, pressed locally, and flavored with various herbs, also of local origin.

"Now we've come to the right place. What beautiful bottles, what interesting shapes and great flavors. Wonderful gifts!" gushed Penelope.

"Great prices too," muttered Barbie. "Do you realize how much per ounce you pay for this 'great' olive oil? You can make flavored olive oil yourself, just stick the herbs in and let it sit!!" She shook her head and browsed some more. Stacks of olive oil soap bars caught her eye and she picked up three to buy. "Hey, Penelope, this is more like it!" she called out, showing Penelope the cheaper, and easier to carry, soap.

They proceeded to other shops, bottles of olive oil clanking in packs as they walked in the streets. They found a shop that carried some of everything, so they all happily entered. Huge flat baskets near the doorway held silver jewelry. The quality was poor, but the heaviness of the pieces was impressive. Bangles, chain mail breastplates, head pieces with attached ear pieces, huge disks with intricate patterns. As Barbie hefted them in her hand, she felt the weight of ages. Young girls wore these outsized necklaces and head pieces to show off a family's wealth, not the beauty of the wearer. She wondered if young Siwan girls were proud to show off their dangling baubles as young American girls were. Jewelry was jewelry, she thought. Whatever was in fashion. She dropped the disks back into the basket and then turned to Penelope who was looking at carpets. They were hung on racks against the wall and Penelope had pulled one out to look closer. "David Roberts!" Barbie exclaimed.

The scene was of men in the covered bazaar. A tableau of three men, two standing, one seated, looked at something on a table. The scene was set in a typical bazaar with tiled floors, wooden windows and a cover over the street. The men wore colorful robes, turbans and their faces represented the variety of Egypt. Barbie could have sworn the scene was stolen from a Robert's painting. "I need this, I really need this," Penelope said as she set out to bargain. She glanced over her shoulder as if to say to Barbie, 'watch me'. Barbie had demonstrated her powers in bargaining to Penelope many times and taught her the skills that Barbie had witnessed while shopping with her mother in Tijuana Mexico and honed herself in India. Show how much you like the product, praise it as lovely, but start by offering NO MORE than half their asking price, or less if outrageously inflated. Stick with a price and force them to come down. They may expect you to raise to match their lowering, but if you are persistent, smile and praise the object, they will come down. If all else fails, be prepared to walk away. There is always another shop just around the corner. Barbie had bought things for ten percent of the asking price using this method. Granted, they were not the best of souvenirs, but they were cheap. She now watched Penelope use the 'method'. Barbie drifted away, letting Penelope work for her carpet.

In the next shop, Barbie sat on a low stool and simply looked. The shopkeeper, a young man wearing jeans and a turban, smiled at her. Silently, he made tea for her in the back of his shop. He brought her a glass and took one for himself.

"Shukran," she smiled, taking the tea, the fifth glass she had had this morning. "You know; I'm not going to buy anything."

"It's okay, I wanted tea anyway," he flashed a gap-toothed grin at her. "How is your stay so far in Siwa? We are so happy to see some tourists here. After the Revolution, things were very bad, now they are just bad. We had NO troubles here, so why should people stay away? But I understand that they must go to Cairo to get here, so what can we do? What hotel are your staying at?"

Barbie mentioned the hotel and the young man shrugged. "Not an eco-lodge, though. These will be the savior of Siwa. High-end lodges, private swimming pools, gourmet meals and lots of dollars. All outfitted with solar panels, water filtration systems that recycle the water, passive cooling systems, everything a rich person wants. All for only $350 per day."

Barbie laughed and said she couldn't afford that. "But it sounds like a good idea. Are there any?"

"Yes, one expensive one, but there are a few that are trying to be mid-price. They are built in old houses with thick salt brick walls, courtyards that have private garden ponds and rooftop dining. But not expensive. Would you like to see one?"

"Yes, I would, but I'm with a group, and we have little free time. Thanks for the tea. I will buy one bottle of olive oil, though, if you have a nice one." Barbie smiled at the young man, both recognizing a sales tactic that was decidedly un-Egyptian, but would work on certain customers. Offer a gift, very politely, then any self-respecting customer would purchase something, so as not to be indebted. The soft sell.

Barbie walked out into the street and back towards where she had left Penelope. No one. She took out her phone and called. No answer. She noted that the battery was getting low. She thought to herself that she needed to take a few minutes and get more juice.

She wandered back to the main square and then spied Mitch and Rachel sitting at a different café on the square. Better coffee? Probably not, but a different angle from which to view the world. She sauntered over to join them. They were drinking cokes this time and Barbie ordered one. "I feel extraordinarily decadent to be drinking this so far from where it is made, and so far from its 'homeland'. I wonder if these kids can afford to drink coke?" she asked no one in particular.

She gazed out at the square, now bright in the midday sun. The traffic had slowed. The buses that had left Marsa Matrouh that morning had arrived, debouched their passengers and departed to get more gas, have their windows washed, interiors cleaned and rest their drivers. They would depart later this afternoon for the return trip of four hours. The small bus kiosk sat on the main square directly in front of the ruined Shali, at the edge of the large mural of the town. Now, the passengers had all left and the small window slammed shut for the rest of the midday rest. It would open a half hour before the afternoon buses departed.

Penelope loped up to the restaurant, clutching a large paper-wrapped package under her arm. She threw it on a chair and collapsed in another. "Something to drink!" she demanded.

"Cokes are cold, is that okay?" Barbie signaled to the waiter.

"So, you bought it!" Barbie commented.

"For $100. He originally wanted about $250 for it. I feel like I stole it from him." Penelope said.

"Let's see it," Rachel urged, untying the string that bound the unwieldy rug. She spread it out on the nearby table, touching and rubbing the thick wool, turning it over to check the back side. "Look at this lovely work, the same on front and back. It looks like the Three Kings of the Bible, three different races, three different styles of clothes, three different attitudes. And so primitive!"

"Is that remark meant to call into question the skill of the weaver? I mean, I LIKE the wonky perspective, it's endearing." Penelope spit back, arching her eyebrows, daring Rachel to dismiss her treasure.

"You did well, supporting the local economy and giving some aspiring artist the chance to learn his or her trade. Never mind the bulging nose of the big guy here, or the cadaver look of the seated seller of what is it? Multicolored baubles?" Mitch pitched in.

"This is my beautiful Siwa carpet, you all can stuff it!" Penelope rolled the carpet back up and retied the string. Her coke came and she sat sipping it, declining to join in the conversation.

Mitch inclined his head, calling attention to a lone figure that sat on the very edge of the café. He had a glass in front of him that looked suspiciously like a beer, although it was neither in a beer glass nor accompanied by the bottle. Mitch looked quizzical and then said, "The Siwans. They want his custom, they want to serve him what he wants, but it would look very bad if this café were to be seen serving alcohol. I'll bet the locals come here to drink beer as well."

"It's the Dutch motorcyclist," Barbie remarked. "Hmm, anyone fancy a beer? I'll go ask him how he did it." She stood and strolled over to the Dutchman's table.

She stood beside the table and cast her smile at the man and his beer. "Is that fizzy brew what I think it is? Is it beer?"

"Nasty stuff, horse's piss. But beer it is," he chuckled.

"Mind if I join you and have one too?" Barbie said sitting down, the question being only a rhetorical one. She signaled to the waiter.

Barbie smiled and said, "I hear you are on a motorcycle and that you are traveling alone. True?"

"True," came the reply.

"Tell me more! Where did you start, where are you going? Where is your final destination? What is the most amazing thing you have seen? Do you take photographs? Are you writing a book?" Barbie shook her blonde curls and bestowed a brilliant smile on the stranger.

He laughed a deep throaty laugh, an indication that he would try to answer Barbie's personal and vaguely rude questions, only because she seemed innocuous and enthusiastic.

He told her he started in Amsterdam, he had been around Africa, he was on his way home the very next week after more than a year in Africa. "There is a ferry from Alexandria to Venice every week. If the sea is not too difficult, the waves not too high, the rain not too bad, and if there are enough passengers, we will go."

"I saw your motorcycle. What a lovely beast!" Barbie urged him to continue.

"Beast, what, an animal, my beautiful machine! Yes, she is a beast. But she has taken me everywhere. This is my fourth long trip." He stopped and took a long draft of beer, finishing his glass. He set the glass on the table with a satisfied 'thonk'. "Do you mind?" he asked, taking out a package of cigarettes.

Barbie looked askance, but noted that the pack was empty. If she wanted to make her escape, now was the time, before he bought another pack and lighted up.

"Oh, damn, but never mind, I will smoke my new one." The motorcyclist from the Netherlands reached over to his shabby pack and stuck his hand into a pocket. He pulled out a long thin white tube. He screwed a smaller red tube onto the end and stuck it into his mouth, sucking noisily. The tip turned red and then a stream of vapor escaped.

Barbie watched in fascination as she saw him smoke an e-cigarette exactly like the one that she had seen Thurman Hall smoking just hours before his death.

Chapter Twenty: Water in the Desert

When the four friends arrived back at the hotel, they found their bus waiting in the hotel parking lot. No one was there yet, but they noted that the bus may not wait for them if they were late. Hurriedly they returned to their rooms, exchanging souvenirs for a light jacket and a water bottle.

When they returned to the parking lot, they noticed the huge motorcycle in the corner, with a few of the local young men hanging around it. Tentatively they ran their fingers along its sleek lines and murmured words of admiration and envy. Barbie thought that her new friend's cycle had been subjected to this treatment many times and she wondered if the owner objected to this violation of his property. If he were a generous and perceptive world traveler, he would understand.

As she got on the bus, she tried to avoid sitting next to Sally, to continue the conversation of yesterday. She suddenly found herself not wanting to pursue an 'investigation' of what had happened to Thurman Hall. He died, she thought. No one liked him, no one would mourn and it appeared as if this group did not care. I wish I could leave all of this behind in Siwa and see the desert and all the sights without thinking of it. Just let us be tourists and enjoy ourselves!

Sally sat across the aisle from Barbie and immediately picked up the conversation from yesterday. She however, was feeling as Barbie did. "Oh, I'm so happy to be on this bus going into the desert. I just love the desert, don't you? I think we deserve to have a good time today, don't you? Did you bring your swimming suit? I think swimming in one of the ancient pools will be fun, don't you? This is a great tour, isn't it?" And on she went.

Barbie realized that only a minor 'yes' occasionally would keep Sally talking and Barbie could ignore her if she wished. Barbie needed to keep an ear out for any information about the 'murder,' but otherwise, she was free to let her mind wander.

They did not pass the Shali and the main square this time, but headed out into the desert to the east of the town. The palm trees that gave shade and color to the inhabited and cultivated parts of Siwa gave way to small orchards of olive trees, some ancient and gnarled, others young and upright. Through the gloom of shade thrown by the trees, Barbie saw small plots given over to vegetable gardens and realized that Siwans could be quite food self-sufficient. Animals wandered the streets and groves of trees, nibbling on the grass that grew on the verges of the sunken fields. Barbie noted, as they passed by the palm groves, the channels that fed water in intricate patterns. Each tree had its own sunken 'field' that was flooded and then allowed to dry out. She marveled at the intricacies of the patterns and the minds that had laid it all out, without benefit of computer modeling, she thought. Humans are so clever, she thought.

Soon, they left the trees and all cultivation behind. The delineation from town to country was abrupt. There was no 'gradual' loss of trees and fields, but one orchard of palm trees bordered the desert. And the desert was a very dry one. Barbie could see nothing growing wild. She felt sure there was something there, but from her position high above the ground, there was absolutely nothing to see. So, she switched her view to the horizon, which was obscured in a haze. A haze that gradually morphed from tan desert to light blue sky. There did not appear to be any hills or mountains, nor any habitation to break up the view. Barbie laid her head back in the seat, ignoring Sally's continuous patter from across the aisle and closed her eyes.

"Oh, we're here," Sally announced, jerking Barbie to an upright position.

The desert had been invaded by a parking lot and a slew of buildings. A large sign announced the "Siwa Bottling Company" as they bumped their way into the almost empty lot. They descended from the bus and were herded into a low building. They were handed small plastic cups of water, a welcome drink in this dry landscape. Barbie looked at the water and decided that it must be some of their very own Siwa Bottled Water and therefore safe to drink. She gulped hers down and then found a seat on a hard bench in the middle of the room.

Cornelius broke off his conversation in Arabic with a distinguished-looking man wearing casual clothes and turned to his charges. "Welcome to the Siwa Bottling Company's main headquarters. Here is the factory that pumps the water from 2000 meters underground, puts it into bottles, that are also manufactured here. From water to finished product, an amazing achievement in modern Egypt. You all drink this bottled water in Cairo, but it is also shipped all over the Middle East and especially to Saudi Arabia where it is prized for its purity and taste. Today we will be given a tour by the manager of the plant who is also the CEO of the company itself. We are so lucky to have this privilege. Let us listen to our host describe what we will see."

All eyes swiveled towards the large man standing next to Cornelius. In excellent English, most likely honed during his college time in the US, he explained the various steps that were necessary to bring the water from far underground, being filtered multiple times and then bottled in small to large plastic bottles. "We shall see it all, follow me."

The small group wove from building to building, awed by the large stainless-steel tanks, the efficient pumps and pipes that whistled and grunted as they walked by. They marveled at the water storage warehouse, stacked with enormous plastic bottles bound for the Arabian Gulf. The square bottles were disposable and shrink-wrapped into groups of eight. Barbie wondered at their weight and then saw miniscule cracks in the cement floor where too many bottles had been stored. Wooden pallets were also cracked and machines for lifting and stacking lined the walkways, abandoned where they had stopped work that morning. Barbie remembered industrial tours she had taken as a child, the chocolate factory, the bread factory, and the same sense of awe and amazement overtook her. She hadn't realized what it took to pull that water from the ground, package and transport it to her kitchen. She vowed she would never waste a drop of bottled water again. If Badboy, her cat, refused to drink his Siwa water, he could just drink foul-smelling chlorine-laced Nile water from the tap. This water was too precious to waste on a finicky cat!

As the group was leaving, another bus pulled up into the parking lot. Barbie watched as the graduate students, including Schuyler Stanford and his groupies, descended. They were quickly whisked away to the visitors' reception area. They are following us, thought Barbie, dogging our footsteps.

The next stop was not far away, the promised swim in a pool. Mahmoud jumped off the bus before anyone else could descend and greeted two of the men who lounged at one end of the pool. The entire surface area was not large, about twenty meters by ten, and the natural contours of the pool had been kept even as the sides had been cemented in, with a lip. The water in the pool was clear as the group passed by, but the sides and bottom were a mass of weeds and growing things. Barbie looked alarmed as this and remembered a time when she had become quite ill after swimming in Lake Dal in India. They said it was clean there, she thought, but the horrible stomach cramps and bizarre headache belied their most fervent hopes and thoughts about the cleanliness of the stream of water flowing into the lake. Never trust the locals.

A few thatched buildings at the rear housed changing rooms, primitive toilets and a small kitchen where tea was being made. Lines quickly formed for the changing rooms, while some of the men who had worn their swim trunks under their clothes prepared to dive in. Barbie watched from the deck as they stepped up to the side and looked in. Barbie noticed a large brown chunk of water plant, reminiscent of bodily waste, float by. She vowed she would not go in. Clean swimming pool water or sea water for me, she thought.

No one else seemed to notice the dirt in the water, so Barbie decided to keep her mouth shut. Let them experience water borne germs, she thought. She ordered tea and found a seat near an umbrella made from palm-thatch. She used her camera to capture the scene and as an excuse not to go in. She watched as Rachel and Mitch enjoyed themselves, jumping in splashing water at each other and generally not acting their age. She tried not to look askance as the brown plants floated by and the water became murky as they were torn apart.

Then the crowd increased as the second bus arrived and the graduate students prepared themselves for their cavort in the pool. The three gradate students spied Barbie and waved. She waved back and smiled. They took it as an invitation to join her, which they did, dumping their gear on the empty chairs near Barbie. "Aren't you going in?" one asked.

"Too old and fat," Barbie said. "Besides, the quality of the water leaves much to be desired." She nodded towards the pool.

"Euwwww," another said and giggled.

"Well, I've come all this way and I am going in," the last one answered and headed off to the changing room.

"Not going in?" Barbie asked the two who remained.

"That's a good line you used, 'too old and fat', I think I'll use that one too. You're right, the water doesn't look nice. Can't any of them see that?"

"It was clearer before they got in," Barbie said.

"I'm sorry, I don't think we introduced ourselves properly. We've met your housemate, Penelope, so we know who you are, but proper introductions are in order. I'm Roxana, and this is Aida and Esmeralda has gone to change."

"Aida?" Barbie looked quizzical.

"My parents were opera fans."

"My mother had one of the first Barbie dolls ever. I guess she never got over it. But what can we do about our names, huh?" Barbie smiled.

"We've all come to study Arabic and the Middle East," Roxana volunteered. "Arabic's a lot harder than I thought it would be. Of course, we have taken our preliminary courses at home, but my goodness, when we got here, it was so much more difficult than we thought. I feel as though this is the first time I've been able to breathe since last September. The other courses, history, sociology etc., are normal courses, but Arabic... We are so in awe of Schuyler. His Arabic is really good. It seems so easy for him."

"And he's really nice, and really handsome, but doesn't know it. What a perfect specimen of manhood." Aida said.

"He's funny too, and so nice and polite to everyone."

Barbie allowed a skeptical look to cross her face.

"Oh, I know; no one believes us. They think we are all 'smitten'. But what's wrong with that? He helps us with homework sometimes, which is so important, and that's why I like him. And when we came back after the Revolution, he was so nice to help us get back into the swing of things."

"You missed the Revolution?" Barbie asked. "That's too bad, it was an experience not to be missed. Oh, bad joke. The atmosphere during the whole thing was electric. So much happened."

"Yeah, we took the opportunity to practice our Arabic. You know, part of the reason why Arabic is so difficult is that the daytime and the nighttime Arabic is different," Aida said.

"Daytime and nighttime, I've never heard of that?" Barbie looked startled.

"Oh, I mean the difference between Standard Modern Arabic, taught to us during the daytime and thus 'Daytime', and the language we hear and speak on the streets, which we only do at night, the local dialect of 'Ameyya. They are so different, and so we practiced our nighttime after the Revolution, talking to people in the streets. Our classes were delayed slightly."

"And because we live in Zamalek, we meet all sorts of people. Egyptians are so friendly and we get to meet people on our field trips too. We've gone to the Khan el Kahlili and the Palace Walk and when we speak Arabic, wow, instant connections."

"Doors open, that's for sure," said Barbie. "Who are your guides?"

Esmeralda returned, suited up, and the three talked about the guides that had accompanied them, knowledgeable Egyptians with excellent English and all willing to answer questions and take the visitors to out-of-the-way places. "The graduate students always go, but sometimes we have extra spaces on our tours, so occasionally a member of the faculty goes with us. In fact, there are a few this time, but one new one on this tour," Aida volunteered.

Roxana added, "She's a loner, doesn't socialize much with us, or anyone else. She said she would NOT go with the faculty, but that she thought we would be a nicer group. She said she hasn't been on many tours, even though she's been here quite a while, a lot longer than us."

Barbie held her breath and waited.

"But you must know her," Aida said. "I'm sure she lives in Zamalek too. I've seen her on the streets. I've seen her getting ice cream from Mandarin's. You know where that is, don't you? So, I assume she doesn't live far from there. And she has this fascinating name, Winter."

Barbie blinked and slowly let out her breath. Winter Doern was in Siwa. She had come on the tour with the graduate students, so she had been here all the time. Barbie had seen her out the window the previous night.

"Where is she now?" Barbie asked, her voice low and as neutral as she could possibly make it.

Aida and Roxana looked at each other and shrugged their shoulders in unison. "Dunno. Haven't seen her lately."

Chapter Twenty-One: A Visit to a Bedouin Village

Beads of sweat gathered on Barbie's upper lip. She felt herself begin to tremble. She felt in her bag for her phone. She needed to get her phone, make a call to David. She found it and fumbled to find the number. The crowd started to gather in preparation for leaving the pool. Barbie stood and tried to grab her belongings, spilling things on the ground. With one hand holding her phone and the other stretched out, scooping up her scattered possessions, Barbie pushed the wrong number. The phone rang fitfully, then she heard a message in Arabic that she recognized as one she knew. Phone disconnected or not working. Desperate to not miss her ride, Barbie tucked her phone into her bag and ran to the bus. She was the last one on.

She hesitated about calling while on the bus and realized that many ears would strain to hear her conversation. She sat, fiddling with her phone, eyeing the other passengers. She felt she couldn't tell Penelope, who sat beside her; too many might hear the conversation. Wringing her hands, breathing deeply to calm herself, fidgeting with her phone, Barbie sat unhappily while Mahmoud babbled on about the next stop.

"Bedouins have lived and traveled in this part of the world for centuries. Although the inhabitants of Siwa are from the Maghreb, to the west, Bedouins are from the east and speak Arabic, or rather Bedouin, an Arabic dialect. And so, these two groups don't mix, or rather they do, but not as easily as you might think. The Bedouin village that we will visit today is one that was built by the government so that this group of people could have a more permanent home. Although the cinder block houses have some good uses, they are nice in the winter when it's cold outside, they are not so good for the summer and they are frankly, not suited for the Bedouin lifestyle. So, in addition to the houses that everyone owns, you will see Bedouin tents pitched in the yards, places where people often do more living than their proper homes. 'You can lead a horse to water, but you can't make him drink.' Ha, ha."

Barbie laughed at Mahmoud's joke and felt herself relax. Just do what you need to do when you can do it, she told herself. She calmed herself by looking out the windows and taking in the desert landscape. She felt the bus penetrate deeper into the desert and began to worry about the ability of her phone to contact David. She knew that towers were limited by line-of-sight and so many places had dead spots if they were not privileged to have a multitude of towers. She watched the power poles as their wires dipped and swayed in the wind alongside the road. At least these Bedouin had some amenities provided by the authorities.

After fifteen minutes, they pulled into the 'square' of a settlement of red brick one-story buildings. There was no neat square of lawn surrounded by a white picket fence that would designate this as a town, but a dusty, divot-marked patch of packed earth, hemmed in on three sides by buildings that had seen better days, or cleaner days. The stamp of poverty marked the cluster of buildings.

The group slowly descended from the bus and gathered in a tight circle around Mahmoud. From the low doorways around the square, a few children peered out. Squeals of surprise and delight met the ears of the group, and children cautiously oozed out of the houses. Then slowly the adults made their appearance. All had something in their hands as they approached the AUE staff.

It was not yet summer in the desert, but the temperatures had warmed up, especially during the daytime. Although the children dressed for the warmer weather, the adults did not. The clothes were traditional, many of them handmade, dirty and in poor condition. The smallest of the children wore no pants, the better to avoid accidents and thus eliminating the need for toilet training. The older children wore clothes that were much too big for them and obviously hand-me-downs from poor cousins or Western charities. The women, for now Barbie noted that no men were about, wore long black and red dresses, their heads covered by black headscarves that were loosely placed on their heads and hung down their backs. The girls wore miniature versions and the younger children wore jeans and dirty sweaters. Barbie felt very underdressed in her three-quarter length blouse and loose khaki pants. The children approached with tiny shell-bead bracelets of their own making, gently holding them out at arm's length. They were silent in their attempts to sell.

A bleating disturbed the scene as a teenaged boy dragged a protesting goat to the group. A kid followed, crying almost as loud as his mother. An absurd grin lit the owner's face and as soon as some of the group approached to pet the kid, the teenager shouted, "Ten pounds!"

Penelope had been only inches away from stroking the surprisingly clean baby goat when the price of a touch reached her ears. She jerked her hand back and stared at the boy. Mahmoud intervened, "One pound is enough." Penelope continued her reach then and touched the thick wiry hair on the goat's back. Before she realized it, she held the kid in her arms and was cooing to it, like the baby it was. Barbie sighed in amazement.

The crowd then began to be subjected to the artifacts of the rest of the villagers. Old coffee makers, dirty carpets, inexpertly done embroidery and other gems that were still owned by the poor villagers appeared for sale. Barbie slowly backed away, attempting to find a quiet place to make her telephone call. When she had gone fifty yards from the group, she pulled out her phone. No signal. Sighing in disgust, she looked into the skyline, trying to spot a tower or relay station. There must be something here, a whole village full of people and no telephone reception??? In the twentieth-first century, this was unheard of in Egypt. It was an indication of how poor these people were. And it might also explain the lack of men. They would work or at least hang out where telephones could be used.

She wandered back towards her group with her phone in hand, hoping to pick up the bars needed. After the initial onslaught, the quality of goods had gone up. Barbie now saw a stack of Bedouin carpets on one woman's shoulder. The colors struck her and she wandered near for a closer look. The woman and a companion began holding the carpets out for inspection. They were short for the traditional Bedouin carpet, but made on a narrow loom, so that a 'carpet' was two or three strips sewn together. The colors were red, dark red, orange red and purple. The patterns were subtle but simple, stripes of various colors. Barbie noticed her hands itching to touch and so gave in to the temptation to stroke the coarse wool. She turned one over and looked on the back side, she inspected the seams, and then asked to see the entire woven rug by spreading her arms out in front of the women. They smiled, large toothy grins and obliged Barbie. Before the bargaining could begin, Barbie pulled herself back and turned around, retreating from the temptation to buy. She needed to make her phone call.

During the time spent in the Bedouin village, the urgency of her phone call seemed to diminish. What do I know? What do I think is so important to convey to David? Maybe he already knows that Winter is in Siwa. The police must have asked for the passenger lists of the buses that brought tourists into Siwa, and surely, they had requested to know who was registered in the hotels. It seemed the local police had made up their minds that this was an accident and so had not done much of an investigation. Would they care if Barbie informed them that a particular person was in Siwa? Suddenly, it did not seem so important. She would call when she could. In the meantime, she would enjoy the Bedouin village.

Keeping the group in sight, Barbie wandered off a little farther. She spied a corral at the corner of a house and turned the corner to see what it contained. A loud 'honk' in her face let her know that a camel inhabited the space. A baby, still wobbly on his feet, stood swaying at his mother's side. Barbie came closer. The adult camel stuck her head over the fence and made to lunge at Barbie, who backed up immediately. Then Barbie felt herself surrounded by her fellow AUE tour members, all trying to get photos of the baby and mother. Another teenaged boy leapt the fence and grabbed at the end of a rope tied to the mother camel's neck. He tugged it and pulled; the camel turned her head. Suddenly, the camel and baby were outside in the alleyway and Barbie inched her way back, avoiding the large beast, and the suffocating crowd. She now realized that others had joined their group. At least five people crowded around the camel and baby that she did not recognize as with her group. Where did these tourists come from, she wondered? When she had freed herself from the tangle, she looked around. Now was the time to try that phone call again.

She walked away from the camel frenzy and looked at her phone. The late afternoon sun glinted off the surface, so she turned her back and tilted it away from the sun. She squinted to see if the phone was on and enough bars showed for a connection. She saw one tiny blip in the upper corner. Something, she thought, and tried to find David's number. The brightness of the sun hindered her search, so she turned the corner and sought some shade. The bar disappeared. Damn, she thought. Where is that signal?

Ahead of her was an open space and she headed for it. The sounds and distractions of the tourists and the camels receded and she concentrated on finding the magic spot with the connection. She had seen people raising their phones to the heavens in an attempt to capture a signal. She tried that. But when she raised her arms, the phone was out of her sight and the blips and lights on the screen were too far away to be seen. When she brought it closer to her face, she seemed to lose the signal. She kept walking until the houses were left behind. Still no signal.

Well, I might as well rejoin the group, go back to Siwa and then call David, she thought, cursing her phone. She walked back through the scrum of dilapidated brick houses until she came to the cross street. She looked down the street and saw no one. Nothing. No crowd, no camel pen, no main square, nothing familiar. She kept walking straight ahead, deserted houses on either side, until she came to the end, another entry to the Sahara Desert. She turned around. The village was not so big that she could possibly get lost, could she? Her heart began to thump in her chest and her breath came shallow and fast. Where are they?

Suddenly, she saw the camel and baby, and a few stragglers of the adoring camelid crowd. She hurried towards them, thinking that she would ask where the AUE group was. When she caught up to two young women, she realized that she had never seen them before. She smiled and then they turned to one another and spoke in a foreign language. German. Barbie thought, who are they? When did they get here? Surely her group was nearby and she slipped on by without saying a word. She headed for where she thought the main square was, but quickly found herself trapped in a dead end, a few houses with corrals now teeming with bleating goats and a few sheep. She stopped to look at two sheep that looked miserable with thick coats of wool. "Baaah," she bleated back at them. She looked one way, then the other. Low houses made of bricks, open doorways hung with tattered cloths, goat dung mingled with loose papers and food scraps littered the ground. Poverty screamed from every opening.

She turned and retraced her steps again. She could hear engines throbbing and squeals of laughter one row of houses from where she stood. She stopped and took a deep breath. You are almost there, she told herself, just beyond the next corner. Glancing at the sky, she noted the changing blue that heralded dusk. She walked a little faster.

Suddenly, she was there, in the main square, lined with the nicer houses in the village. Clumps of carpet sellers were scattered about and the children raced after one another, the lucky ones holding up candies and coins as their prizes of the afternoon. However, there were no foreigners around. Where is the bus, she asked herself? There can't be more than one square, could there be? She twisted herself around to one side, then the other, catching her scarf in her face as she whipped herself in a frenetic whirl of confusion. Where are they?

A roar then came to her from a distance and she saw a thin rising stream of dust. Gears ground and the cream colored twenty passenger bus roared into the desert. "Noooooooooooo," she wailed.

Behind her, another cacophony arose. The gunning of engines by young, or not so young, testosterone roared in her ears. Squeals of mock fear accompanied the increasing roar and three jeeps wheeled into the square from parking places out of sight. Stuffed with young females, a few of whom Barbie recognized as the young German speakers, the jeeps dashed by and flung themselves into the sands of the desert. Within half a minute, all noise had ceased. The sounds of silence oozed into the dusty square.

No one remained. "No," Barbie shouted. "Don't leave me!"

Chapter Twenty-Two: Missed the Bus

"How can they do this to me? How can they leave me here like this?" Barbie said aloud to anyone who would listen. No one did.

She struggled to find her phone and found Penelope's name. She punched the phone hard. A thin 'ring' could be heard, but the line crackled and hissed. Just as she thought she heard a voice say, 'Hello', the phone died. Barbie looked at the bar indicator. Nothing. This inability to get a signal was the cause of her missing the bus and she could think of nothing to do about it. She had transited the village, walked out into the desert and nothing had worked. She had stood in the middle of the center of town, gotten a faint signal, then lost it. What more could she do?

She looked around. All the people seem to have left the square. Now that the money had rolled away, there was no need to hang around. Barbie began to walk the perimeter, looking down the lanes to see if any vehicles remained. Dust curled up around her feet and her throat began to itch with thirst. She ignored both and continued to search for a serviceable vehicle with which to return to the small town of Siwa. It now appeared as a metropolis compared to this small settlement. She spied a car and ran down the street. As she neared the vehicle, she noted the heavy layer of dust that lay over the rusted blue paint job. All four tires were flat. Obviously, this car was going nowhere.

She retraced her steps to the main square and saw a man loping across the barren ground. She called out, but he ignored her and walked even faster. "Jerk," she said, spitting out the word as if it were something much worse. She kept looking down alleys and into fenced off spaces in back and side yards. She noted two sorry-looking jeeps, not ones she would trust to go the twenty or so kilometers back to Siwa and once she saw a bus. It had been converted into living quarters; its seats torn out and half the windows blackened. Nothing, she muttered to herself, nothing.

She turned to go back once more to the square when she happened on a house that was different from the others. A coat of paint adorned all the front bricks and a modest yard boasted a few flowering plants in pots. A set of cement blocks created a walkway to the front door, a wooden plank that had also been painted, in blue, and sported a doorknob. A house, a proper house, Barbie thought. She unlatched the front gate and stepped inside. Mindful of customs different from her own, she called out to the inhabitants, "Masa al heer. (Good afternoon.)"

She was answered by a loud 'woof' and a huge mastiff appeared from the side of the house. His mouth was open, saliva flew out and his long legs carried him forward towards Barbie. Without thinking, Barbie leapt backwards over the short gate and held it shut with both hands. She screamed. The dog stopped six feet from the gate and continued to bark furiously, his voice booming from a deep bass to tenor in each bark. Terrified after her first initial leap, Barbie stood her ground next to the gate and screamed. Loud terrified screams. No one came, no one noticed.

Gradually, Barbie stopped screaming and began to sob quietly. The dog stopped barking, but stood his ground and glared. So much for asking for help, she thought. She backed away and continued down the street, occasionally checking over her shoulder to see if the dog had moved. Eventually, he dropped his head and tail and trotted back to the space beside the house from where he had come.

Back in the main square, she tried a general shout, "Hello, hello". The cry sounded similar to the French 'Alo' which was the normal way to answer a phone in Egypt. She switched to the Arabic for Good afternoon, but neither call elicited a reaction. From anyone. Barbie felt abandoned. Why had they left her in the first place? Couldn't they have counted? Why hadn't Penelope alerted them to the missing Barbie? She hadn't said anything about wanting to be abandoned here, had she? No, Barbie thought. I did not want this and never said anything of the sort. She may have been tired and occasionally ditzy, but not that crazy. She tried calling out again, but her voice floated away into the air, sounding thin and weak.

Phone, she thought, try the phone again. She clicked it open and checked the bar again. One faint bar showed, which meant that there was some sort of tower or transmission device in the vicinity. A small box, a dialogue box she remembered it being called. "Dialogue be damned," she said to the phone. "this is a one-way message, not two way speaking. And what do you think you are telling me? My battery is low? As if there is anything I can do about it." She scrolled through the names until she came to David's. Cautiously she tapped the number. The telephone rang, similar to the previous call to Penelope. But this time there was no answer. She let it ring as long as she thought it possible that David might answer. Nothing. Finally, she stopped. Turn it off, she thought. I need to save the battery. But if I turn it off, no one can call me. Which do I want? Why would they want to call me, why not come and get me? They are the fools for leaving me.

Barbie saw movement out of one eye. She turned off her phone and put it in her back pocket. Looking up, she saw two young men, gallebeyas flowing, crossing the square. She thought that maybe the man she had seen before thought that she was not properly dressed, a she-devil, and decided that he could ignore her. Maybe she should try being more 'modest'. Speaking to a strange man may be immodest, but there are ways and means, even in this strict society. She unraveled the scarf from around her shoulders and pulled it up and over her bouncy blonde curls. Compared to the village women and girls, she was still incredibly immodestly dressed, but at least she had her offending hair under control.

"Hello, hello," she called. The young men hesitated.

"The bus, bus, gone," Barbie accompanied this with gestures of a bus running off. "Please help me!"

The young men looked at her, but Barbie dropped her gaze to the ground, trying to be modest, but not sure if it was the smartest thing to do under the circumstances. "I need a bus, a jeep, a car, go to Siwa," she continued.

The young men looked around the square, looked at each other and shrugged. They ambled on.

"Thanks, Shukran," she shouted after them. They ambled faster. This total disregard of her plight puzzled Barbie. Usually Egyptians were welcoming and helpful. Maybe they distrusted her because she had come with an Egyptian, and these people were Bedouins, a minority within Egypt, not overly fond of the overbearing Cairenes.

Women, she thought. Women will help me. I need to speak to them in my best Arabic, though. What can I say? She ran through all the words she knew like a menu in her head. Then she plunged down a street, looking for a woman, or better, women. They should be around this time of day. Sunset always brought women out of their stuffy houses and into the street, sitting or standing together, gossiping about the day, waiting for the menfolk to come home, or if at home, to demand food. They gathered on street corners, on front stoops, or here, in front yards. She looked down each street. No one.

Finally, she spied two women down a street, walking away from her towards the desert. She followed them, trying to catch up with them. They stopped at a house and she heard them call, presumably to a friend inside. Barbie took the short hiatus to check her phone again. A weak signal showed, but almost immediately dimmed. Damn, she thought, shoving the offending machine away in her pocket again. When she turned to find the women, they had disappeared. She walked the length of the street, but did not see them again. She walked back one street over and passed the two jeeps in the street. On second glance, she noted, although dusty, they were perhaps roadworthy. She stood near one and peeked inside. A dusty sweatshirt lay on the front seat. Gingerly, she reached in and lifted it. By the dust that did not fall off of it, she concluded that it had not been sitting there long. She dropped it and looked around, fearful of being caught intruding, but also to see if a driver were to be found.

"Hello, hello, Masah al heer. Asalam aleikum!" She called out again and again. She looked again at the shadows in the street and realized that they had started on their daily growth. They now covered half the street in shade. "Hello, hello!" she called again.

She looked at the sky and the shadows and tried to determine by the angle of the sun where she was in relationship to Siwa. She knew she couldn't walk, but she certainly did not want to go off in the direction opposite the town. Did they come directly into the town from the road, or was there a turn? More than one turn? Was it a real road, or a dusty desert track? Would there be any more traffic today, going towards Siwa? Or only coming back. Any vehicle was okay, she reasoned, she could presumably cajole someone into taking her to Siwa for money.

This line of thinking led her back to the reason why she was stuck here. Someone had forgotten her, or deliberately left her here. Who would do that? Why? The anger welled up and tears sprang into her eyes. Why did this happen to me? She wandered on some more, talking to herself in a low voice, cursing her fate, cursing her friends for losing sight of her.

She reentered the square and then decided to head back to the street with the two jeeps. They were the best shot she had, unless some other vehicle came into town. When she approached the place where the jeeps had been parked, she noted that one had gone, the other had been moved. This startled her as she had heard nothing. The settlement was so quiet, she must have heard the engine rev, the rumble of a vehicle, even from one street over. But there it was, one jeep.

And it was not in the same place. Someone must have moved it.

"Hello, hello!" she shouted. "Hello, anyone here? Anyone!"

"Don't be so pathetic!" came from a voice behind her.

Barbie almost fell down in her attempt to turn and see the speaker.

"Winter Doern."

Before her stood the woman that she had met the first day in the building at Hatshepsut's Mansions in Cairo. When Barbie and Penelope said hello to her, she had hung her head and twitched a little in greeting. Mouse brown hair hung lankly on either side of a face devoid of makeup. Sharp elbows protruded from a shapeless dress that hung loosely on a frame made too thin by fret and worry, or a poor diet. Small rimless glasses perched on her beaklike nose. She made a strange, incongruous sight here in the small Bedouin village on the edge of the desert.

"What…" Barbie started to say, but then stopped when she saw what Winter held in her hand. This was a totally new experience for Barbie. She knew what was happening, somewhat, at least the gesture was very clear. Winter held a gun. The small, round black hole pointed directly at Barbie's head.

Chapter Twenty-Three: Kidnapped

"What is this?" Barbie croaked, staring not at Winter's face, but at the gun.

"Drop your bag, put your hands out where I can see them. We are going for a ride," came the answer. Winter jerked her head towards the jeep.

Out of nowhere a gallebeya-clad, turban-wearing figure had appeared in the driver's seat. Barbie could not see a face and had no idea whether it was another foreigner, or whether the driver was an Egyptian.

Winter pushed Barbie towards the back seat. She held the gun in one hand and opened the door with the other. When Barbie stood closer to the jeep, Winter quickly grabbed Barbie's bag, all the time pointing the gun at vulnerable parts of Barbie's anatomy. Winter rummaged in the bag.

"Where's your phone?" she demanded.

Barbie looked startled. "Isn't it in there? At the bottom, or maybe in the top pocket?"

Winter rummaged some more, sticking her hand into the small top pocket. "It's not there, what have you done with it?"

Barbie's face went ashen and she mumbled. "Oh no, I've lost it. Maybe I dropped it somewhere!" she hiccupped.

As Winter continued to rummage, turning the bag upside down, spilling personal items on the dusty street, Barbie remembered her phone in her back pocket. She continued to look frightened as the thought of Winter finding out she had lied swept over her. "I don't know what happened, it was right there."

"Never mind," Winter said finally, "It's not important, you don't have it. Get in the car!"

Barbie turned sideways and slid into the back seat, trying to keep her right hip hidden from view in case her phone began to stick out of her pocket or bulge into view. Winter followed her into the back seat, all the while pointing the gun in Barbie's direction. Winter touched the driver on the shoulder and the jeep jerked into life. It lurched forward a few feet, then slowed to a rumble and a slow pace.

"Look forward, look like you are enjoying this ride," Winter commanded as they slowly went through the main square, now populated by a number of people. Winter waved and smiled at them, the gun held down low and out of sight.

Barbie thought it unfair that now the square buzzed with people whereas fifteen minutes before, she could find no one to ask about transportation, or a phone.

Within two minutes they were out of town and the desert had swallowed them. Winter leaned back in the seat, but held the gun steady.

"Why are you doing this?" Barbie whispered. "Why me? What have I done to you?" All the while, Barbie had this horrible feeling that she knew why she had been kidnapped. She had a sick feeling in her stomach that the bus leaving without her had been orchestrated by the woman sitting beside her holding her hostage with a gun.

Winter relaxed and threw her head back with a maniacal laugh. "You are stupid and inept. Questions to everyone, conversations with the police. What business does a well-educated English-speaking policeman have in Siwa? That one is just so out-of-place in Siwa. Don't you think it's weird? And why so many? And why consultations with Professor Smythe? What did he have to say? Nosy, nosy, nosy. You have to disappear."

"What? Nosy? Why do I have to disappear?" Barbie cried.

"You know why! You have known all along, haven't you?" Winter said with a little-girl sing-song voice.

Barbie thought that Winter hadn't been around. That she couldn't have heard or known about any of Barbie's conversations, consultations and questions. But now she knew she had been very, very wrong. Barbie hadn't seen Winter, except for the very brief glimpse through the window. At the time, Barbie wasn't sure whether to believe her own eyes or not. But Winter had been in Siwa from the very first evening. And now she was faced with her own naiveté. They had all said that it was Winter Doern who was the prime suspect in the murder of Thurman Hall. Even she had admitted that the bare facts were damming. She had also been reminded that a poisoner need not be present to be a murderer. She had assumed that the murderer had been, if not nearby, at least in the vicinity. It would have ben so much easier that way.

These thoughts swirled through her mind as they picked up speed thundering into the desert wastes. Barbie twisted her head and looked through the dusty window. Barbie saw nothing, so she turned back to Winter in the seat beside her. Winter had let the gun droop beside her, but when she noticed the movement at her side, she switched into an automatic 'gun up' mode and shook the pistol in Barbie's face. Not knowing if the gun was loaded or not, safety on or not, in working condition or not, Barbie chose to assume that the gun could hurt her if she stepped out of line. She decided to keep within limits.

"But, where were you? I didn't see you, except at the lecture, through the window. No one had seen you. We were all certain that you were not in Siwa. So if you were here, all along, where have you been?" Barbie ventured to question.

"In plain sight, dearie, right in front of your eyes. You were too busy ogling young men, cozying up to tired old has-beens, asking those silly girls inane questions, spying on everyone to notice. But I was watching you," Winter sneered. "I've seen you, I've watched you. The great Sherlock Holmes, with your sidekick Watson."

Barbie turned to the window to hide her blush of embarrassment. Barbie looked out and saw desert streaking by. There were no buildings and the road was bare and dusty, only one lane, hardly more than a track through the desert. The tire tracks that had been laid down before were the guide to the road now.

"So, what does this 'disappear' mean?" Barbie asked tentatively.

"Aha, you are catching on quickly here." Winter readjusted her hand on the butt of the small pistol, loosening the grip, which must have been cramping her hand. "Well, we are going on a journey…ooph!"

The jeep had hit an obstacle or a pothole in the road and they all flew towards the roof of the jeep.

The jeep slowed considerably and the driver looked in his rearview mirror at Winter, as if asking for pardon or checking to see if she was okay. They proceeded at a more sedate pace, but continued to penetrate the wasteland.

The sun abruptly flared directly into the jeep from the front window, momentarily blinding Barbie. Now, she thought, grab the gun, change the equation. She twisted, reaching for Winter's arm with both hands. Sparkles of dust and brilliant sunlight made it difficult to judge the exact placement of Winter's arm that held the gun. Barbie missed, her hands falling short and instead of an arm, Barbie's hands grabbed a handful of swirling colorful skirt.

"No, you don't," came a shout as the car slowed even more. "Get back, hands off me."

Barbie felt something hard hit her head and she saw stars. She slumped back into the seat and moaned as she wondered why she had never 'seen stars' before, as it was such an apt phrase for the aftermath of a blow to the head. "Ooooh," she moaned.

"You brought it on yourself, you silly witch. What were you thinking? Sit back, no need to think. In fact, not thinking is the best thing for you. You have been doing too much cogitation for your own good. I am the one to think, I am the strong one. You are the weak one, you are the one who needs to obey."

Barbie sat quietly, trying to concentrate on the passing scenery and the unfolding events.

"Tell me again, what does 'disappear' mean?" Barbie asked plaintively.

Suddenly, the jeep hit another pothole and they all bounced upwards. Barbie, from long experience in bumping jeeps, put her hand up to protect her head. Winter grabbed the door handle to keep from being thrown around, dropping the gun in the kerfuffle. Out of the corner of her vision, Barbie noticed the flying gun, and from a great distraction, heard it hit the floor, somewhere below her. Before she could recover and find the gun for herself, Winter had lurched forward and recovered it.

"Aha," she crowed. "You are still my prisoner."

"So why am I your prisoner and what will you do to make me disappear?" Barbie persisted, even as she felt the driver slow down again.

"You thought maybe that I would lose the gun and you could get it for yourself. You thought maybe I would lose vigilance and let you grab it or recover it from the fall. No, you silly thing, I am strong and you are weak. I am so intelligent and you are unaware. We are not made of the same cloth, you and I. Hah."

Barbie sensed that Winter was losing it. The strange laugh, the disjointed thought patterns, the obtuseness, the avoidance of legitimate questions; or what Barbie thought of as legitimate. To a crazy person, to one who had gone off the rails, maybe legitimate was not the right category. But that last rant, 'I am strong and you are weak', Barbie thought, appeared to be more of a self-help mantra. Too pat, too strong, too over-the-top to be the thoughts of a person who lived in the here and now, instead of one who had lost herself in the past. Maybe she could not let go of the hurt from the past? Obviously, Barbie told herself. She murdered Thurman Hall in revenge for that. Now, she is going to 'disappear' me.

Barbie did as she was told and allowed herself to close her eyes and sink into the seat. The constant rolling motion of the jeep was uncomfortable and she began to feel carsick. Her eyes snapped open and she tried to look through the front windscreen, a good cure for her life-long tendency to get nauseous in a car. Boats were worse. But the bright sun in her eyes and the blow to the head were making it worse. "Oh, stop! I'm going to throw-up," she mumbled.

"No way, you'll just have to keep it down." Winter growled.

She then said something in Arabic to the driver and they veered off to the left of the setting sun. The slowing of the lurching, the absence of the sun and her closed eyes, helped to settle Barbie's stomach and she began to feel better. By now, she had lost her sense of time and thought she would check her phone. In the nick of time, she remembered that Winter did not know she had a phone and so she needed to keep it hidden. Could she ask Winter what time it was? No, she thought, it doesn't matter. I know the sunset by the angle of the sun and the change in the air.

She heaved a sigh and sat up straight, with a thought. "Why did the bus leave without me?" She turned to look directly at Winter.

The now disheveled and dusty Winter stretched her neck and twisted to face Barbie, still keeping the gun level. "Aha, I managed that!" she smirked.

"How? Who did you lie to? Why did you do that?" Barbie's righteous anger flashed.

"Sit, sit," Winter cooed. "There was a message. From you to your friends. You wanted to buy a carpet. Doesn't that sound like you? Wander off by yourself, buying yet another carpet."

"But why would anyone believe that? I have too many carpets already. I swore that I wouldn't buy any more. And Penelope knew that. Everyone knew that."

"Oh, you said that you had found a ride back with another tourist group and you were in the midst of bargaining for them. So, you needed more time!" Winter beamed.

"No, I'd never do that, I'd never just walk off," Barbie defiantly spat.

"Oh, yes you did. One of the local boys delivered a hand-written note from you. Why wouldn't they believe that? It's just like you. Independent, arrogant, stubborn, foolish. It will be your downfall, Miss Barbie Doll." Winter laughed. It was not a chuckle, or an amused laugh, or a laugh from sheer delight. It was the laugh of madness.

Barbie shuddered but tried to cover up her fear. "So, where are we going? Why don't you shoot me here and let my blood be spilled all over you and your car? Why go out here? Where are we going?" she demanded again.

"Oh, no, I don't have any intention of shooting you. This is only to scare you into doing what I really want. I intend for you to get lost in the desert and die by yourself. It will not be my problem. I will be gone before they find you!"

Chapter Twenty-Four: Lost in the Desert

Barbie felt out of control. She didn't know where she was, where she was going, what was happening to her. This was distinctly not how she liked to operate. She wanted to be in control. She wanted, always, to know the answers to all the 'wh' questions (who, what, when, why, where and how). She did not like not knowing. Her father, who wanted a son and not a 'Barbie doll,' was close to her and imparted some of his Boy Scout wisdom to her. She could use a map, and better yet, she knew how to figure out where she was by the sun, the time of day by the angle and where to find the North Star in the sky. Now, she casually looked around her and noted that the setting sun was directly behind them. Oh no, she thought, we're heading east, away from Siwa. The Bedouin village had been to the east of Siwa, and now they were going deeper and deeper into the desert, and further and further away from mankind.

She noted that the faint track they had been following now veered towards the right. The arc of the sun swung around and the sun light rested on her right elbow. Barbie stared at it, trying to use the moments she had to focus herself. She gently swiveled her eyes towards the gun, still resting in Winter's hand. Gradually she turned to look more closely at it and with a start, admitted to herself that it looked very cheap and plastic. Was it a fake? They made guns of plastic nowadays, she knew, but this looked like a cousin's toy pistol.

She had never been allowed to have a toy gun, so the fascination of seeing and then touching and playing with her cousin's gun was magic to her. She had never seen the gun after that one day, and seldom played with her cousin again. Now, the vision of the toy gun melded with the current plastic gun. Better to pretend it was real, just in case it was.

"Stop," Winter said loudly. The jeep slowly stopped. The driver cut the engine. It took a few seconds for the engine's whine to desist and the desert silence to intrude. "Out," Winter commanded.

Barbie looked at Winter, not sure if the command was for her and what was meant.

Winter shook the gun at Barbie with annoyance. "Get out of the car!" she shouted. "Dense, really dense!" she muttered to herself.

Barbie slowly reached over to the door handle and gingerly pushed down on it. She had to push three times, each more forceful than the last, before the door popped open. Barbie looked over at Winter to see where Winter's eyes were focused. She knew that the phone in her right back pocket had probably inched out with the ride and the jostling and she didn't want Winter to look at her backside as she stepped out of the car. Barbie pushed open the door and slid sideways until her right side was all of the way off the seat. She reached around quickly, found the top of the phone and pushed, all the while oozing her body out of the car. Finally, she stuck her rear out and pushed off with her hands on the seat. She watched Winter at every move.

"Now, back up where I can see you, watch yourself girlie!" Winter slid across the seat and exited by the same door Barbie had used. Barbie backed up, still staring at Winter and the gun, but at the same time using her right hand to push her phone deeper into the pocket of her baggy trousers.

When both of them were standing on the sand, the jeep started and proceeded to turn around. Barbie understood that this was the place, the destination of their journey and perhaps the scene of her demise. Not if I can help it, she thought. She kept her face towards Winter, but used her swiveling eyes to check out their surroundings. They had stopped between two large sand dunes, with lower dunes on the third side. The entrance to the cul-de-sac was the way they had come and the way that the car now faced. The valley was in shadow as the sun sank quickly in the west.

"Walk!" Winter demanded. She had retrieved Barbie's small daypack from the jeep and she now hitched it up on her shoulder. She pointed with the gun uphill. "Go, you stupid cow!"

Barbie thought furiously. She reached to either side and pulled her knit shirt down as far as she could. It was one of the short variety and Barbie wished that she could have found one of the new style down-below-the-hips style. She had no weapon other than her phone. *And my* voice, she thought. How can I use either one? This is very close, one-on-one, and Winter has the upper hand. She started up the hill, but pretended to slip with every step. She turned her hip with the phone in the pocket towards the uphill side, away from the prying eyes of her captor. "Ouph!" she complained.

"Keep walking, straight up this hill. Don't give me that 'I'm a weakling' because I know you are not," she growled.

Barbie exaggerated her huffing and puffing, slowly making her way up the hill, stalling for time. Time to think of a way out of this. My 'voice', she thought. How can I use my voice? Her father's lessons in ventriloquism had proven to be useful on many occasions. Being smaller than most of the boys and only average for a girl, she had faced many bullies by distracting or frightening them with imaginary enemies. Packs of dogs, fighting men, squealing cars, all were grist for her ventriloquist's voice. Frightening, especially at night.

Barbie stopped and turned to look downhill, exaggerating her breathing. She squinted to get a good look at the driver, who now stood beside the jeep, waiting for someone's return. She still wasn't able to make out his face, but she saw dark skin and a glowering stare. Who was he? How was he allowing Winter to do this? Was he paid? How did Winter think she was going to get away with this? She may not have had a witness to her poisoning of Thurman

Hall's e-cigarette, but this was kidnapping. He was a witness, an accomplice. How could he allow this to happen? She might be crazy, but what was he?

Talk, make her talk, thought Barbie. She's obviously obsessed with something, maybe more than one. She is 'off.' Barbie thought that one way to distract her and gain the upper hand was to force her to tell her story.

Barbie huffed, trying to 'catch' her breath. "So you killed Thurman, what do you do now?" Barbie asked innocently.

"I didn't kill him; I didn't poison him. He poisoned himself and drowned!" Winter countered.

Barbie's face scrunched into a mask of disbelief.

"No one will ever be able to prove it. There are no traces. I wasn't even near him when he went into the pool. I have people who can say for certain that I was a long way away." She smiled. Her chin lifted in the air like a child caught, but imagining that no one saw.

"But you did poison him, didn't you? And a poisoner doesn't have to be present. Everyone knows that. So alibis of 'I wasn't any where near that place!' don't mean a thing. There are other ways of proving poisoning." Barbie countered, but thought to herself that it all sounded a bit lame.

Winter cackled again. "What a pathetic narrative! Now, move, move, keep going, to the top!!" She brought the gun closer to Barbie and jabbed it in the air that separated them.

"The police know," Barbie continued, half turned towards Winter as she slowly ascended.

"The police know only what you told them," Winter sneered.

"No, the police told me. They told me that Thurman Hall's e-cigarette was poisoned. That's how he died, not by drowning in the pool." Barbie wanted to cross her fingers as she told this half-truth, but then realized that it only mattered if you want to stay clean and look good in the eyes of God, or your teacher or your mother. It did not matter if you were talking to a maniac bent on killing you.

"They can't prove anything." Winter dropped her voice and whispered menacingly. "And you will not be around to tell them otherwise."

Barbie stopped and turned to face Winter. "They know you did it. They know it was you who put the nicotine in the cigarette. They know you are capable."

"Hah! What do you or anyone know? You are all such innocents, such pathetic dolts. Who was first in her class in high school? Who graduated summa cum laude in Chemistry from Harvard? Who won awards for her Master's Thesis? Who had profs falling all over themselves to be her PhD supervisor? Who? Who? Not you, not any of them! Move, shut your mouth and keep going!" came the answer.

"They will tie everything back to you, they will!" Barbie almost shouted.

"No, sweet innocent Barbie Doll. You are going for a long walk and you will never make it back to civilization. You are going to die of dehydration in the hot Egyptian desert." Winter produced a water bottle from out of Barbie's pack and dangled it in front of her, but out of reach. "Move, turn around and keep walking!" Winter's voice had a new edge to it that pushed Barbie upwards.

Barbie continued to pretend to be out of breath and slowed as much as possible. She hoped that Winter could not see her phone that she knew was inching upwards out of her pocket. She tried to concentrate on how this was going to end. And what she could do to end it in her favor, not in Winter's.

Abruptly, they arrived at the top of the dune. The sun's setting rays spread in a glorious arc in the western sky. Small clouds broke the even light and scattered it in dozens of uneven rays that turned colors. Red, orange, yellow, and the fading blue of the sky created myriads of hues and delicate variations. It was one of the most magnificent sunsets Barbie had ever seen. She may have been frightened, afraid she would die within a few minutes, suffer pain and loss; but she still had an appreciation for the beauty of nature. "Oh," she murmured.

"'Oh', is right. Sit down, here where I can see you!" Winter said.

Barbie tore her thoughts from the sunset in realization that this might be a good place from which to place a phone call. The Bedouin village had been much lower, but here, she sat on top of things. The phone towers worked on direct line of sight. It didn't matter if they were far away and so you couldn't 'see' them, as long as the phone could.

While Barbie was distracted, Winter had taken her pack and turned it upside down, letting the contents fall to the sand and slip down the opposite side side of the dune, much steeper than the side they had climbed up.

Barbie, realizing that all her belongings, and some potentially very useful ones, were being dumped out, gave a squeak.

"You won't be needing these things," Winter cooed.

"Stop, don't do that. Put them back," Barbie cried, heedless of the fact that Winter had the upper hand, and a gun.

Winter laughed and pushed a few of the recalcitrant items over the edge with her foot. They both watched the items gain speed in the sand and slide downwards. Barbie bent over to try to retrieve them and again pleaded with Winter, "Stop, please, no."

Winter held up the water bottle to Barbie's gaze. With exquisite slowness, Winter drew her hand back and then launched it into a long arc over her head and far down the sandy slope in front of them. Barbie watched in dismay as it fell and then tumbled end over end down the dune. "No, you can't do that!" she wailed. Barbie turned to Winter as they both stood on the narrow ridge of the sand hill.

Winter pointed the gun at Barbie's midsection, poking her hard in the solar plexus. Barbie kept her balance, but flinched away from the lethal weapon. Winter poked again, this time depriving Barbie of some of her breath.

Barbie breathed deeply, but had to bend over a bit to keep her balance, catch her breath and so was not in eye contact with Winter. With a loud, crazy laugh, Winter pushed

Barbie again. This time Barbie tumbled backwards and followed her water bottle down the slope.

Barbie watched her feet fly over her head, sand spray into the air and felt the sand punch her in the shoulder. Just before she blacked out, she heard a laugh. Maniacal, out of touch, otherworldly. Like a ghost, a wraith, a devil or a mad woman.

Chapter Twenty-Five: Nightfall

Barbie felt the sand in her mouth, her thumping head, her unnaturally twisted shoulder. She tried to think where she was, why she was eating sand and why her head was going downhill. What had happened?

She rolled over and tried to sit up, but she was lying head downhill and that was an extraordinarily difficult thing to do, so she tried to swivel around, putting her feet downhill. The thumping in her head became better. Her eyes had not yet focused on the surroundings, so she laid back onto the hard sand and breathed deeply, trying to fill her lungs with air and ease the discomfort in her diaphragm. She reached over with one hand to massage the shoulder that had hit the sand first. Bruise, she thought, but I'm still alive.

She pushed up and looked around. She listened. Silence. The blue sky was much darker to the east, but to the west, an orange glow diffused the gently undulating sand dunes that stretched to the horizon. As she watched, the glow faded and the purple-blue sky darkened. When Barbie looked down, it came to her that night was falling, fast. She could barely see the sand under her hands.

"Oh stars above, what has happened to me?" Barbie sat in the sand and felt the evening breeze gently against her skin. The day had been warm, but she knew the nights here could get cold and she wore only a thin shirt. She looked at her feet and was thankful that she had worn shoes, not the sandals that

Penelope had urged her to wear. They were still on her feet and tightly tied. She ran fingers through her hair, and caused sand to trickle down her neck and under her shirt. Nothing was torn, or bloody, she was in one piece. Then she remembered exactly why she was here. She turned and looked up to the top of the hill, now at least a hundred feet above her. Silence met her ears, nothing met her eyes. Had she gone? Had the car, waiting below facing in the direction from where they had come, now left, carrying them away? What had Winter said, "You will die of dehydration in the hot Egyptian desert." She was meant to be abandoned here. That's why the stuff from her bag was dumped out, why she was pushed so hard down the hill. Alive, but far away, and nothing with her except the contents of her pack.

Tears sprang to her eyes and as she wiped them away, sand and dust mixed with her tears creating a gritty line on her face. She allowed the tears to run as sobs threatened to overcome her. "Stop," she said out loud. "No time for tears."

Pack, where was her pack, where did those contents go? Quick, she told herself, find them now before all the light is gone. But wait, she thought, I need to get back to civilization, now, before all the light is gone! "Sit," she said to the wind. "Sit down and think. What can you do? What needs to be done first? How will I get out of this mess?"

She sat, took a deep breath, feeling a twinge in her shoulder, but otherwise unharmed. No broken bones, no blood, shoes on both her feet. What was in her pack? A granola bar, her water bottle? Wallet, a lightweight jacket? She licked her lips and thought, some water would be in order.

Phone, where was her phone? She stood quickly, and felt dizzy. Reaching behind her, she thrust her hand into her pocket. No phone, lost. Spilled out? It could be here on the sand. Look for it! It could be your only chance! Pack and contents, as much as you can find, now! She found the pack above her head; it had been unzipped and the contents dumped. A granola bar met her fingers when she checked the top pocket. The side pocket revealed a small notebook and pen. At least she could write a note and let them find it with her body implicating Winter. This thought cheered her and sent her looking for other items. All the other pockets were empty except a stash of tissues. I can wipe my nose and my backside. Wow! she thought.

Putting her head down, cutting out as much light as she could from the brilliant sunset, she let her eyes adjust to the darkness. She used her hand to shade her eyes as she scanned the sand for other objects. What was in the bag, where might it go?

The wind swirled up and a black crow-like object fluttered only ten feet away. "Eeeek," she screamed. Then she recognized the thin black material with red zip ties. Her jacket. She lunged for it, grabbing and slipping it on. Her hand brushed her back and she felt something hard sticking into her back. She shivered in anticipation of what horrors it could be.

She reached her right hand around and felt the pocket. A hard, thin rectangular object, smooth to the touch. Her phone! She had checked the wrong pocket. A huge sigh whooshed from her lungs and she sat in the sand. For the first time since she had gotten lost in the village, she felt a sense of relief and hope.

She held the button down and waited to see the screen. The opening bars of the jingle came to her ears. She had always hated the silly jingle, but now it seemed like a lifeline. Love it now, she thought. The screen was dim, but she managed to register two things. One, there were no bars showing on the connectivity section. Two, the battery was at 1%. She quickly turned it off.

The light from the screen had temporarily blinded her and she pinched her eyes shut, trying to recapture her night sight. Find the other objects from the pack. They are here, not far away. She stowed the phone in the top pocket of her pack and zipped it closed firmly. She put the granola bar back into the side pocket and looked around for the water. She saw her little paper diary with all her appointments flapping in the breeze. She found her wallet, still intact, not far away. She looked for her water bottle, twisting around in a circle.

She spied a lump on the hillside below and stumbled down, only to discover it was a piece of wood, stuck deeply into the sand. Perhaps a tree? How did it get here? Who brought it? Did it grow here? Never mind, she told herself, you are looking for your things. Specifically, your water bottle. For precious minutes, she continued to search the steep hillside, until she realized the slope had softened and she was effectively at the bottom of the hill. If I were a water bottle, where would I go? she asked herself.

Barbie looked up the hill and tried to estimate the arc of the bottle and its trail down the hill. Then she turned and faced the flat desert in front of her. A small rutted train snaked away from her. At the end of the trail a faint lump morphed into a water bottle, lying on its side in the sand.

"Halleluiah," she screamed as she pounced on it and thrust it into her pack.

She turned her face towards the top of the hill. She needed to get there and see if she could use her phone. What if they were still there, waiting for her? She scanned the hilltop and saw nothing. She would have to take the chance that Winter and her companion had left. She slowly climbed through the fine sand. She had thought she was making far too much noise on the way up. She thought she was pretending to struggle with the sand and the climb on her way up the dune, but perhaps it was harder than she originally thought. She seemed to slide backwards at least a step for every two she went forward. At one point, she slipped and she found herself sliding face down in the sand. She reacted by instinct, digging the heels of her hands into the sand, pushing her butt in the air. Ice-axe arrest, learned at her father's side in the glaciers of the Sierras. She slowed and stopped. Barbie rolled over and sat, waiting for her breathing to slow and her heart rate to return to normal. She took a deep breath and checked to make sure that all her possessions were still intact in her small backpack. Okay, one more try.

Carefully she climbed and just before she reached the top, she fell face first into the sand, creeping slowly up to the edge to peek over the top. Blackness greeted her below. As she scanned the short valley, she realized that the jeep had gone and there did not appear to be anyone around. Gone, left her alone.

A small sense of jubilation ran through her, giving her courage and hope. She looked towards the west, now almost completely black, only a trace of orange sky remaining. Stars were beginning to show and she picked out the evening star on the horizon. Moon, she thought, where is the moon? I need light!

A lick at her lips revealed a powerful thirst. She thought about the last time she had had anything to drink. Maybe lunch, she admitted. Barbie wasn't big on 'sipping as you go', as her mother was wont to say and do, but more of a chug-a-lug like her dad. Now, she needed a big drink, but she needed to save some for later as well.

She pulled the water bottle from her pack and in the dimmest light looked at it. It didn't feel right; it was shaped differently. The top was different. This wasn't her water bottle; it must have been the one Winter had with her. Shrugging, water is water, she thought.

She unscrewed the top, sloshed a little around to see how much the bottle held, tipped her head back, and brought the rim towards her waiting lips. Anticipation of quenching her thirst ran through her like a beacon of hope and salvation. I am going to get out of this. Just as she heard the faint gurgle of the liquid descending towards the narrow mouth of the bottle, a flash of understanding came. Hastily, she jerked the bottle from her lips, spilling some of the precious liquid down her shirt.

Water. Is this just water? she thought with panic. Why did Winter leave her with this bottle and not her own? What did Winter say? That she would get lost in the desert and die by herself of dehydration. What was this water? Could this be poison? Could this water contain some chemical that would suck moisture from her body rather than give it? Barbie held the bottle out at arm's length and slowly screwed the top back on. She couldn't risk drinking any of it, but it might come in handy, just in case it was water. She needed to keep it, but right now, she would have to go thirsty.

She rummaged around until she found the granola bar. Make your own saliva, she thought. One bite of the sugary, salty bar disabused her of this. But as she slowly chewed, the sugar raised her spirits slightly.

Phone, time to try the phone again. She gently took the small machine out of its pocket. She held it tightly, because she had far too often let the precious thing slip between her fingers. Here, it could get lost too easily and at the moment, it was the only link to civilization she had.

She pressed the button to turn the phone on. The silly jingle sputtered, but the phone's face lit up. She tried to discern if there was any charge left and also, if there were any bars showing in the connectivity band. As she stared, trying to turn it right and left, the bar appeared and when she held it high over her head, one bar flickered on and off. Stay on, she willed it.

She brought it back closer to her and found David's number. She held the phone up and pressed the 'call' space. She heard faint ringing, but also pops and cackles. Snap, snap, it said. After four incomplete rings, someone answered. The fuzz faded in and out. "David, David,' she screamed into the phone. "I'm here in the desert. Come and…" the call abruptly ended.

Penelope, she could try her number. Penelope would be able to sound the alarm. Maybe David wasn't in the good place either, but Penelope should be in Siwa with decent reception. She found Penelope's number and pressed. She held the phone far over her head, trying frantically to find and sustain the signal. After five or six rings, again obscured by crackles and buzzing, Penelope's voice came through. "Barbie!"

The shock of getting through startled Barbie and she was momentarily at a loss for what she might say. "Penelope, I'm here, in the desert. Kidnapped by Winter. Help me!"

"Barbie, come back! …. What are you doing …. Where….?" Barbie only heard parts of this weird conversation, but she knew she hadn't gotten her message through.

"Send help, in the desert," Barbie yelled at the phone. She looked at the face of the phone, now faded to blackness. No battery life, no connection, no Penelope to the rescue.

She sat then and cried. She let large tears streak down her face until they ran into her mouth. Tasting the salty water made her even thirstier and caused even more sobs and tears. When she was thoroughly miserable, she let out a howl of absolute wretchedness, a wail that sent a snake of chill up her spine. It was in the midst of this raucous keening that Barbie heard another sound, not one made by her.

She stopped abruptly and listened. A hum that gradually became a low-throated growl came from the desert towards her. A vehicle! A jeep or dune buggy?

Was Winter returning to see if Barbie had drunk the water and died? Was it someone to rescue her? If so, how did they know where to go? She had only moments ago made her seemingly useless phone calls. It was too soon for help. Maybe someone else? Someone who had seen Barbie being snatched off the street at the Bedouin village? Looking to her left, towards the sound, she saw a flickering light. She sat in misery, not knowing if this was friend or foe. Was it someone to trust, or fear?

Chapter Twenty-Six: Savior or Satan?

Barbie slipped her phone into the outside pocket. It was useless in any case, but she didn't need to lose it in the desert. Then again, this might be the end Winter had promised.

She sat down behind the top of the dune and peeked over the top. She felt torn between fear of the Satan that had taken her and ecstasy that this might be a savior. Should she, could she, trust this person or persons? What if it was Winter coming back? What should she do? Play dead? Fight? Run? If it was someone to save her, she should shout out, now before they, too, turned around and left. She hunkered down below the top and waited. Lights accompanied the noise; a beam, weaving back and forth threw light on the ground. It was easier for her to see them than it was for them to see her, as she sat high above the closed-in valley below.

The vehicle stopped and the noise died down soon thereafter. Someone had turned off the engine. The lights were still on, but dimmed now that there was no engine to supply electricity. Barbie strained to make out who it was. One or more? No one talked, so maybe it was one person?

The silence was pregnant with tension. Why was someone standing there? Soon the lights flickered off and the valley was once again drowned in blackness. Barbie let her eyes adjust and tracked the movements. Soft sounds, not voices, but sounds of movement rose from below. She saw only one figure moving around the small vehicle. She leaned out over the edge to see better and dislodged a berm of sand. She held her breath and listened as a whoosh of sand slithered downwards. She pulled her head back, but curiosity grabbed her and forced her to look again. Now there was a flashlight, a small dim one, but a light. It swooped and played on the undulating dunes that moments before had spoken of her presence. Damn, she thought, now I've got to find a place to hide. Where?

She slipped backwards as carefully as she could and found herself in a small depression of hard packed sand. She remembered the piece of wood she had found and thought that this dune might have once held vegetation, creating bumps and dips. She flattened herself into the shallow space, gathering her belongings around her. She put her face down to hide the whiteness of her skin and then remembered the blonde hair on her head. She struggled to pull her jacket over her blonde curls.

She lay as quietly and unobtrusively as she could, keeping her breathing to short, shallow, and she hoped, quiet breaths. The desert was so quiet, she heard the buzz of tinnitus in her ears. She was used to traffic noises in the city; birds, crickets and creepy crawlies in the country. But this was different, so quiet. Like a graveyard she thought. And shivered.

The soft sounds drifted and at first Barbie wasn't sure that they were anything but the sand and wind. Then they came closer, "Huuuh, huuuh, huuh, huuh." They were the sounds of labored breathing, like a human climbing a sand dune. Barbie turned her face and slipped back the jacket to have a peek. She saw the flash of the small light over the top and to her left. She pulled the jacket over her head again. Hopefully, the sound couldn't be heard over the hiker's breath. She heard the resumption of the climb, now coming closer. The breath, the soft swish of sand, louder and louder, closer and closer.

If this person is my savior, why doesn't he or she call my name? If he's looking for me, why not call out? It's got to be Winter returning to check on me. She knew exactly where she left me and now she is returning to make sure. That's why she hasn't called, she is going to look for me and finish the job if necessary.

But I've got the advantage, I know where she is, but she doesn't know where I am. I can attack, I can surprise her and grab her and… She remembered the gun and lapsed back into despair. The sounds came to her ears again, closer and closer. But I'm hidden, she doesn't know where I am. I've moved from the spot where she pushed me. That is my weapon. Throw her off the track.

The sounds of the climber neared the top of the dune and the light was brighter now, moving in an arc, someone trying to follow footprints in the sand? But there were so many. Think, think, she chided herself.

When Barbie was young, she loved to sing like many little girls, imitating the sounds and words of the songs on the radio or on her little record player. Her parents realized long before she did, that she had perfect pitch and a marvelous range in her voice. Barbie liked to sing, but was not interested in lessons or trying to harmonize with others. But her dad discovered another ability she had. He was an amateur magician and ventriloquist. He entertained at Barbie's friends' birthday parties and at the school fair. He was superb at making balloon 'weenie' dogs and his simple card tricks thrilled the other kids. He had a ventriloquist's dummy, but everyone laughed at him because they could see his lips move, the worst possible outcome for a good show. Until one day, the dummy talked by himself. True, his voice was more soprano, but that was the best show he had ever done. After two or three minutes of the dummy's patter, he noticed that his little girl Barbie, sitting in the front row and off to the side, was grinning ear to ear, when she didn't have her hands to her mouth cupped like a megaphone. That was when he realized that Barbie possessed a truly magnificent gift. She could throw her voice anywhere. And because she had such good pitch, and an extensive range, she was easy to train as his assistant. Later Barbie leaped forward on her own, learning to imitate the sounds of animals and humans, natural phenomena and supernatural beasts. She could make sound appear from anywhere and everywhere. She practiced by finding rooms, alleyways, anywhere there was something to bounce sound off of, and she honed her skills.

Now was the time to use those amazing abilities. She wasn't able to see, so she took a leap of faith that the sand was firm and even not far from where she lay. "Amuuuuun, Amuuuun. Sssssss." The sound slithered along the sand, human and hissing snakelike at the same time. The whispering noise was so soft, though, that the figure huffing and puffing up the dune couldn't' hear it. She tried again, this time a little louder, and more like a snake than a human, "Amuuuun sss, Amuuuuun sss." She created a curling sound that spread across the sand, fell down and away, and then disappeared. She kept up this sound until a figure could be seen standing on the top of the dune.

The figure hesitated briefly and the light clicked off. Barbie held her breath. The light from the flashlight came on again suddenly and moved across the sand. Barbie had just enough time to cover her head again. Was she sufficiently sand dune like? The light raked over her prone figure and moved on. Barbie raised the jacket covering her head for a quick peek out. The light veered off to the far side of the dune, away from her. Should I try again? She took a deep breath and threw her voice as far as she could in the direction of the light. "Amuuun sssss." She saw the figure hesitate, but flash the light in the direction of Barbie's sound. She watched and then tried again. "Amuuuuuuuuun. Ssssssssssssssssss." The voice ended in a whisper.

The figure with the light, Barbie was sure now it was a lone person, shined the light further down the slope, but did not move. Stupid, thought Barbie, who would be attracted to a snake sound?? Most people would run from it, not towards it. What was she thinking? The light revealed for the first time to Barbie, the outline of the person who had climbed up the dune. The light was dim, but the thin figure seemed familiar to her.

Wearing leather motorcycle gear, thin hair sticking up and catching the light like a halo, the man swung his light once more down the hillside, looking for the origin of the sound Barbie had made. It was the motorcyclist, the crazy Dutch motorcyclist. Barbie didn't stop to think what he was doing here and how he got here, only that he was her savior. She rose from the sand and shouted. "I'm here, I'm saved!"

Suddenly, the man whipped around and shined the light in her eyes. Barbie quickly turned her face away. He faced her and played the light over her figure. Barbie couldn't understand what he was doing. Didn't he know that the light was blinding her, that she couldn't see? What was he trying to do?

Then he shouted, "No, no!"

Barbie, startled, slipped in the sand and fell forward onto her face, her arms caught up in the sleeves of her jacket. Sand filled her mouth, now being sore and cottony with lack of water. She felt strong arms wrap themselves around her and pinned her to the ground. "No, no," he shouted again.

Have I just made a horrible mistake? Has he come to recapture me or save me? Had Winter sent him to 'make sure' that I was lost and dying in the desert? Instead of being my savior, could he be Satan? Would this be the last I hear before the eternal blackness descends?

Chapter Twenty-Seven: The Desert Savior

Light shone in Barbie's face. It was too late now if he was not her savior. The motorcyclist shouted again. Finally, Barbie understood it to be a warning. A warning about the 'Amun snake'.

"Don't worry, there isn't any snake, that was me," she said to the Dutchman.

He grunted in reply but Barbie wasn't sure he understood. Never mind, the snake wasn't real, but he was.

He looked over his shoulder in the direction of the reptile sound as he backed away from her. "Are you okay?" he asked in a heavily accented voice.

"Yes, yes. Do you have water? A phone?" Barbie rasped. The thirst that had plagued her for the past hour now overwhelmed her and she felt the raspy ache in her mouth and throat. The addition of sand complicated the situation. "Water," she croaked.

"Water in my machine. Phone here," he reached into his jacket and produced a phone from some inside pocket. "You can use, please," he proffered the small machine.

Barbie took it and pushed on the side, then thrust it towards the Dutchman, "How do I turn it on?" she croaked with a wheeze. She coughed as she tried to spit out some of the sand, but the grating of the grains on her tongue and mouth hurt, adding injury to insult.

He took the small phone and within seconds, it lit up and played a merry jingle.

Damn, she thought, I don't know David's number, only my phone knows that and it is dead. Penelope, I'll call Penelope and she can call him. Hopefully she knows how to get ahold of him. "God, I hope this works," she grunted huskily.

She fumbled with the phone, trying to read the numbers and remember Penelope's number at the same time. She began to feel faint and sat down in the sand before she embarrassed herself and fell. "Pene, Pene, where are you?" she whispered, wheezing and grunting with every breath now. The phone lay inert and quiet in her hand. What was wrong, isn't there a signal here, she asked. She looked at the bar and saw nothing. If I can't get bars here, I can't get them from anywhere, she thought and tears welled in her eyes, except that she had no liquid inside to make tears, only the feeling of them.

"We go," said the motorcyclist. "Up here, maybe we have signal." He reached down and grabbed Barbie under one shoulder, forcing her to her feet. Barbie pushed herself to rise, and was grateful for the help. She needed water badly. Together they struggled to reach the top of the sand dune.

Unsteady on her feet, Barbie focused her eyes once more on the tiny lighted screen. Only one small bar showed, but Barbie smiled anyway. She punched in Penelope's number one more time. Holding the phone to her ear, she listened as the ring sounded, broken and crackling. In the middle of a fizz, she heard Penelope's voice.

"Penelope, are you there? Listen to me," Barbie shouted.

"Where are you? Barbie, where did you get to?" the voice sounded far away and tinny, not like Penelope's at all.

"Shut up and listen! Winter, it's Winter. She kidnapped me. Call David, tell him!"

"Barbie, David's not here."

"Call him, tell him!"

"Tell David or Ali Rafiq? I can't hear you, where are you?"

"I'm in the desert. Call David, or Ali Rafiq, call him and tell him it's Winter. She kidnapped me."

"Winter is kidnapped? Wow!"

"No, she kidnapped me."

"Barbie, I can't hear you. What are you saying?"

"Winter murdered Thurman Hall. Tell David."

"Thurman Hall, what's that? He's dead. Where's Winter?"

"That's what you need to tell David. She is the one, arrest her!" Barbie shouted, not knowing if that would make the message go through better.

"Barbie, where are you? David's not here."

"Call him. Call David."

"Barbie I can't hear you." The phone fizzled and buzzed and then the connection was cut. A flat tone met Barbie's ear.

Should I try again? Would the call go through if she persisted? No, she thought, let Penelope call David. She would trust in Penelope's intelligence. Even if she didn't hear everything, thinking Winter had been kidnapped, but at least some message would go through. She could sort it out when she got back to Siwa. She tried to laugh at the thought of Siwa being the center of civilization and being anxious to arrive back there.

"Water," she said again, her voice weak and soft.

"In my machine," her rescuer replied, pointing downhill. He turned on his light and focused it on the space below them. Barbie's eyes could hardly focus to see, but she knew it was there. She straightened up, struggled to thrust her arms into her small pack and began to walk.

Immediately she fell and started to tumble. Strong arms reached out and stopped her slide down the dune and pulled her back upright. "Thanks," she muttered. She allowed herself to be helped the rest of the way down.

When they reached the motorcycle, the Dutchman swiftly retrieved a bottle from the hard carry case mounted on the rear. Wordlessly he held it out to her. Barbie took it and struggled to unscrew the top of the plastic water bottle. Her savior reached out, grabbed it and with a mighty twist took the top off. He held it out to her and helped her tip it up to pour the cool liquid into her mouth.

Barbie gulped greedily and within seconds had emptied it. It had only contained a few ounces of water. It was not enough, but immediately Barbie began to feel the life return to her limbs and the clouds dissipate from her brain. She sat down suddenly in the sand. "Maybe some food," she muttered to herself. She rummaged in her bag, throwing items into the sand around her. When she found the crumpled granola bar package, she brought it to her mouth and found a morsel of chocolate covered oatmeal with her tongue. The sugar and chocolate felt like heavenly nectar on her tongue. "Mmmmm," she moaned, closing her eyes.

When she had recovered somewhat, she opened her eyes and looked around. Her rescuer had left the light sitting on the seat of the motor and the dim light illuminated a small circle around her. She absently watched the motorcyclist as he bent to pick up some of the detritus Barbie had scattered around in her attempt to get at her granola bar.

"Water?" he asked, holding up the water bottle that had fallen from Barbie's pack.

Her brain was still clouded and confused. She couldn't remember this water bottle. Why ask for water when she already had this?

As he lifted the bottle to his lips, she remembered and with a great cry, she launched herself at him, knocking the bottle out of his hands, and in the process throwing them both to the ground. He scrambled backwards out of her reach and jumped to his feet. "Who are you, crazy woman?!"

"It's poison. She left it for me to drink and die. You can't touch it, it will kill you," Barbie cried, not sure if she believed this or not, but unwilling to suffer the consequences if it was not true. "Don't drink it!"

They both looked at the bottle, now on its side, pouring the clear liquid into the sand. He bent to pick it up gingerly, screwing the lid on, trying not to touch any of the spilled 'poison'.

"Better we go now," he said, sliding the offending bottle in the case in place of the water bottle Barbie had drunk from.

"Wait," Barbie said anxiously. "How did you find me? Why?"

The Dutch motorcyclist smiled tersely. "Curious. I am always curious. I saw the jeep in the village of Bedouins. There are three people, going off to the desert. Then, later, it passed me, going back, but there are only two. So, I followed the small road and here I am. There are tracks, something is here. You are here. Now, let us go back to the civilized Siwa."

The light above the door of the police station illuminated the porch and spilled into the courtyard. Barbie nearly toppled from the motorcycle as she dismounted. She stretched her hands and arms, cramped from hanging on to her savior. She needed more water, a chance to sit or lie down in a place that was quiet and not vibrating and bumpy. And she needed to be reassured.

At the sound of the motorcycle, Ali Rafiq appeared on the porch, his trim figure dressed in police black, a small smile lurking on his face. He stood and waited for Barbie in the shadow of the porch. She wanted him to help her mount the steps, she desired some recognition of their special relationship, but he waited. Other police and the tea boy appeared, helping both of the travelers to climb the steps to the office. Tea appeared, baladi bread and a dish of ful was placed on a small round table that magically appeared on the porch. Barbie smiled at the helpers and muttered, "Shukran, water??" A small bottle of 'Siwa' water appeared and was thrust in her hands. She drank half of it in one tip, then brought it down and sighed. She reached for one of the glasses of tea and sipped gingerly. Water and sugar, she thought, the restoratives I need.

A small stool had been placed at her side and Barbie attempted to sit on it, but missed and almost met the floor. Strong arms grabbed her before she made contact and pulled her upright. David's grin met her. "I'll take you inside. You need to rest."

He led her into the office while the men stayed outside. The small door in the corner was open and her led her into a small bedroom. It was spartan. A bed, small wardrobe, a dressing table, one straight backed wooden chair, wooden floor with a few Bedouin rugs, bare walls except for a small picture of the Pyramids with flood waters in the foreground. "Please freshen up," he said, walking to a doorway, and switching on a light. A small clean bathroom greeted her.

She used the toilet, washed her hands and face and dried them on a small white towel that hung on a nail. When she returned, he took her hand and indicated she should sit on the bed. He took the chair and sat near her. As she sat down, she felt herself falling into a comfortable prone position. She closed her eyes, but immediately opened them. She was afraid of what she might see in the darkness.

"Winter did this. She kidnapped me and left me in the desert. She tried to poison me. She admitted to me that she killed Thurman Hall. You have to catch her." Barbie sat up and stared wildly at David. "She's dangerous, she has to be stopped."

"Don't worry. We have already taken steps, but I will call and make sure. Stay here, rest." He left the room and reentered his office.

Barbie lay in the bed calming her wildly beating heart. The room was cool and she realized that two small very high windows were open, allowing the night breeze to flow through. Another window held a new air conditioner. Comfort, she thought, but not what he was used to. Here was a man who had an apartment in Zamalek, one of the toniest neighborhoods in Cairo. He had owned an antiquities business, rubbed shoulders with academics, writers, the intelligentsia, and maybe even politicians. He had an education, friends all over the world; he had a life! Now, he was reduced to this. Tears started to her eyes as the enormity of her adventure came to her.

She heard him speaking Arabic, on the phone, to someone? Then he returned and closed the door firmly behind him. "All is well, you are safe. It is being taken care of.

Nothing for you to worry about now. Why don't you close your eyes and rest?"

Barbie opened her mouth and let out her breath that she had been holding for minutes, or was it hours? She felt safe and now happy in David's company, lying in his bed, in his room.

He leaned over and adjusted the pillow under her head and gently kissed her forehead. Barbie felt the kiss and opened her eyes to stare directly into his deep brown ones. She reached up with her arms to encircle his neck and he leaned over again. This time their lips met.

The phone rang and David reached over to pick it up. "Alo," he answered. "Aywa, aywa," he muttered repeatedly. He stood then and walked away from Barbie.

She lay on the bed, listening to David's one-sided conversation. She understood little beyond the 'yes' he murmured. He now began to pace the room in agitation. Finally, he threw the phone down and ran to the wardrobe. Within minutes he had done a Houdini-wardrobe change and emerged from the shadows as a well-dressed Egyptian man in a white gallabeya, brilliant white turban, new slip-on sandals. He threw things into a small bag, underwear, shaving kit, a clean pair of slacks. When he turned to face Barbie, the gallant Ali Rafiq was gone, as was David the antiquities dealer. Her David had transformed himself once again. In their stead was a conservative, middle-class businessman from a provincial town. His face was a mask, only his eyes betrayed emotion.

He sat on the side of the bed and gathered Barbie in his arms and embraced her. "I'm so sorry. Ali Rafiq has been found out. All this business, you see, meant I was thrust into the limelight. And then my enemies... I must leave again. This time, I must leave Egypt." Emotions skittered across his face.

Barbie once again that evening felt tears well in her eyes. "I just found you, really found you. And now..." she couldn't finish her thoughts. She began to blubber as she did as a child when she was disappointed in anything.

"Stop, stop." His emotions matched hers as they clutched each other in a final embrace. He kissed her with such passion that she was sure a mark would remain long after he was gone.

"Here," he pressed a small piece of paper in her palm. He kissed her again and then was gone, leaving Barbie alone in his bed.

Chapter Twenty-Eight: Coming Back to Earth

The police car pulled into the circular drive at the Siwa tourist hotel. Barbie climbed out of the back seat gently and slowly, holding herself upright for fear of falling. She turned to close the door, but the driver had anticipated her and was standing by to close it for her. The reception desk was manned and the receptionist stared at her from behind the desk.

Barbie thought to herself, Oh, I look that bad? She put her head down and walked towards her room. Immediately a uniformed man stepped out of the shadows and blocked her way along the path, staring at her. Barbie abruptly halted and stared back. The wild look in her eyes and her tousled blonde hair must have spoken for her legitimacy to be at the hotel. He stepped aside and let her continue.

Before she even reached her room, she heard the voices of her friends. She hesitated briefly outside the door, then gently turned the handle. Inside, the three friends jumped to their feet at her appearance, shouting at once, "Barbie! Where have you been all this time? Have you heard the news? You look terrible, I mean, dirty and tired. Come, sit down."

"Euww, I really need a shower," she said, avoiding the crowding around her. She hoped that what they smelled was the sweat and dirt of the desert and not the sweet men's cologne smell that she hoped would linger longer than this. "I'll be quick!"

True to her word, five minutes later she emerged from the bathroom, presentable.

"Tell us!" Penelope demanded.

Barbie sat on the edge of the bed and uttered a deep throbbing sigh. "Where do I start?" She recounted losing herself in the Bedouin village and seeing the bus leave without her. She told them about being kidnapped, at gunpoint, by Winter.

"I got a little message from one small boy in the village. It said, 'Buying a carpet and got a ride back, see you later. B.' I knew that it wasn't exactly your handwriting, but it was all crooked and written in pencil, so I figured you didn't have a hard surface to write on, or something, so when you didn't show up, I wasn't exactly worried. But then later, I thought it was weird. But at the time, Barbie, it sounded just like you! So I said that we should go and not wait for you. I guess that Winter had written it and slipped it to a boy to deliver."

"Diabolical!" Barbie spat. She went on with her story, trying to recall the most important parts. The climb at gunpoint, the topple at the top of the sand dune and falling down the other side were hard for her to retell, even though she had already done it once that evening. "I tried to phone, did you get my phone calls? I heard you, but I don't know if you heard me at all. It was so terrible. We think that our mobile phones will always save us, but that's not true."

"We were beginning to worry when you didn't return later. We had our dinner and I know that you'd be really mad to miss that, but we couldn't have done much else. I contacted the police station, finally. I got Mitch to go to Cornelius Smythe to do it. I knew that if Cornelius contacted them, they would take it seriously," recalled Penelope.

"But then when Ali Rafiq arrived," Mitch said, "and went into consultation with Cornelius, it was then that we knew something big was happening. We didn't have much say in it, it was all Cornelius and the police and of course, the university administration."

Barbie continued, "And then I was rescued in the desert and of course I phoned then. I borrowed the phone of the

Dutch motorcyclist. He was fabulous. But then there was the water. That evil woman left me with a bottle of poisoned water. She thought I was going to drink it, but I'm made of stronger stuff than that. But I did have to keep the Dutchman from drinking it. So, you know all about Winter and what she did. You know, she confessed!"

"Well, not exactly," Mitch said reluctantly. "She made a statement."

"They found her? They caught her? Thank god. I didn't know that. I feel so much better. They can get her now."

"She's already on her way out of the country," Rachel added.

"What? Why are they sending her out of the country? I mean, the deed was committed here and they need to do something here, not 'out of the country'. And where out of the country?" Barbie's voice rose in anxiety.

"We haven't been told the whole story," Penelope added. "But it appears that AUE has done a deal with the Egyptian government. I mean, she is protected, we all are, by the university. And I guess that they didn't want a fuss. So, out she goes."

"So, they'll try her in the States? I mean, the university is a foreign entity, it's American, sort of, but aren't the police and government of Egypt somehow involved? Isn't that a bit hasty, sending her out of the country? Why do that?" Barbie almost screamed in distraction.

"Barbie, sit down. I mean if you don't really understand, we can get Cornelius to explain it to you. But I think it is a matter of protecting the university," Mitch's voice was soft and smooth.

"But she killed Truman! She killed the head of her department. She said so, she confessed to me. And there is the evidence, the e-cigarette, the…"

"Ah, the evidence. What evidence? If you look at it all, you will see that they have nothing, the police that is. No one has anything," Mitch said diplomatically.

"Confession. She confessed to me, she said she got rid of him. And she threatened him, didn't you say that everybody heard that? So isn't that good enough?" Barbie's words tumbled out of her mouth in her frantic attempt to convince her friends.

"She didn't confess to the police. Or at least that is what Cornelius could gather. No last minute mea culpas. What she may have threatened and what she may have said to you didn't enter into the equation. It was a matter of discretion, I believe."

Rachel chimed in, "Yes, you see Barbie, she was very distraught and she did admit to leaving you in the desert. So you had a big part in her punishment and in resolving this whole mess."

"Oh, so she will be punished?" Barbie asked.

"Well, she has been sent home. You know our contracts are such that if we are found to be misbehaving in some way, then the university can cancel our visa. Which is what they did," Mitch said.

Barbie stood and turned to face Mitch. "They cancelled her visa? They kicked her out of the country? And that is it? She misbehaved, poisoned her colleague, so they cancelled her visa?"

"She also forced you out into the desert and abandoned you. In fact, I think that is why her visa was cancelled. She admitted that, and there were some locals involved, so they could make that stick. But the poisoning, they can't prove that, and she didn't confess."

"So why did she kidnap me? Why did she give me poisoned water, abandon me? She tried to kill me!!" Barbie screamed her frustration.

"Barbie, settle down," Penelope stood next to her and patted her arm. "I know, it was awful, but you aren't hurt, are you?"

"She had a gun, she threatened me," Barbie continued.

"What kind of gun?" Mitch asked quietly.

"What do you mean, what kind of gun? It was a black gun, it had a hole in the front of it where bullets come out."

"Was it loaded? Was it even a real gun? Where is it now? Think, Barbie, could it have been a fake one? A toy gun?

What do you know about guns?" Mitch used his 'teacher's voice' with its reasonable overtones.

"I know guns. I know what a gun looks like, I have seen guns, lots of guns. I watch TV and movies and I have been to toy stores and I know what a fake gun and a real gun look like and I know guns. I know what I saw." Barbie sputtered; a defensive look came onto her face.

"Did she shoot you? Did she shoot anything? Did she pull the trigger at all? Was the safety on or off?" Mitch asked quietly.

"I don't know. How should I know? I didn't sit there and ask, 'Is your safety on or not?' She pointed a gun at me!!" Barbie shouted.

"Barbie, quiet!" Penelope said gently. "Mitch is just asking. You know, he is right in asking. We all know that it is really, really difficult when someone points a gun in your face, but the gun that they found, that she had with her; well, it was a fake one. It wasn't real. And so it looks bad for her to threaten you with it, but she couldn't have hurt you. And she didn't touch you, did she? Hit you?"

"She pushed me down the sand dune! And she tried to poison me. She took my water bottle and she gave me hers and she said my body would be found dead, lost in the desert and…"

"That water bottle, the one the Dutchman brought back? That one? That only had water in it. They checked." Mitch looked at Barbie with sadness.

"So, all those threats, pushing me down the hill, all that leaving me in the desert, she is not punished. She 'loses her visa'. This is justice?" Barbie sat and tears welled in her eyes.

"Well, according to you, she confessed to Thurman's murder. And if she did do it, then we should be upset about that," Rachel pointed out.

"But you said that they can't prove it!" Barbie countered.

"And they don't want to prove it," Mitch added.

"They don't want to prove it? Who are they? And what do you mean, don't want to prove it?" Barbie sounded confused and very unhappy.

"The university for one, the Egyptian government for another. It would be quite inconvenient to have a murder of a university professor, especially by one of our own. You see how bad it looks?"

"Especially after last January's murder. That was covered up as well, wasn't it?" Barbie demanded, reminding them all of the murder of their colleague during the Egyptian Revolution.

"That was best for his family," Mitch countered.

"And for the reputation of the university and the Americans and other foreigners who live here. At the invitation of the Egyptians. We need to be nice to our hosts." Penelope added.

"So, we cover up murder!? How does this help our dead colleagues?" Barbie demanded.

"Thurman Hall will be missed by no one here, that is for sure. So, his death is helping some of our colleagues. Lisbon Truegood will undoubtedly become head of the department, much better for all of us. And our young Master's student Schuyler will get the recognition he will need in the years to come. Banishing Winter will remove her from the scene. The messiness will disappear." Mitch made it sound reasonable.

Barbie stood and looked at all of them. They had had a few more hours to let all of this sink in, and they had decided to accept the decisions made by the university and the Egyptian officials. How could they do this, Barbie asked herself. How could they let murder go unpunished?

"What about justice?" Barbie asked furiously. "What about justice for a dead man? What about punishment for taking a life? The man is dead!"

"So is Winter. At least academically. She will never work in academia again. Her life is over, so to speak. Who would hire her? I mean, getting a job after being denied tenure is hard enough, but being denied tenure and then being fired in the middle of the year for attacking a colleague. Oh boy, no one would dare touch that one! She's dead." Mitch shook his head in melancholy contemplation of the tenure-denied academic.

"So, that's it? Justice denied." Barbie sat in resigned agony.

"Well, look at it this way. The university is willing to let this incident die, sorry about the pun, because, and this is in confidence, tell no one on pain of… Well, do not tell anyone. Cornelius let slip that the administration was unhappy with Thurman anyway and were looking for ways to get him out. This seemed to be convenient. That is a horrible way to put it, but we need to look at things differently. This is Egypt. In some ways, our university is more Egyptian than we think. There are more important things than avenging the death of one person. The matter has been taken care of. We should look at this as a benefit to the university, whose reputation and standing in the Egyptian community can benefit the whole country. Sorry, Barbie, but our 'American' sense of right and justice must sometimes bend to another viewpoint."

"Well, I'll have to think about that one. I guess I am too 'American' and in my book, a life is sacred," Barbie shook her head in confusion.

"We are leaving in the morning. We're going to stop at one more place on the way out of Siwa, and we get to spend a lovely last night in Marsa Matruoh," Rachel said. "I will try to have a good time! You should too. Try to put all of this behind us. Just think, the end of the spring semester is coming and then it's summer. Holidays and family. Think of that!"

Penelope and Barbie groaned, thinking of family, but they thanked Mitch and Rachel and shooed them out of the room.

When they had gone, Penelope turned to Barbie. "You were gone a really long time. Do you know what time it is? Are you hungry? Did anyone give you any food?"

Trying to deflect too many questions about her whereabouts, Barbie greedily accepted the offer of another granola bar and a bottle of unopened Siwa water.

"Yeah, I guess I really needed the rest. After all the things that happened and the motorcycle ride back from the village, I was truly exhausted."

"So, do tell me about David?" Penelope grinned mischievously.

"He's gone. So is Ali Rafiq. He got a phone call and presto-chango, he whisks out wearing a gallebeya and apologizes, again. He said that his enemies had found him out. You know, this business, so he had to leave. This time, he said it was out of the country. So, nothing to tell. Alone again."

"Ah, too bad. You two just never had a chance."

Barbie turned her head to hide the tiny smile that crept to her lips. She bent to pick up her discarded jeans that had landed on the floor and retrieved a small piece of paper. She looked at it and memorized the post office box number in Monaco. Only three numbers, so it was easy. She tore it into a few pieces and threw it and a used tissue into the trash.

"While you were out and all this stuff was coming down, I got onto the internet. You know how we are always kinda looking? There are a number of ESL teacher sites and I found jobs. You know, we really need to get out of Egypt. The Revolution and all. Too many deaths. So, I found this great job in Turkey, in Ankara. I mean, I guess that Istanbul would be better, but listen to this, they help find housing and they have a great program. The pay is not so great, but Turkey!!! So, listen to this, 'Experienced English teachers wanted at the….'"

Barbie listened and as Penelope read on, she began to see the advantage of trying a new place. They hadn't been to Turkey yet, but everyone raved about the food, the dynamic economy and the ad did sound good. "Yeah, mark that one. When we get back, I'll explore. Shall we go together??"

They discussed the job prospects for it, then Penelope cocked her head. "I have a question to ask. You know that 'trick' in the Amun temple? The one where Schuyler was pretending to be Alexander and the 'god' answered him? That was you, wasn't it?"

"Of course, it was me. Who else could do something like that?" Barbie smiled at Penelope. "Silly girl."

"Then why did you tell me that it wasn't you? Why lie about it?" Penelope said angrily.

"Oh, my friend, there were ears listening. And that special talent of mine? It's only on a need to know basis. And those ears didn't need to know." She grinned. "Turkey, huh? Whirling dervishes, kebabs, and where is that place with the fantastic rock formations? Cappadocia I think."